the Juniper Gin Joint

Lizzie Lovell

ALLEN&UNWIN

First published in Great Britain and Australia
in 2018 by Allen & Unwin

This is a work of fiction. All characters and events have
evolved from the author's imagination.

Allen & Unwin
c/o Atlantic Books
Ormond House
26–27 Boswell Street
London WC1N 3JZ
Phone: 020 7269 1610
Fax: 020 7430 0916
Email: UK@allenandunwin.com
Web: www.allenandunwin.com/uk

A CIP catalogue record for this book is available
from the British Library.

Paperback ISBN 978 1 76063 269 4
Ebook ISBN 978 1 76063 986 0

Text design by Lindsay Nash
Printed in Great Britain by Clays Ltd, St Ives plc

10 9 8 7 6 5 4 3 2 1

For Eloise, my first gin-drinking pal
and most excellent cousin

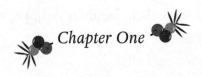

Chapter One

A Sunday afternoon in late September, a sniff of autumn in the air, a change in the light. Sunday afternoons used to be about the roast dinner and the lawn, me cooking, Mike mowing. Now it's all veggie sausages, joss sticks, and rapper dudes banging on about stuff I don't even understand. The joys of living with an eighteen-year-old. Only not for much longer.

'Come on, Lauren, get a move on!' I have to yell to be heard above the 'music' pounding from her bedroom.

No response.

Just the shoutiness of DJ Nobber, or whatever this one's called.

Back upstairs then, for the sixty-fourth time today. It doesn't feel like two ticks since I was trudging up these very same stairs to settle her of an evening, what with her colic and Harry's toddler gymnastics. I could've done with a Stannah Stairlift. Which isn't such a bad idea now I come to think of it. Not for me. I'm only a few months off fifty. (I have to whisper this number, even in my head.) It's Dad I'm worried about. He's doddery on his legs and I'd hate for him to have another fall.

I take a deep breath, steady myself, prepare to enter Lauren's room.

'Get a move on, Lolly.'

'Calm down, Mother. We've got ages yet.' She's on her hands and knees, searching for something: DNA? A murder weapon? A dead body? It's hard to tell with all her crapaphernalia. Meanwhile, Bob, our creaky old Jack Russell, is languishing on his back in a patch of sunshine on Lauren's unmade bed, oblivious to the fact that his number-one fan is about to abandon him.

'I don't want to get caught in the rush-hour traf—'

'It's Plymouth we're going to, Mum, not Manhattan.'

Plymouth most definitely isn't Manhattan, but it's got a university and that's where I'm taking my daughter. If she ever gets her bloody act together.

'How much more of that stuff are you bringing? My poor old Polo's already crammed.'

'Stop stressing,' she says, using the voice that makes me stressed. She gets up off her knees, her search forgotten, in order to survey her room, hands on hips, hair in plaits, dirt on cheeks, like she's Pippi Longstocking. 'There's just this suitcase. And my sleeping bag. And that lamp. And those Yankee candles I got for Christmas... and... oh, yeah, this box.' She nudges the box with her foot. There's a hole in her sock and a glittery toenail pokes through.

'You really need a box of cuddly toys?'

'I might get lonely.' She slumps onto the bed and pulls Bob towards her, nuzzling her freckled nose into his neck.

'Plymouth's barely an hour away.' I'm doing my best to be a model of calm but sometimes, right now, it's not easy. 'Why don't you just take Mrs Pink?'

Mrs Pink, the one-eyed bunny with grubby fur and worn-out ears. She's always been top toy. Goes everywhere with Lauren. School residentials, sleepovers, festivals. Now she's going to be a frigging fresher.

'But Mrs Pink needs Tinky Winky. They're best friends, remember.'

I take a deep breath. I want to say in a very firm voice, *Lauren, you are eighteen years old, about to embark on a chemistry degree, not infant school*. But I can't. 'Just bring Mrs Pink and Tinky Winky. The others can stay here and guard your bedroom from the Bogeyman.'

This does the trick. I go on to say she won't be allowed smelly candles because the powers that be don't want drunk students setting fire to the halls of residence.

'You sound upset, Mum. Are you going to miss me?'

'Course I am, Lolly, but you're going to have the best time. I'm so jealous. Me and your dad never got further than Dingleton Comp. You've done us proud.'

'Where is Dad, anyway?'

'No idea. He said he'd be here to wave you off.'

'He's probably busy with *her*.'

I want to agree. I want to say yes, he's probably having some afternoon delight with your chemistry teacher, Miss Melanie Barton. Yes, he's probably right at this moment showing her his Bunsen burner. But, no. I am the sensible parent. And Lauren's the last of our babies to leave the nest. Harry's been gone a whole year, bartending his way across Canada. I've adjusted to his being away, to his random middle-of-the-night messages, the occasional FaceTime. But this is my little girl.

It's only Plymouth.

'Let me grab Granddad from the shed. We're leaving in ten. At the latest. Text your father.'

She follows me downstairs, Mrs Pink under one arm, a wriggling Bob under the other, texting her father with her wizard fingers. The fingers that can turn magnesium into gold dust and Snapchat in the dark.

Mike pings back his apologies. Says Melanie needs some emotional support because her cat's gone AWOL. I feel like texting him to say I've kidnapped her bastard cat and it's currently boiling away to a pulp on my stove. But I like cats. And I'm the grown-up.

'Never mind, Lolly. He'll pop down and see you when he's on the road. He's in Plymouth a lot.'

4

I release Bob from her grip and shoo him out to the garden for a wee. He can't half bark for a little dog.

Lolly stays put, at the bottom of the stairs, pouting. She's five years old again, standing in her Mulan PJs, sucking her thumb, Mrs Pink's ears nestled one against each side of her nose, waiting for her daddy to come home from work. 'Where's Granddad?' she asks, wiping away a rogue tear.

Here he is, Granddad, wandering out of the kitchen into the hallway like he's forgotten something, or is maybe looking for it. He's not got dementia. He's always been scatty. But now that he's spotted Lauren, a smile spreads over his wizened face and he looks his seventy-four years and yet he's also my dad from when I was a little girl, the spark in his cornflower-blue eyes still fizzing away with awe and wonder.

'Here she is,' he says. 'The brain of Britain.'

'Granddad. Don't,' she half-heartedly protests. 'It's only a degree.' She blushes but she loves it. Laps it up and milks it for all it's worth.

He hands her a bottle of his home-made damson wine. 'This'll make you friends and influence them.'

'Thanks,' she says.

'It's stronger than that cider you drink.'

'You're a legend.'

'I certainly hope so.'

She kisses him and he slips a wad of cash into her

hand. 'A little something to help you on your way.' He winks. 'It'll buy you a snakebite and a packet of condoms.'

'*Dad!*' He is *so* embarrassing sometimes.

He shrugs.

She stashes the notes in the back pocket of her ultra-skinny ripped jeans that remind me of the venetian blinds we had in the front room back in the day.

'We don't want any surprises. Not till you've graduated and won the Nobel Prize in Chemistry.'

Sexual-health advice from my father to my daughter. What next? I must sigh or look pained as he says, 'Get a move on, Lollipop. Your mother's hit that time of life where she's likely to explode at any given moment.' He hugs her. She hugs him back, tight, so tight she might fracture one of his ribs.

'Don't go losing that money,' I tell her, heading back up to her room. 'You can buy a heck of a lot of condoms with fifty quid.'

Dad does his Sid James laugh.

I can't see my daughter's face from here but I know it'll be the colour of that damson wine.

AFTER SEVERAL MORE trips up and down those bloody stairs, and after much faffing and flapping, after she's said her emotional goodbyes to the dog, to her grandfather and to all the rooms and bits of furniture, we get going, Dad and Bob waving us off until we can no longer see them even though they're standing in the middle of the road.

'Bye, House,' Lauren whispers. 'Bye, Road. Bye, Park. Bye, Library. Bye, Museum. Bye, Train Station. Bye, Sea—'

'Why don't you put on a CD, Lolly?'

She tuts, like I've suggested she winds up a gramophone, then connects her phone to my car stereo.

Despite DJ Nobber blasting my ears, despite Mrs Pink and Tinky Winky making it tricky to see out the back window, and despite the fact that I keep bashing the lamp with my hand every time I go for a gear change, we've done it. Me and Dad. We've got Lauren on her way. Our little girl's all grown up.

'What's a "snakebite", Mum?' she asks, fingers flying over her phone as she Instagrams every moment of our epic journey down the A38. 'How can you buy a snakebite?'

God, I feel old. God,

THREE HOURS LATER and I'm driving back up the A38, alone in an empty car. All that's left of my daughter is the smell of ylang-ylang and a Quavers packet screwed into a ball on her seat. At least I can listen to the radio. Leif Garrett is singing 'I was Made for Dancin'', a proper tune. I used to have a life-size poster of the gorgeous one, blew kisses at him from my bed, before I even knew what a proper kiss was. That happened a few years later, school leavers' disco, July 1984.

Now I'm officially an empty-nester, Harry and Lauren off on adventures, and while I'm pleased for them, proud of them, this isn't how I imagined my future panning out. Thought we were doing all right, me and Mike, not bad for a couple with just a handful of O levels and CSEs between them. We were on course, two relatively functioning children, a semi-detached house with off-road parking, permanent jobs, three more years to pay off the mortgage, and a cruise booked. I never expected to be driving home to my dad in a rattling old Polo, worrying about student loans and pension funds and a marriage breakdown. But then I never thought Mum would go first or that Mike would be such a tosser.

'I'm well annoyed with Dad,' Lauren said earlier once we'd reached her halls and started to unpack the car.

We'd lugged all her stuff – the suitcases, the rucksack, the bedding, the crockery, the sleeping bag, the lamp – into her new room, just Lolly and me between us. And her room, her room is all right. A pod with a desk, a bed and an en-suite. I've never had an en-suite but I don't begrudge her that. She's worked hard. Extra tuition. Which is where Miss Melanie Barton entered stage left and exited stage right with a middle-aged man who happened to be my husband. A man I'd been with ever since school.

'I'm well annoyed with him too, Lolly. Well annoyed. But you've got a fresh start and it's going to be bloody brilliant.'

I gave her a hug and left her organizing her Sharpies and make-up and socks to go back up the A38 to my increasingly empty life.

'Forty-nine years old, Lief.' I say this out loud, in the safety of my car. 'Forty-nine!'

Lief carries on singing. He's not bothered.

But I am.

THE SUN IS setting by the time I get home and our street is Sunday-night quiet. There's a van on the driveway. Mike. I pull in next to it. Twice the size of my rust bucket and yet he couldn't take his daughter to university. Couldn't even wave her off. Wait till I get my hands on the little ratbag.

I turn off the engine and sit for a while, eyes shut, hoping that when I open them, his van will have disappeared.

It hasn't. I'll have to go in. Besides, I'm gagging for a G and T. Better still, Dad's got a bottle of sloe gin from last autumn. He'll be happy to crack it open. It's almost time to make this year's batch. And today's rite of passage should be marked somehow.

I get out of the car, knees clicking, back sore. I'm

reaching for my bag on the back seat when I notice
something, someone, left behind on the floor. Mrs
Pink.

Bugger.

I pick her up like she's a newborn, hold her tight,
sniff her, and have to resist the urge to suck my thumb,
though I do rub those worn-out ears. They feel like silk.
I feel like bawling. But I will not let Mike see me upset.
Oh, no.

MIKE IS FRATERNIZING with my father in the shed. It
was newly constructed by Mike last year as an attempt
to lure Dad to move in with us after his fall. He didn't
break any bones but he was shaken up and riddled with
grief because it happened within a few weeks of Mum
dying. The existing shed, Mike's, wasn't big enough for
Dad's stuff so this clinched the deal for my eccentric
father to sell up the old house. When Harry left to go
travelling, Dad moved into his room. Not so long after
that, Mike moved out. And now Lauren.

I'm not going to mope though I do have the right to
feel narked.

This shed might be huge but it's stacked with Dad's
stuff: books, vinyl, fossils, mysterious scientific objects,
Kilner jars, recycled bottles, an old nappy bucket filled
with corks. A home-brewing/distilling aficionado who

thought nothing of roping in child labour when needed. It's entirely clear where Lauren found her interest in chemistry. Watching her grandfather turn fruit into moonshine, hooch, cider and gin was like being in the presence of an alchemist. A magician. She always loved a trick. The coin behind the ear, the nose in the fingers. She wanted to be Hermione Granger and use real magic, not just sleight of hand or misdirection. Dad's booze-making intrigued her. His ginger-beer plant was the stuff of legends and watered the whole of Dingleton at one point. Chemistry was the closest she could get to this. Though I have no doubt she'd have taken a degree in brewing and distilling if she could have.

I turn my attention to Mike, slouched in a deckchair, one of a pair we used to take on holidays, a traitorous Bob curled up tight on his lap.

'Drinking tea?' I ask, surprised, seeing as he's normally on the beer when he's with my father.

'I'm driving,' he says.

'So you are.'

I wait for him to carry on.

He coughs, that clearing-his-throat cough he does when he's embarrassed. 'Sorry, Jen,' he mutters. 'About the mess-up earlier.'

Apparently the scraggy cat returned at teatime, smelling of lavender and smoke. Mrs Baxter, who lives up the road from the dirty lovebirds, is number-one suspect. I tell him, all calm like, that I don't give a flying monkey about Mrs Baxter and her personal habits. But I do care that he wasn't here for our daughter. I tell him Lauren was disappointed and he'd better visit her soon. He says he'll go mid-week.

'Make sure you do.' I am so annoyed I can't look at him so I busy myself hunting down that remaining bottle of sloe gin. It's in here somewhere.

And now Mike's moaning to Dad, about Melanie, about how she nags him which is something I never did. Probably should have. Though I am now. Which is better late than never. And how dare he? How dare he grumble about Melanie, the woman he left me for? It's no use Mike offloading onto Dad. My father's not listening to a word; he's gone elsewhere, deep inside his head. He'll be thinking about stuff most of us never will, such as how many smells your nose can remember (fifty thousand) and which day of the week you're most likely to have a heart attack (Monday).

I do not want to hear about Mike's troubles.

Though I do confess to a certain smugness.

All is not rosy then.

'Ah, gotcha.' I hold up the bottle in a moment of triumph.

'The secret is to use decent gin,' Dad says, back in the room, when I pull the cork out of the precious bottle. 'The sloes are all the happier for it.'

'Yes, Dad,' I say. 'You get what you pay for.' Life advice from the man who forages in hedgerows and loiters around bottle banks. The man who makes booze that can knock your head off: elderflower fizz, damson wine, blackberry liqueur, and my favourite, sloe gin. I might be the owner of depleted hormones, a diminishing family and zero sex life, but I've got Dad and his home comforts.

I grab a couple of dusty tumblers from the shelf, look in my bag for a tissue and there she is, Mrs Pink. I pull her out, a rabbit out of a hat, hold her up for my audience of three, give them a moment to absorb the significance.

There's an intake of breath.

'Bugger,' the men say in unison as Bob whines.

I use Mrs Pink to wipe the glasses, pour a generous one for Dad and an even more generous one for myself.

Mike looks up, expectant. 'What about me...?'

'You're driving,' I remind him.

'So I am,' he says.

'You'd better take Mrs Pink with you, Mike. Your daughter needs her. She needs you.'

We watch as Mike struggles out of the deckchair and makes for the door, off to his home, Melanie the Moaner's home, Mrs Pink clutched in his hand. If I were a kinder person I might feel a teeny-weeny bit sorry for him. But obviously I'm not and I don't.

'Cheers, Dad.' I chink my glass against his.

'Bottoms up,' he says.

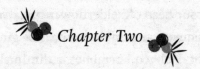

Chapter Two

I LOVE THE twenty-minute walk to work. It takes me from our house on the edge of town, past the bunga-lows and retirement flats, down onto the high street, with its pound shops and cafés, then into the park, past the immaculate bowling green, the tatty bandstand, the half-arsed crazy golf. Along the footpath that edges Dingleton Water, a brook famous for its black swans. On past the amusement arcade where I had my first summer job, under the bridge that carries the trains to London, the Great Western Railway carved out of the sandstone cliffs by our hero, Isambard Kingdom Brunel, and down to the seafront with its kiosk, cockle hut and boat trips.

Next to the two-platform station stands Clatford House, a once elegant, now shabby Regency building, overlooking the beach with its red sand where, from the big sash windows, you can watch the sea in its whole spectrum of glory, from stormy grey through to spar-kling blue. On a clear day you can see the Jurassic Coast as far as Portland Bill. It's a little hazy this morning, the sun yet to burn off the sea mist, but you can smell the ozone, as my mum used to call it.

The house was built by an infamous sea captain, harbourmaster and profiteer, Thomas Clatford, who turned a blind eye to smuggling in return for a cut of the profits. This was back when Dingleton was thriving, fish were plentiful and booze tax was sky high. This was the town's heyday and Clatford House was a symbol of its wealth. At the turn of the last century, Captain Clatford's granddaughter bequeathed the house to the people of the town and it became our museum. I've been full-time assistant manager since the implosion of my marriage. Working here has pretty much saved my life, thanks to my brilliant colleagues. Brilliant, if slightly insane.

We're busy this morning. As well as the usual visitors, there's a run on the computers in the archives room out the back. Upstairs, there's the weekly course on family ancestry run by the manager, Jackie (Exhibit A of brilliant but slightly insane colleagues). Meanwhile, Carol (our part-timer and Exhibit B) is holding the fort at the desk while I am sorting the window display behind her. Across the way, in the Captain's Parlour, there's a school visit, a Year Six class from the local primary where Harry and Lauren went – and Mike, Carol and me before them.

Carol nods towards the class of ten- and eleven-year-olds who are sitting cross-legged, listening to Tish, our faithful volunteer and local historian (Exhibit C). She's telling them all about Dingleton's smuggling days of yore, hamming up a Devon accent, dressed like a pirate, complete with a stuffed parrot on her shoulder and a patch over one eye. They are slightly terrified of her. Especially the teacher.

'He's a bit of all right,' Carol says in a stage whisper, nudging me in the ribs.

'Who?' I can only see old Mr Bailey filling his carrier bag with leaflets and Trampy Kev outside on the pavement, picking up fag ends, which at least means we don't have to.

'Not Mr Bailey, you numpty. And definitely not Trampy Kev. *Him*.' She points ever so subtly at the teacher, with a stabbing motion. 'That's Mr Winter. The Silver Fox.'

'Is he new?'

'Retrained as a teacher when he hit fifty. Fancied a career change.'

'What did he used to be?'

'Some kind of do-gooder.'

'Oh, right.'

We both linger a while, checking out the Silver Fox, then while I'm balanced on a chair putting up a poster – is Hallowe'en really next month? – Carol attempts to make a spider using pipe cleaners.

'By the way,' she says. 'I saw your Mike last night down the Co-op.'

'He's not my Mike any more.'

'Maybe not, but he was proper sheepish when I accidentally ran into him. Actually more like mutton.'

'What?'

'He was wearing a hoody.'

'A hoody?' I nearly slip off the chair. 'He hates hoodies.'

'I know.' Carol shrugs like she can't understand how such a thing could happen. 'He looked like a right twonk.'

'He is a right twonk.'

'I can come up with a stronger word if you want.'

'Nothing I haven't called him.'

Carol laughs, lobs the spider at me and I scream so loudly that the class of children look across at me, petrified. However, the Silver Fox smiles. Quite a nice smile.

'It's a mid-life crisis is what it is,' Carol says for the thousandth time.

'Can we change the record? I'm fed up of talking about bloody Mike.'

'Keep your wig on.'

'Sorry, Carol. I'm missing Lauren, that's all. It's making me grumpy.'

'She'll be fine. She'll be out on the town with all

those freshers having the time of her life. You, on the other hand, are a miserable cow and need some spice in your life.'

'Thanks.'

'We should go out tonight, take your mind off.' She gives me a quick hug and it feels nice, the warmth of another human. It's been a while. 'Let's talk about Dave instead.'

'Dave who?'

'You know exactly Dave who.'

'Oh, you mean Dave-Dave?'

'Yeah, I mean Dave-Dave.'

'Do we have to talk about him? He's another twonk I'd rather forget.'

'Yeah, we do, actually.'

'Really?'

'Yes.'

This is how it always goes between Carol and me, this bickering banter; *me to you, you to me*, like a flipping Chuckle Brothers ping-pong match.

'Why do we have to talk about Dave?'

'He's called a meeting after work. Didn't Jackie tell you? We can go straight for a drink after that. I'm sure it's something or nothing. The bins or seagulls.'

I feel the need to look out the window and steady the buffs. Where Dave is concerned, it's more likely to be something rather than nothing.

Dave-Dave, aka Councillor David Barton, uncle to Miss Melanie Barton, was at school with us, Mike, Carol and me. He was in the same year, but we were in different classes as he was considered 'academic'. And, for whatever reasons, we weren't. Dave fancied himself, thought he was the mutt's nuts with his Morrissey quiff and slim hips. He was good-looking, I'll give him that, but he was also a plonker. A really self-assured good-looking plonker. It's no surprise he ended up as our local councillor, not just because politics (in the broadest and loosest and most Machiavellian sense of its meaning) ran in the family, but also because he was always a leader, always wanting to be in charge, even when he clearly wasn't the best candidate for the job, like the year he was debating captain and the Dingleton team were up against Appleton and the chosen subject was 'Blondes Are Stupid' which ended up with Carol giving Dave a black eye and being suspended for a week.

Bloody controlling show-off.

It was Dave who told me the news about Mike, almost exactly a year ago. He came in here one afternoon and asked to have a word. I assumed it was something to do with work; I was acting up that week, as Jackie was on annual leave. But he had this weird smile hovering around his lips. The lips that were the first lips I ever snogged. Leavers' disco, 1984.

I took him into the office, grudgingly made him a coffee and somehow resisted the urge to pour it over his head.

'I have some information for you, Jennifer.' He helped himself to a ginger nut and dunked it in his Nescafé. 'Shocking coffee, by the way.'

'You're welcome.'

A moment's silence while he finished his biscuit.

'What did you want to have a word about? Is it the bins? I mean, those seagulls are a right pest but we're doing our best to keep on top of the situation.'

'No, Jennifer. It's not the bins. Or the seagulls. Though if I had my way, I'd shoot every last one of the little bastards.'

'You can't. They're protected.'

'That was a joke, Jennifer.'

'Ha, ha.'

He smiled that smile and I was a schoolgirl again, the burden of virginity weighing me down, him happy to relieve me of it, a snog at the school disco turning into something far more, deluding me into thinking this was as important to him as it was for me. Until he binned me for Sharon Shaw. And I turned to Mike for consolation.

'So what did you want a word about?'

'Your husband.'

'Mike?'

'He is your husband?'

'You were at the wedding.'

'What a day that was.'

'We can't all have our reception at the Palace Hotel.'

'Indeed not.' He grimaced at the coffee, but persevered. 'Some of us have to make do with the RAFA club.'

'Mike's dad was in the RAF. He was a war hero. Your dad was a banker. And we all know what that rhymes with.'

'Spanker?'

'Ha, bloody ha.'

'Don't be like that. You know we have this "thing" between us.'

'I wish that thing would drop off.'

'Very good. I'll make a note of that.' And then he laughed. I meant to dazzle him with my cutting wit but he bloody laughed at me, a rip-roaring laugh, like I was an idiot. The bastard.

'Enough of this joshing,' he said, serious all of a sudden.

'What is it, David? Get to the point.'

'I thought it my duty to inform you of something that's cropped up. I speak with authority not only because the person in question is a relative of mine, but also as chair of directors at the Academy.'

'Just because you call it an "academy" doesn't change it from being the very same comp we went to.'

'There's great importance in a name, Jennifer. Miss Barton, for instance.'

'What about Miss Barton?'

'You know her?'

'Of course I know her. She's your niece, poor thing. We used to babysit for her, remember. Plus she's Lauren's chemistry teacher, gives her extra tuition because she says she's got potential. Which we pay for, as your academy won't.'

'You should know that Melanie is also being paid in other ways.'

'What are you talking about?'

'Your husband.'

'Mike's paying her too?'

'Not quite, though there's an exchange of sorts.'

Talking in flaming riddles as always. 'What the hell are you going on about?'

'Temper, Jennifer.'

'Well?'

'He's having an affair with her.'

'Who's having an affair with who?'

'Mike. With Melanie.'

'Don't be ridiculous.'

'I'm not being ridiculous.'

'She's far too young.'

'And?'

'She's Lauren's teacher.'

'And?'

'Mike's not like that.' I heard all these words falling out of my mouth, I acknowledged them, but even so I felt the need to sit down on my chair for a moment. 'Mike wouldn't do that.'

'Every man would do that. They'd do her anyway. Not me, obviously, she's my niece—'

'Don't be disgusting, you sexist pig. And don't judge every man by your own shoddy standards.'

'Can you honestly tell me you have a good marriage?'

'My marriage has got nothing to do with you. And anyway, what do you know about marriage?'

'Quite a lot. I've had three of them, remember.'

'And three divorces.'

'I'm very happy to advise if that's the path you choose.'

'Get out.'

'I'm going. Got a round of golf booked.'

'Of course you have.'

A year ago. He was right. I was wrong. Bloody harbinger of doom. Whatever he's got stuffed up the sleeve of his designer shirt can't be any worse than that.

ONCE WE'VE LOCKED up, we head upstairs to the meeting room. It's cramped what with all the staff gathered and Dave manspreading on his chair. I force myself to look at his double chin rather than his crotch. He's put on weight. Golf and tennis aren't keeping the pounds off. Nor are the late hours he keeps or the women he chases.

'Councillor Barton. What can we do for you?' Jackie is polite and formal; this is a work meeting and she is the manager and the council pay our wages.

'I'll get straight to the point,' he says. 'We need to close Clatford House.'

The room fills with a collective gasp and a lot of what-the-hells.

'But you can't,' Tish says. It doesn't help that she's still dressed like Captain Pugwash. 'What about the museum?'

'We'll incorporate Dingleton museum with Appleton's. They've got a state-of-the-art building, all mod cons, and it's only three miles away so we're keeping it local.' He gazes around the room, making eye contact with every one of us. We've known each other for years and yet he can look us in the face and be so blasé about our future. 'I'm sorry,' he says. 'But this place is decrepit. It's just not feasible to keep it going.'

'Clatford House is listed.' Thank goodness for Tish. She knows her stuff. 'You have to do the repairs, surely?'

'It is listed, yes. Thank you, Tish, for bringing that up.' He gives her a charming smile that I want to rip off his face. 'But we can't afford to get this place up to speed so we'll have to sell it.'

Sell Clatford House?

'There has been some interest from a national company,' he goes on, all chirpy as if he's our saviour but I know where there's a Barton, there's a cunning plan to make money. His dad was the same. And his dad before him.

'What about us?' I ask him, throwing daggers. 'Will we be incorporated into Appleton?'

'Well, Jennifer, realistically that's not going to be possible for all of you.' Here it comes. 'You'll be offered early retirement or redundancy.'

And that's when he clicks opens his briefcase and hands over the letters of mass destruction.

So Jackie, Carol, Tish and I end up down the Thirsty Bishop, sitting outside on one of the picnic benches that overlooks the green because it's a balmy evening and because Tish smokes like a 1940s starlet, constantly and glamorously. We share a bottle of Pinot that turns into two, then three, going round and round in circles, trying to get to grips with this news, not only the prospect of unemployment but also the loss of a vital part of our community. And I know David; there'll be something dodgy at the heart of the matter.

'Can I join you?' It's the Silver Fox.

'Course you can,' says Carol, a little too keenly.

'I couldn't help overhearing your conversation.'

'Oh, girls, we've got ourselves a stalker,' Carol screeches. I kick her in the shins. She shoots me a frown and shifts her bum away from me, tapping the spot on the bench between us with her scarlet acrylics. He squeezes in, careful not to spill any of his pint or brush against any stray body parts. He has dirty fingers and I find myself wondering if this is because he's a gardener in his spare time, or just a dirty bugger.

'Is it true?' he asks, conspiratorially, checking all around for spies or whatever. 'About the museum closure?'

We look at Jackie. She's our manager. It's up to her to say. She's been quiet all evening. She's not the most talkative, but she's a plodder, a dependable plodder who can step up to the mark when needed. Actually, that's a little unfair. She can be a warrior. A dependable warrior. She wasn't camped out on Greenham Common with her mum for nothing, standing up to one of the biggest superpowers in the entire history of the world.

She reaches into her bag and shows him her letter. I'm surprised, she's normally so discreet, but I can see a fire burning away inside her and I know that she will not let this lie. 'I hear you used to be a campaigner before you started teaching, Mr Winter,' she says.

He raises his eyebrow. His silver eyebrow. I think we all raise an eyebrow and prick up our ears.

'Call me Tom,' he says.

'Well, Tom?' I ask him. 'What did you campaign about? Brexit? Page Three? Boaty McBoatface?' I know I'm sounding cynical but I can't bear the thought of another man thinking he's God's gift and feeling the need to mansplain everything.

'Er, well, I've worked for Amnesty. Free Tibet. And Mind. Oh, yeah, and a stint at Battersea Dogs and Cats Home.'

He has me at dogs. I feel so completely stupid and infantile. Boaty McBoatface. My excuse is that I've had bad news. And much wine.

'What you need is a campaign,' he says. He's on the verge of saying something else but then shuts up.

Tish notices this. 'Go on, Tom. What is it?'

He checks from side to side again. 'There've been rumours,' he says quietly. 'About a certain pub chain who like to buy up historical buildings and sell cheap booze.'

We know exactly who he's talking about. They took over the Wesleyan chapel in Newton, the old cinema in Tormouth and the family Grace Brothers-type department store in Appleton where I used to buy the kids' school socks. Are we next on the list?

'They'd never get planning permission,' says Carol. 'Not in Dingleton. We're all about local pubs and indie cafés here. People won't put up with it.'

'People like cheap booze.' Tom shrugs. 'You'll have a fight on your hands.'

'We can fight, can't we, team?' Jackie is fired up.

We all are. We nod. We even give a little whoop that could be mistaken for a battle cry.

'I'm happy to help in any way I can,' Tom says. 'You don't have to give in to this. You could buy it. Get an investor.'

'What, keep the museum going?' Jackie sounds surprised, optimistic for a moment.

'Maybe. Maybe not. But you could stop it being a chain pub. Keep it independent. Keep your jobs going somehow. You might just have to come up with something unique, though. Something that will make you stand out and bring added value to the town.'

The four of us slump again. We had hope there for a while.

'What's so unique about a bunch of menopausal women?' Yes, I've said it. The M word. Out loud. The ground did not split asunder. The sky did not fall down.

'Nothing a bit of HRT can't sort out,' says Jackie.

'That's the spirit,' says the Silver Fox and the five of us bump fists like we're in an American movie, not a shabby seaside town with its best years behind it.

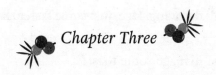

Chapter Three

I HAVE A lie-in the next morning, Saturday. No one to get up for. The word 'redundant' floats around the bedroom. My head pounds. My heart is heavy, like it's been marinated overnight in cement.

Redundant. Though there's Dad, of course. Mum used to say he was a full-time job but mostly he's self-maintaining, just needs regular feeding and an occasional reminder to put on some normal clothes when in public.

And there's Bob. I can hear the pint-sized menace barking in the garden. I contemplate putting the pillow over my head and trying for more sleep but the yapping goes on and on. I'll have to get up.

Dad is sitting at the kitchen table, drinking tea. He takes one look at me and pours me a mug, two sugars. 'I suspect you need this, Jennifer Juniper.'

Jennifer Juniper. My childhood nickname. He and Mum were Donovan fans, used to sing the song to me when I was a baby.

'Thanks, Dad.'

'You look like you've been dug up.'

'Again, thanks, Dad.'

'We're all decaying, love. Just some faster than others.'

'*Dad*.'

'Can you manage some toast?'

'Just a slice. With butter. And Marmite.'

'That bad, eh?'

I'd nod my head but it hurts too much so I muster a weak smile.

'After you've had some brekkie, and a shower, I'm taking you and Bob out.'

Bob has stopped yapping. He's still in the garden but has given up on the squirrel or whatever in order to wait patiently at the patio door, steaming up the glass with his slobbering breath.

'Really, Dad? I was hoping to spend the day in my pyjamas feeling sorry for myself.'

'Don't be daft. You're not going to waste your weekend. We've got things to do.'

Oh no. 'Things'. 'Things' means we're going foraging. It's that time of year. And whereas I usually love it, I'm not in the mood right now for scratches and rashes and I certainly can't face the usual embarrassing situation – an angry landowner, a couple having it away, me falling arse upwards into a ditch.

I don't have the energy for shenanigans.

DAD INSISTS ON driving. My car, because he doesn't have one any more. Bob perches on my lap, head out the window, ears flying, doggy heaven. It's a beautiful day, the sun is low and the sky soft blue, a cool breeze wafting down from the hills, which is where we're heading. This could mean we're in for bad weather. It can catch you out up there, but Dad reckons we'll be fine. He has a sailor's knack of forecasting though he's a total landlubber, never ventured further than the ferry to Exmouth.

We head up the Devon lanes; narrow, high-hedged lanes we know by heart, every dip and turn, lanes that horrify BMW drivers worried about scratches on the paintwork and no idea how to reverse. We park up in a small clearing and as soon as I open the door, Bob is off, that three-legged run that Jack Russells do so well, slipping under a gate and vanishing in a field of maize, no sheep for him to worry. He never goes far; we track him by the movement of the crop. And there's no point calling him back because he won't come until he's ready.

'Right then, Jennifer Juniper. Sloe time.' Dad nods at the hedge, hands me a basket, an old one of Mum's. 'Pick until you can carry no more.'

The blackthorn is awash with green leaves, hiding clusters of blue-black sloes. You used to have to wait until the first frost to get the best out of the berries, so they'd crack open, but now we pop them in the freezer overnight and the skins burst. Then we put them in Kilner jars with a load of sugar and fill to the top with Plymouth Gin. Stored in Dad's shed for three months, we have the perfect delicious dark liqueur to accompany the Christmas pud and it gets us nicely through the Queen's speech.

We work in companionable silence. Every few minutes Bob tears back to check up on us, tongue lolling, panting vigorously. You'd never know he was fourteen.

I'm glad Dad's brought me up here; the clean air and the big sky have buoyed my spirits and I've managed to forget, briefly, my absent family, my perilous job, and that sod, Councillor David Barton. This is part of our routine, our natural annual rhythm, but I miss the kids. And Mum. Though I know how lucky I am to have my dad. Even if he is from another planet.

After an hour or so we're done and my hangover has cleared. We wedge the baskets into the boot and get ready to head back home for a cuppa and stage two of the gin distilling.

'Where's Bob?'

'He won't be far,' Dad says.

We look around but can't spot him. Anywhere. I call his name. Listen. I whistle. Listen hard. There's his yap, far off. And a different bark, another dog. And a big shouty man's voice.

'Bob!' I yell as loud as I can. Listen again. Another distant Bob-woof. 'What's he up to, Dad?' I scrabble over the gate and into the field and scan the horizon. I can make out a bloke waving his arms, some way off. A tall bloke up to his midriff in maize. Hopefully not the farmer, though there's a public right of way through this field, so probably a hiker. Maybe a dog owner. Bob's harmless but his yap can make people nervous.

'Bob!'

'Over here,' the man shouts. 'Quick!'

Oh God, no, please don't let Bob be hurt. Please don't let Bob be hurting another dog. 'Bob!'

I stumble through the crop, my eye on the tall man so I don't lose sight of him, though it's tricky as the maize is up to my chest. As I get closer, his mop of hair catches the slipping sun and turns almost white. Bloody hell, no. It's the Silver Fox.

'Hi!' He's shouting at me, a booming teacher voice, not quite as friendly or comradely as last night in the Thirsty Bishop. 'This your dog?'

'Bob? A Jack Russell? Where is he?'

He points downwards, towards his hidden feet.

I'm not near enough to see anything, but it's gone all quiet. 'What's happened?' My words come out stuttered and breathless but I'm nearly there. Please let him be OK. 'Is he all right?'

'He's fighting fit,' he says, just feet away from me now so I can see his grim smile.

'He's been fighting?'

'Not exactly fighting, no...'

'What then?' I've reached them now and can see for myself what's going on. Two Jack Russells, locked together. My dog and his bitch.

'Oh, no, oh, God, no. Bob!' I go to grab his collar but the bloke – Tom – yanks me back, firm not rough, but a yank all the same.

'You'll not separate them now,' he says.

I pull my arm away, on the verge of having a proper go at him, but he's obviously trying to help and my dog is locked inside his. I know I'm blushing from the run, the cringeiness of the situation, him touching me, the Silver Fox. So I take a deep breath. 'I'm really sorry. He doesn't normally go around humping strangers. Is she on heat?'

''Fraid so,' he says. 'That's why I brought her up here. Thought it would be quiet and she'd be safe.'

'Safe? You shouldn't really let her off the lead then, should you, if you want her to be safe.' Like a mother sticking up for her child, I have to defend Bob's behaviour.

'I realize that.' He puts his hands up, a gesture of conciliation. He's softening. His battleship-blue eyes are kind and a bit crinkly, a life lived on the edge perhaps, a sort of world weariness. There's colour in his cheeks.

34

Maybe he's embarrassed too. Who wouldn't be with their pet rutting at their feet? 'Sorry I grabbed you. I didn't want you to get bitten.'

'Bitten?'

'They both seem... involved. I don't think I'd be too pleased to be interrupted. I mean, if it was you and me, we wouldn't want to be interrupted now, would we?'

'I beg your pardon?'

'Oh, no. No. I didn't mean that! I meant in general. Having sex...' He falters. 'I'll shut up now.'

'Probably for the best.' He is squirming. I am squirming. If this were Dave he'd be loving it but Tom's clearly as mortified as I am. 'What do we do then?'

'Nothing,' he says. 'We can't separate them while they're tied.'

'This is proper awkward. How long will it go on for?'

'It can last quite a while.'

'You sure I can't get Bob off her?'

'No, you really can't. You could injure them. We'll just have to wait.'

So we wait. In silence. Somehow it's hard to make small talk. But the quiet is too much and I have to say something. Anything. 'Have you done this before?'

'Er, what, watched dogs having sex? No,' he says. 'It's not my thing.' He watches me have a hot flush, takes pity. 'Growing up, we had Labs. One of them had puppies and

35

my older brother told me all about the mating part in graphic detail.'

'But they're facing different ways. How is that even possible?' I don't want to look but I can't help myself. 'Is she in pain?'

'I don't think so. She's moved her tail aside and everything.'

'I don't even know her name.'

He laughs then. 'Would that make a difference?'

I'm such an idiot. I have to laugh too. At myself. At the situation. From mortification.

'She's called Betty,' he says, more kindly, gently. He can see how embarrassed I am.

'After Betty Boop?'

'No, Betty Boothroyd.'

'Oh, that's nice,' I say. And oh, how inadequate those words are for this situation and I conjure up Betty Boothroyd with her curls and glasses and accent but then I remember where I am – in the middle of a maize field with a man I've met just the once who happens to be rather attractive. A man who has a dog like my Bob, another Jack Russell, a dog who is currently mating with him in an intimate encounter – much like tantric dog sex. I shake my head to shift the sight which I will never un-see. 'I'm Jen, by the way.' This seems important to establish as I don't think there's any sign of recognition in his eyes which are far too full of other stuff anyway.

'Tom.' He reaches out his hand.

Mine is clammy but I shake his all the same. Nice, firm grip. 'I remember.'

'You remember?' His expression is blank for a sec, then the light switches on. 'Oh, my God, the Thirsty Bishop? I'm so sorry.' His turn to redden. 'I'm hopeless with faces. I remember you now.'

'How do you cope being a teacher, not remembering faces?'

'How do you know I'm a teacher? Do you have kids at my school or something?'

'I did. A long time ago.'

He's waiting for me to answer so I put him straight, don't want him imagining I'm some kind of lunatic stalker. 'I saw you in action with your class. In the museum. Earlier in the day.'

'Oh, right.'

I clearly made a huge impression on him. Though not as huge as the impression Bob is making on Betty. They are still tied.

'I'm assistant manager there,' I bumble on. 'For the time being, at least.'

'Were you the one standing on a chair and screaming?' He raises that silver eyebrow and his eyes twinkle. They actually twinkle.

'Oh, yeah. That was me, mucking about with Carol.'

'Carol?'

37

'Carol with the... you know.' I mime an hourglass figure like I'm playing pervy charades.

'I didn't notice.' He looks away, can't meet my eye.

Of course he noticed – who wouldn't? – but I let it drop. After all, my dog is humping his bitch.

We stand there for a few more minutes, that silence again, wrapping around us. Surely it can't get any worse?

Then Dad appears, a little out of breath. 'I see there's life in the old dog yet,' he wheezes.

'*Dad!*'

'YOU'VE GOT A nice place here,' Tom says. He's sitting at our kitchen table, thanks to my father who insisted he follow us back home for a cup of tea. I'd be happy to never see him again. Not that I don't like him. I mean, he's a bit worthy, makes me feel judged somehow, though I don't reckon he means to. It's not as if I fancy him. He's not bad-looking but he's really not my type. I don't actually know what my type is. Maybe I don't have one. My choice in men hasn't exactly been the best. And right now, I can't be doing with any more hassle. What if Betty's pregnant? What if he sues me? And yet. It's quite nice seeing him here, feet under my table.

Dad gets on with sorting out the sloes, scooping them into plastic bags. 'Stay for lunch,' he says. 'We need to use up some of the frozen stuff to make room for these small balls of merriment. Do you like fish fingers?'

'I love them.'

'Fish-finger sarnies it is then.'

My heart bounces. Really, Dad? Lunch? That's just prolonging the agony. I'm going to have to stop this now. 'Shouldn't you be getting Betty to the vet, Tom? Google says you can get the morning-after pill.' I show Tom my phone.

He takes it off me, scans the information, fiddles about with it for a while, not as quickly as Lauren, but pretty deft for a middle-aged man. 'To be honest,' he says, 'this is embarrassing, but I'd rather let nature take its course.'

'Oh, right. And what if she's pregnant?'

'Betty would love puppies.' He laughs, like he can't believe he's saying such a thing, like he's going to be a grandfather. Which would make me a grandmother. Which I'm really not ready for. I don't even know if Tom's an actual father. Of human children. I don't know much about him at all and yet here he is in my house, talking about having Bob's puppies.

'What's Bob's pedigree?'

Dad laughs, unhelpfully. I flash him a look that swoops over his head and smacks against the wall.

'Well, he's never won Best of Show. He came off a farm,' I say. 'But he's a proper Jack Russell.' Here I go again, bigging up Bob.

'That's why his tail's docked?' Tom asks.

'I suppose. Farmers don't like their dogs getting their tails caught in hedgerows. When they're ratting. And stuff.' I run out of steam, feeling judged again. A woman who drinks too much, mucks about at work, mentions Boaty McBoatface and lets her dog with the docked tail ravage his bitch. But, wait a minute... 'Didn't you used to work at Battersea? Shouldn't you be against unwanted pregnancies? Shouldn't you own a rescue dog?'

'Betty *is* a rescue dog,' he says.

'Oh?'

'Not from a dogs' home. I inherited her off my Uncle Jim when he went into residential care.' He sighs, then checks himself. 'And I've always wanted puppies.'

'You have?'

'I sound like a ten-year-old girl, don't I?'

'There's nothing wrong with ten-year-old girls. I used to be one.'

'I'm surrounded by them at school, remember. Tough little buggers but they go soppy over puppies. That's all I'm saying.'

I examine him closely, his body language, his expression. He's hard to gauge. But I don't think he's a sexist pig like Dave and Mike. How can he be when he's had such a do-gooder past? 'But—'

'It's hypocritical, I know, but it would be great for the kids in my class. We could do a whole project on it. Plus

I'd love to keep one as company for Betty and you could have pick of the litter.'

Dad's faffing around, putting the finishing touches to those sarnies, a sprig of watercress and slices of beef tomato, then plonks a plate in front of each of us. It smells comforting, like childhood, the whiff of Captain BirdsEye and the tang of tartare sauce. He chooses this moment to get involved. 'Everybody loves a Jack Russell.'

Dad!

'Imagine having another little Bob running around,' he goes on, mouth full of fish finger and a trail of watercress stuck to his bottom lip.

Old Bob is now curled up in his basket, not a muscle twitching, out for the count. Betty is under the table, resting her chin on my left foot. They are ignoring each other like a married couple.

I'm wondering what else to say when my phone rings. Tom's still holding it – is he really looking at puppy pictures? – so he hands it over. 'Someone called Lolly Lol Lols for you,' he says, the twinkle intensifying. But my heart bounces again. A bad feeling. Is Lolly OK?

BACK IN THE car with a Jack Russell perched on my lap, pelting down the A38. This time it's Tom's Prius and Tom's Betty. My car wouldn't start, I couldn't get hold of

41

Mike, and Tom offered to drive me to Plymouth. I was so worried about Lauren that I said yes, please. And here we are, whizzing past Ashburton.

'Thank you so much for this.'

'No problem,' he says, all chirpy like he's trying to keep me positive.

I'm less worried now that the distance is shortening between me and Lolly. She poured her heart out down the phone; none of it made much sense as it was mostly high-pitched and snotty. I managed to confirm that she's not in a hospital bed or in a police cell or tied up in a serial killer's basement. But she is upset.

'You don't have to hang around for me. I can make my own way back on the train.'

'I'll drop you off and head into the city centre. I have some things to do. You can text to let me know if everything's OK – which I'm sure it will be – and we'll take it from there.'

Hmm. Things.

'What about Betty?'

'She'll be OK in the car for a bit,' he says.

'Why don't I take her? Lauren and I can go for a walk.'

'OK, great. If you're sure?'

'Course. It's the least I can do.' I try to convey both my humiliation and my gratitude in a smile, though it feels like a tortuous grimace. 'So... take your time. Though... don't you have someone to be getting back for?'

'Nope.' He shakes his head, a little forlornly it has to be said. 'There's just me and Betty.'

'I'd have offered for Betty to stay at ours but, well, there's Bob.'

'Really, it's fine. She likes a car journey.' He switches on the radio. Radio 2. We're of an age. 'What about you?' he asks a bit later.

'Do I like a car journey?'

'No,' he says. 'Do you have someone to be getting back for?'

'Just Dad and Bob.'

'So... what's your, um, family situation?'

My family situation. That's a new one. 'Harry, my oldest, he's in Canada on a gap year. Lauren's a fresher, as you know. And last, but certainly not least, there's Dad.'

'He lives with you?'

'Since my mum died last year.'

He gives me a sympathetic smile, understands there's no need for words. Betty takes the opportunity to lick my face. 'She likes you,' he says.

'I have no idea why after what my dog put her through.'

We manage a coy laugh between us.

'And your husband... partner... doesn't mind your dad living with you?'

'It was his idea.'

'That was generous of him.'

'It was. But he spoilt it by buggering off with Lauren's chemistry teacher two weeks later.'

'Ah.' A small word full of meaning.

'Ah, what?'

'You don't like teachers then?'

'I never said that.'

'I'm teasing. That must have been shite, though.'

'It was at the time. I was getting my life back on track. Only then we're given those redundancy letters and suddenly everything's up in the air again. And now Lauren...'

'She'll be fine. Just wants to see her mum and cadge some money.'

'You're right, I'm sure.'

TOM IS INDEED right.

I knock on Lauren's door which is already covered with stickers and Post-it notes with emojis.

'Come in,' she says, her voice wobbly.

I poke my head around the door. She's lying on the bed, wearing her fleecy Batman pyjamas, cuddling Mrs Pink. This isn't unusual for a Saturday afternoon but her face does look pale, her freckles almost disappearing into oblivion.

'Dad delivered Mrs Pink safe and sound then?'

'He came yesterday.'

'Yesterday? He took his time.'

'Yeah, I know, right. But he did take me to Aldi and paid for a bag of shopping. Have you brought Bob?'

I enter the room which smells of daughter. Joss sticks and patchouli. The little hippy.

'That's not Bob,' she says, as if I haven't realized this. 'What have you done with Bob?'

'He's at home, don't panic.'

Betty wags her tail round in circles like a little propeller. Lolly pats the space next to her. Betty doesn't need much persuading. Once I've let her off the lead, in less than a moment she's up on the bed, licking my girl's pale face. She takes it on the chin. And the nose. And the mouth. She doesn't care, lets Betty get on with it. Once the dog's had enough, Lolly is able to ask, 'What's going on? Why the dog swap? Are you sure Bob's all right?'

'He's tired.'

'Is he OK?'

'He's had a very busy morning.'

'Oh. Who's this then?'

'Betty.'

'Hello, Betty. Who does she belong to?'

'The bloke I got a lift off. My car wouldn't start, I couldn't get hold of your dad, and he offered.'

'A stranger?'

'Not quite a stranger. I've met him before. He's the

Year Six teacher at your old school.' I then explain how I met Tom and what's been going on at work.

'Poor you,' she says and she holds out her lanky arms for a hug, and I lean down to embrace her, a cuddle that reminds me why it's good to be a parent, which can be hard to remember at times.

'What's going on, Lolly? Why the crying?'

'I miss home.'

'Have you made any friends? Been out?'

'Yeah, I've met like loads of people. They're really nice, mostly, and we went out last night. Apparently they won't serve you snakebites any more. We stuck to Jägerbombs instead, seeing as it was two for one.'

'So basically you've got a hangover.'

'I s'pose.' She has the decency to look contrite. 'But I did feel low, I really did.'

'Right, how about we go out for something to eat? It's five o'clock. We could get pizza?'

'What about Betty?'

'There must be somewhere we can eat outside?'

'Yeah, I know a place.' She hauls herself up off the bed. 'What about your... friend?'

'Tom?'

'Tom.'

'I'll text him. See if he wants to join us?'

'He's not some weirdo, is he, Mum?'

'He's all right. Besides, we might be getting a puppy.'

'A puppy?' She squeals with delight, almost loses her balance as she struggles to insert a lithe leg into her venetian-blind jeans. I can't help smiling. She's still a child. A woman-child. And I explain how I happen to be here with Betty rather than Bob.

'Embarrassing, or what?!' she snorts. 'Naughty Bob.'

'Naughty Betty.'

Betty woofs and wags her undocked tail.

WE'RE FINISHING THE remains of our pizza, sitting al fresco at a nice place on the Barbican, the old part of Plymouth not blitzed by the Luftwaffe, Lauren smuggling crusts to Betty who is lounging on her lap, when Tom arrives loaded with bags. He texted me earlier to say he was meeting a friend and would grab a bite with them. I'm assuming it's a woman friend, a hunch, despite the firm, sad shake of the head earlier in the car, when I asked him if there was someone he had to be getting back for. Did he go shopping with her?

'I didn't have you pegged as a shopaholic.'

'Why?'

''Cause you're a Green and that.'

'I buy as ethically as I can. Good quality, as much as I can afford, and then not very often.'

'Oh,' I mutter feebly. He has an answer for everything. 'So you've eaten, then?'

47

'Yes, thanks. Thai. Very nice.'

Is it me or is he a bit dismissive, like he doesn't want to go into detail, some kind of secret? Which he's perfectly entitled to. I hardly know him. We're practically strangers, not that I'd tell Lauren that or she'd be back to worrying about her poor old mother's safety.

'It looks like Betty's eaten too.' He removes a stray pizza crumb from her doggy head. She's clearly not as pro as Bob; he'd never let a pizza crumb, any crumb, go awry.

'Whoops, yeah, sorry about that,' Lauren giggles. 'I couldn't resist those eyes.'

'It's not easy,' he says, chuckling. He's actually chuckling. 'I'm Tom, by the way.'

'I'm Lauren,' she says, best behaviour, reassuring to know she can step up to the mark and be polite when required. 'Thanks for driving Mum to see me.'

'No problem. So... is everything... all right?'

'Yeah, it's all good. In fact, I was just about to duck out and meet some friends at the union. There's a band. They sound all right.' She gives me a hug, looming over me. My Pippi Longstocking. Then she gives Betty a bigger hug, plonks a kiss on her snout. 'Love you, Mum,' she says, that easy way teens use those words. Life is all love and hate, up and down, crap or lush. No in between. 'Kiss Granddad and Bob for me.'

'Will do.'

She's turning to go, WhatsApping her friends, already

48

on to the next thing, when she remembers. 'Soz for dragging you down here, Mum.'

'Any time, Lolly. Except maybe not *every* weekend.'

She blows a kiss which I have to 'catch' and then she's gone, loping away from me, blonde plaits looped into buns, one on each side of her head. I watch her weave through the Saturday-evening crowds of young people, out on the town when I'm ready to be going home to my bed. Alone. No babies. No husband. Redundant.

'Shall we go?' Tom says. 'You look like you've had enough for one day.'

'You're not wrong.' I swig the last of my Chianti. 'Do you need a hand with those bags?'

'You're all right, I can manage. You could take Betty, though?'

'I'd love to take Betty. We're bezzie mates now.'

'I can see that. Mind you, she loves anyone who'll give her pizza.'

'Well, she could be eating for... How many pups in a Jack Russell litter?'

'Er, about four, I think. Though possibly as many as eight.'

'Eight?'

'Probably four.' He shrugs, hands me Betty's lead. 'Hold on tight,' he warns. 'We want to be clear who the father is.'

'Great.'

And we head off, across the quayside, past the May-flower Steps – though the steps aren't there any more – where those Pilgrim Fathers (and Mothers) left Blighty behind, and where Betty does a poop that Tom disposes of. Then we carry on, the smell of ozone in our noses, and chips, past the Mayflower Museum, yes, the museum.

Sigh.

I don't want a pub chain invading our town. A place like that would make our town more like any other town when what I love about Dingleton – what Dave is fighting against – is its character and grit. And I don't want the museum to close. And I really don't want to lose my job.

'I love my job.' I watch the words float out into the darkening evening. 'I know I'm not a doctor. Or a social worker. Or a teacher.' I nod at him, acknowledging his profession. 'But I believe what we do is important for our community. It gives us a sense of identity. We're not just any old down-at-heel seaside town with its amuse-ment arcades and caravan parks. We have a heritage the town should be proud of. We get passed over all the time down here. No decent trains. No decent jobs. But I wouldn't swap it for all the money in London.'

'Get you! Spoken like a true campaigner.'

'Ha, ha.'

'No, really. I'm being serious. You're passionate about your work, that much is clear. It must be stressful. Not knowing.'

'If there's one thing I know, it's that Councillor Barton won't let this go.'

'Does he have a history of being a bastard?'

'He comes from a long line of bastards. His father. And his grandfather. All the way back to the beginning of time.'

We're on Southside Street now. It's busy, young people on the razz, couples on dates, some straggling holidaymakers. The sun is slipping behind the chimney stack of Black Friar's distillery, home of Plymouth Gin. Betty stops for a moment to have a wee in the gutter.

'I could do with one of those.'

'A wee?'

'No! I mean a big fat G and T.'

'Come on, then,' he says. 'What are we waiting for? There's a gin bar in there.'

'But you're driving.'

'I'll have tonic, don't worry. Just let me check if it's all right to bring Betty inside.'

While he's checking – what is he doing in there? – I have time to think about how weird life is. One minute you're chugging along quite nicely and then something happens and everything changes. And you get used to that change, that new life, and then it changes again. So I feel surprised to find myself here, outside a gin distillery, holding another man's dog. A man with silver hair, a nice man, but one I can't quite fathom. Usually men are simple. You can suss them out pretty damn quick. Though I was surprised at Mike, but maybe not that surprised.

Tom's back. 'Yes, we're allowed, if she's well behaved. It's members only after seven p.m. on a Saturday but the bartender said it was OK seeing as it's still early.' He ushers me inside, upstairs, to the Refectory Bar. There's a table and a deep leather sofa and it's really nice in here. He hands over a gin menu. The Gimlet. The Pink Gin. The Marguerite. The Pennant. 'What'll you have?'

'I'm not sure. Which one's the strongest?'

He concentrates on the menu, holding it at arm's length. 'How about the Pink Gin? Plymouth Navy Strength Gin, a dash of Angostura bitters with a lemon twist.'

'If it's good enough for naval officers, it's good enough for me.'

'It's fifty-seven per cent?'

'Excellent.'

He goes to the bar while I sit with Betty by my feet, conked out now. I feel like having a sneaky rummage through his shopping bags but that would be too much. It's probably all Oxfam and Neal's Yard.

I have a look around instead, soak up the atmosphere. It's like going back to the time of the Pilgrims, some of whom actually stayed here on their very last night before setting out on the biggest adventure of their lives, according to the leaflet. I don't suppose they drank gin, what with being Puritans.

He's back, handing me my cocktail which comes in a stemmed Martini glass with a gold rim. The drink is more orange than pink, from the bitters. I've had one of these before, mixed by Dad, so I know they're good. Dad says even people who don't like gin (incredibly, such people exist) like a Pink Gin. Something to do with chemistry. Must ask Lauren.

I take a sip. It's definitely gin. A very strong gin. But surprisingly smooth. A bit flowery. And earthy. A hint of liquorice. Or is it fennel? Dad would know. His nose is far sharper than mine.

'Good?'

'Very good.' I chink my glass against his tonic water.

'Cheers,' we chime in unison.

The alcohol warms my insides and is calming my head. One of these is certainly enough if you want to keep your wits anywhere near you.

'Anything interesting in that leaflet?'

'Very. Who knew there was so much history connected to gin?'

'Tell me,' he says.

So I tell him what I've discovered. That this used to be a monastery and the monks distilled gin, believing juniper to prevent the plague. That they use Dartmoor water which is soft and clear and makes Plymouth Gin one of the smoothest in the world. That the botanicals include coriander seed, orange and lemon peels, green cardamom, angelica root and orris root, which has a hint of violet and is a natural preservative.

He's leaning in, listening intently as I read to him, until I start to get self-conscious and wonder if I'm going on too much.

'Am I going on too much?'

'Not at all. It makes a change to be read to.' He smiles at me. He has an overlapping front tooth with a tiny chip which makes him seem the teensiest bit vulnerable and raises all these questions in my head. What lurks in his past? Why is he single? Is he single? Does he have kids? What music does he like? Does he have any hobbies? Any skeletons in the cupboard? Disgusting habits?

I must be squiffy. I'm staring at him like a demented lush. Back to gin.

'I wish there was a place like this in Dingleton. I mean, our pubs are great, the Thirsty Bishop will always be my local, but this is lovely. And this gin is blooming gorgeous.'

'As good as your dad's?'

'Almost.' I take the last sip, savour it, swallow it. 'I suppose we should be getting back.'

'I think so. It's been a long day.'

'It really has. I'm just popping to the loo.'

Going to the ladies gives me a chance to take a breather. I'm feeling light-headed and although I'm trying to ignore the full-length mirror, I can see I'm flushed, and unfortunately not in a pretty way, but in a menopausal, boozy way. I splash some cold water on my face which makes my mascara run so I have to do a quick repair job. What I really need is a good night's sleep but such a thing has been harder to achieve of late.

Tom is waiting for me by the entrance with Betty and his bags. 'So,' he says. 'I bought you something.' He's grinning like a shy schoolboy who's done his good deed for the day but who's not entirely sure if he's done the right thing.

'Did you?'

'Thought you needed cheering up.' He hands over three tickets. For the distillery tour. 'Next Saturday. Half past two. You can bring Lauren. And your dad.'

'Really? That's so sweet of you. Thanks.' I am now blushing violently so it's a huge relief to get outside into the cool evening, to be walking, quickly, to the car park. Better still once we're obscured in the dark interior of his Prius.

And on the journey home, I'm most definitely going to do some digging. I need to excavate his family situation. Not for any other reason than that we might be having puppies. Some people might not think it any of my business but I reckon I really ought to know.

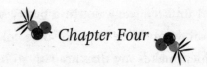

Chapter Four

SUNDAY IS A quiet one and the first day of October. I almost miss the vibrations of drum and bass from Lauren's room and can't muster the energy to make Sunday lunch for just Dad and me. We make do with potato-and-leek soup and a cheese-and-pickle sandwich. Dad eats his in the shed where he's busy reading a magazine article and making notes. He's in one of his thinking moods and is best left alone when he's like this. I have mine at the kitchen table, Bob on my feet, where yesterday it was Betty.

A lot has happened in the last forty-eight hours. I've had my job possibly taken away from me. The town is losing a museum. I've had a run-in with my nemesis. I've visited my daughter in her new environment. And I've met a bloke who doesn't appal me. Actually, a bloke with a sad story.

'So what's your family situation?' I asked him last night as we made our way back to Dingleton.

'Do you mean why am I single?'

'Not just that, no. But yes. Also, I mean, do you have children?'

'I was married,' he said.

And I thought, ah, just another middle-aged divorced man. Two a penny in Dingleton. Two a penny anywhere.

I looked across at him. His eyes were focused on the road. It was dark by then and still a fair amount of traffic. 'Go on, let's have it.' I tried to encourage him, a bit jokey because he knew all about me and maybe we were in the same boat.

'My wife got cancer and she died three years ago.'

'Oh.' What an idiot. What a great big, fat, silly idiot. 'I'm so sorry.' Thoughts flashed by so quickly, I could hardly grasp them, like catching a dream once you've opened your eyes. 'I hope I didn't come across as flippant?'

There was a small gap where he didn't reply which made my heart thud. I'd put my foot in it. And I should've known better, being well enough acquainted with loss to understand that it's different for everyone and I shouldn't transfer my situation on to his. Sometimes I should keep my trap shut.

'No, it's fine, don't worry. Well, it's not fine. It's shit. But I try not to milk the whole widower thing. People fuss and feel sorry for me. It happened. It was horrible. But I can't change it. I loved her. Still love her. But I'm trying to live my life now.'

'Is that what the new career's about?'

'Partly, yes.'

'That's great. I mean, it's a great job. A vocation. Those kids need some decent male role models. In this town you're usually a Dave Barton or a Mike.'

He laughed. There he was telling me about his dead wife and I somehow made him laugh which was, depending on which way you look at it, either good or wildly inappropriate. This was about him, not me.

'Tell me about her?' I asked tentatively, not being nosy for once, actually, simply wanting to share a moment.

'OK,' he said and I heard his intake of breath. 'We met in Africa. Sierra Leone. She was a doctor for Médecins Sans Frontières. We lived in France for a bit. Then London. She was always here, there and everywhere. We didn't live in each other's pockets. But when we were together it was magical. We learnt to make the most of every moment. And when she got sick, we did the same. One of the last things she said to me, apart from *Don't forget to put out the recycling*, was *Live your life for me too*. So that's what I try to do. But a bit half-heartedly.'

'And you never had children?'

'They wouldn't have fitted in with our nomadic lifestyle. Only I wish now we had. Then I'd have something to remind me of her.'

'That's so sad.' I wanted to touch him but had enough sense to realize that a reassuring pat was probably not a good idea, despite the niceness of those thighs.

'You wouldn't be feeling sorry for me now, would you?'

'No, definitely not. Well, maybe a bit. I know the pain of losing someone, what with Mum going last year. And I suppose you could say that very soon after that I lost a marriage. But I can't imagine losing the love of your life.'

'So Mike wasn't the love of your life?'

'No. He wasn't. I've never actually had one of those, to be honest. Not like my mum and dad. It's the marriage I'm grieving over, not the husband. It's the life I thought I had.'

We didn't say much after that because by this time we'd reached the end of my road and the street lights were brighter and we were both swamped with a sudden onset of shyness that put the kibosh on any more intimate conversation.

And now, while I'm contemplating yesterday, I'm wishing I'd said something different. I'm wishing it hadn't been all about me, when he was telling me about him. I wish I'd said something wise and uplifting. But all I have to hand is Facebook platitudes and they're not good enough, are they, though maybe better than nothing.

I finish the soup and sandwich then grab my coat and gloves, all the while forcing myself to be mindful of small wonders, but I'm snapped out of any chance of

Buddhist practices when there's a knock on the door. A jaunty knock so I know it's Carol. Dad, shooting out of nowhere, reaches the door before me and lets her in, shows her into the kitchen, the perfect host for once, concentrating on the job at hand and making her tea. He has a soft spot for Carol. Been like a father figure to her ever since her dad absconded to Dundee in 1978.

'You going somewhere, Jen?'

'I was about to take Bob out for a walk.'

'Don't let me stop you, I'll stay and keep your dad company.' She settles herself in a chair and delves into her handbag for her sweeteners. 'Is that all right, Reggie?'

'Absolutely,' says Dad. 'I'll show you around my shed after you've had your tea.'

'Is that like showing me your etchings?'

'I haven't done an etching in my life. I can show you my collection of *New Scientist* magazines if you like.'

'Is it big, your collection?'

'Extensive. I've kept every issue since 1956.'

'I'll leave you to it then,' I say.

'We'll be fine, won't we, Reggie?' she says. And I love her for taking care of my dad as if he were her own.

'We will indeed be fine,' he says. 'I can tell you all about monkeys, Carol. Did you know they can see faces in inanimate objects?'

'What, like seeing Jesus in a piece of toast?'

'Exactly.'

She winks at me.

He's in safe hands. Time to go.

THERE'S A LOVELY warm breeze, our friendly south-westerly, so Bob and I walk up to the woods where he can go off the lead and I can clear the cobwebs. It's proper autumn now, a softening light, the wind whistling through the treetops, leaves turning, falling, spinning down, and nuts underfoot. The smell of woodsmoke and the subtle mustiness of decay. A stray, lucky pheasant honks a warning as Bob hurtles past its vantage point on top of a hedge. Then into the woods. Bob is loving life, sniffing and peeing and generally hyper-excited. Mike and I used to bring the kids up here all the time. It was our go-to cheap day out. A walk in the woods and a picnic at the top with views over the River Exe, the cathedral blinking in the sun on the horizon.

Now it's just me and Bob.

Which is fine.

Completely fine.

I whistle for Bob and he comes belting towards me, little legs galloping, ears pushed back, regaling south Devon with his high-pitched doggy yap when I put on his lead. He winches me back down the hill, showing no sign whatsoever of his age, which is ninety-eight in human years and older than my father, who has more than twenty years on him. But my father is not young. Every day he is getting older, as we all are, and I worry about him. I know how much he misses Mum. Because so do I.

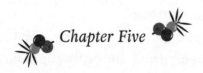

Chapter Five

MONDAY MORNING. A pewter sky with ominously leaden clouds, a whipped-up wind and the smell of rain to come. The walk to work is not as pleasant as usual, not with the prospect of what lies ahead. By the time I reach the park, it's drizzling. School kids are running, old biddies donning their plastic bonnets, Trampy Kev using the *Dingleton Gazette* as an ineffective brolly. This is now technically rain so I get a jog on. By the time I reach Clatford House I'm drenched and the last person I need to see is Dave who's standing under the shelter of the veranda, shoulders hunched against the weather. Smoking.

'Morning, Jennifer. A bit wet and breathless, are we?'

'Put that fag out. It stinks.'

He does as he's told, which is a first.

'I thought you'd given up.'

'Given up?'

'The cancer sticks.'

'I'm a social smoker.'

'Even when you're on your own?'

'But I'm not on my own, am I, Jennifer. You're here now. Do you want one?'

I'm tempted, but I'm not going down that road. It ends up with me drunk and getting up to no good where Dave Barton's concerned. 'No, thank you.'

He ushers me in through the front door as if he owns the place. That's him all over. Thinks he owns the town.

'Can I help you?' I stand next to him inside the entrance, dripping onto the floor.

'I'm here to see your boss,' he says.

'Do you have an appointment?'

'We both know Jackie will see me.'

'I'll go and check.'

'Don't bother, Jennifer. I'm sure you have work to do. You open at nine, don't you?' He checks his watch. 'It's five to.' And with that he strides past me and climbs up the magnificent old rickety staircase to Jackie's office. I want to follow him. I want to rugby tackle him, rip his trousers off and hoist them onto the flagpole at half-mast. Only he'd take that as a come-on so I'll make a coffee instead. And have a moan with Carol.

'He's a tosser,' she says, consoling.

'I know. But he's up to something. We need to be one step ahead.'

'We have to find out what he's up to before we can do that.' She takes a good look at me. 'You're soaked. Go and get changed. There's bound to be something in lost property.'

She's right. I'm feeling chilly now. So I have a rummage in the lost property bin in the staff room. Nothing I'd be seen dead in. In fact, it smells like death. There's nothing for it. I put on Tish's pirate blouse which is actually more Adam Ant than Captain Pugwash so I reckon I might just get away with it.

By the time I'm ready and back with Carol who gives me a once-over and says, 'Stand and deliver,' here come Jackie and Dave. A quick meeting. The expression on Jackie's face tells me she's none too happy.

'You look swashbuckling, Jennifer,' he says before slickly letting himself back outside into the spitting bastard rain. I watch him offer Trampy Kev a fag which he declines. I want to kiss Kev but I know better. I'll buy him a pasty and a cuppa later on.

Meanwhile, Jackie, in warrior mode, shuts the front door a little fiercely, flips the 'Open' sign to 'Closed'. It's only nine fifteen.

'What's up?' Carol asks.

'Emergency meeting,' she says.

Carol and I troop after Jackie into the library, the smartest room in the house, the only one to have been refurbished. Like the Captain's Parlour next door, it has large dimensions and a high ceiling. Plus it's big enough to accommodate a full-size snooker table with space to spare. Not that there is a snooker table. But there's a wonderful collection of leather-bound books on curious subjects with titles such as *Exotic Animals in England*, *Horse Medicine* and *How to Mix Drinks and Serve Them*. It's been done up in keeping with its Regency beginnings but with a modern twist. Farrow & Ball paint and a few Cath Kidston cushions on the window seat. The sea is busy doing its thing out there, bubbling with white-tipped waves. My stomach is doing its thing too, bubbling with nausea. What on earth is going on?

'We're closed,' Jackie says. 'As of now. The building is dangerous and a public liability.' She wipes at one of her eyes. 'Hay fever,' she says. In October.

'We can't just close,' says Carol, her voice reaching a pitch I didn't think possible. 'We've got a school visit this afternoon. And the memory café tomorrow.'

Carol's right. We're more than a fusty museum. We're a hub for the town. We can't just close. 'What's so dangerous about the building?'

'The plaster is falling off in chunks. The roof tiles are dodgy. Some of the windowpanes are loose. With winter on its way, something could fall off and flatten someone.' She sighs a wobbly sigh. 'Shall I go on? There's quite a list.' She hands round the letter that Dave dumped on her.

Bloody Dave with his smug face, his overbearing presence, his interfering ways, his need to control. Well, he's got a fight on his hands.

THE RAIN HAS cleared by the time we leave the museum and head our separate ways, with a plan to meet down the Thirsty Bishop this evening for a confab.

I spot Trampy Kev lurking outside the bakery so I dive in and buy him a steak-and-onion pasty and a cuppa. He nods in thanks and wanders off towards the bandstand, swearing enthusiastically at an over-zealous seagull.

The sun might be shining but it's doing nothing to cheer me up. I can't believe this is actually happening. Maybe I should talk to Tom? He might have some ideas. But after last night, I don't want him thinking I'm after him, the handsome widower with the nice thighs. Because he is handsome and he does have nice thighs.

I'm almost at the front door before I notice Mike's van in the driveway. Has he forgotten he doesn't live here any more? And bugger, now the tears are gathering and threatening to fall.

I let myself in quietly, hoping Mike's in the shed with Dad so I can creep upstairs unnoticed and have a lie-down. Maybe run a bath. Maybe have a gin and tonic in the bath. For elevenses.

'Jen.'

Damn. I've only got one foot on the bottom stair and Mike's appeared in the hallway.

'Hi, Jen. You look, er, nice.'

'What, this old thing?' I'm still wearing the ruffly blouse.

'It's sort of Lady Di,' he says, mesmerized by my flounces. 'You OK? Have you been crying?'

'Course not.' I can't let him see me cry. I will not.

'Jen, come here.'

I should go upstairs and run that bath and pour that gin but I don't. I follow him meekly to the kitchen, let him sit me down at the table, and I watch him make me a cup of tea, just how I like it, almost like the old days. But those days have gone, quite gone, ever since he decided he'd rather make cups of tea for Melanie.

'Here you go,' Mike says. 'Tell me what's happened.'

And suddenly, against my will and better judgement, he's my husband again, for a moment, and it's easy to open my mouth and let the words tumble out into the space that used to be filled with the noise of our children, clamouring for food, whining about homework, arguing about who got the last Rolo. I tell him about how I miss Mum. And Harry. And Lolly. I'm about to say that I even miss him, Mike, but I don't know if that's actually true. After all, it's not really Mike I miss. It's the family unit, the roast dinners and the lawnmowing. So

I tell him about Dave and the work situation and how I was getting on with my life but now it's been bloody scuppered. And I tell him my dog, who was *our* dog, has probably got another dog pregnant and there could be puppies galore and Dad isn't getting any younger. And nor am I. And I'm pretty sure I've hit the menopause and I'll have to get some HRT which is supposed to hold back the wrinkles and give you energy and stop the flushes.

And he listens and he listens and he lets me pour out everything, nearly everything, without interruption, and then he says it. 'Let me come home.'

This is followed by a silence which holds so many possibilities. So many opportunities. So many regrets. So much bitterness and angst and bloodiness.

'No. No, Mike, no.'

I have to get outside. I can't breathe. He wants to come home. He still thinks of this place as his home. I leave him there at the table and escape to the shed in search of some sanity.

DAD IS LYING on the floor of the shed, doing yoga whilst talking to Bob.

'Ah, Jennifer Juniper. There you are. Mike is skulking around somewhere.'

'I know. I saw him.'

'He wanted to talk to you about something.'

'Did he tell you what it was?'

'Did you know that the longest-living cells in the body are brain cells which can live an entire lifetime?'

'Yes, Dad, I knew that. Did he tell you?'

'Did you know that the only letter not on the Periodic Table is the letter "J"?'

'No, I wasn't aware of that.'

'Did you know that Hawaii is moving towards Japan four inches every year?'

'*Dad.*'

'Sorry, love. What did you say?'

'Can you get up a minute? Have a sit-down. You'll get aches and pains lying down there in the draught.' I hold out my hand and help him to his feet. He flops into the depths of his ancient and tatty armchair with an old-man moan, then hunts for his glasses. I point to his head.

'Let's have it then,' he says.

I sit down in the deckchair. A small pause for dramatic effect and then I say it. 'Mike wants to move back in.'

'Oh, that,' he says. 'Yes, he told me.'

'He told you?'

'I said you were highly unlikely to let that happen. I thought he'd gone home in a huff.'

'No, he's still here.' Which is weird now I think of it. He knows I work Mondays. Was he going to wait all day for me to get back? What was he going to do with himself? Cook a meal? Help himself to the contents of my fridge? Use my loo?

'He wasn't funny with you?' Dad asks.

'Funny?'

'Shirty?'

'No,' I say. 'He wasn't funny or shirty or even shitty. Actually, I thought he was going to cry. Or beg. And then that made me realize something.'

'What was that, love?'

'Just how much I don't want him back.'

'Ah.' Dad hunts in his pocket and produces a Werther's Original. Offers it to me. I might be forty-nine but that doesn't mean I'm ready for one of those, thank you very much. I shake my head. Dad pops it into his mouth, sucks for a bit, then thinks of something, checks his watch. The one that has all the time zones, and temperatures, and latest football scores. 'Why are you back so early?'

I tell him about the museum closure and he says not to worry, it won't happen. It'll be a mix-up. There's no way one councillor can have that much influence.

'Unless he's crooked,' he says as an afterthought.

'We're talking about Dave Barton here.'

'Oh,' he says. 'Yes. Well, in that case, have a word with that Tom fella.'

'I suppose. I'm meeting the girls tonight at the Bishop. I could text him and see if he'll come along.' I let out a massive drawn-out sigh. Bob pricks up his ears, leaps onto my lap and licks my chin. 'I'm going for a bath.'

'Take a sloe gin with you.' Dad winks. 'There's still a drop left.'

'Thanks, Dad.' I lean down to give his forehead a peck and take the bottle from the table next to his chair. The level has depleted somewhat. I'm turning to go when he stops me.

'Did you know that there are sixty-two thousand miles of blood vessels in the human body?' he says. 'Laid end to end they would circle the earth two and a half times.'

'Funnily enough, Dad, I didn't know that.'

'Jennifer,' he says, back in the room. 'Never forget that we human beings and this world we inhabit, well, it's all remarkable.'

'Yes, Dad. In the words of David Coleman, "quite remarkable".'

'That's my girl.'

I give him a look.

'Woman,' he corrects himself. 'Woman.'

TOM'S ALREADY THERE when I arrive at the pub, sitting in a nook next to Carol who's wearing one of those gypsy off-the-shoulder blouses that gives her the look of a serving wench from a Dickensian tavern. Which is ungracious of me. Since her divorce a few years back, she's regressed to her teenage years, which were also my teenage years, and not a good thing. But maybe it's better second time around. Though I very much doubt it. Your problems just get bigger.

Jackie's at the bar but she clocks me as I come in, flushed from the walk. 'What're you having?'

'G and T please, Jackie. Lots of ice.'

'Right you are. Sit yourself down.'

I do as I'm told and sit in the space opposite Tom seeing as Jackie has already taken up the other half of the pew with her briefcase and fleece and a stack of papers. I pick up a handful of them and waft myself as it's so flipping hot in here.

The mood is sombre.

'Here you go.' Jackie plonks a tray of booze on the table and we help ourselves, each of us taking a slug without bothering with the usual niceties of 'Cheers'. The familiar, comforting taste, the lovely shock of ice, the slice of lemon are just what the doctor ordered though I can't help but compare it to the cocktail I had in Plymouth. The Pink Gin. If they sold them here, I'd have one. I'd buy a whole round. But I'm not sure June the barmaid is up to mixing anything fancy. They don't even serve diet Schweppes. At least I've got the distillery tour to look forward to this Saturday, with Dad and Lauren. I might try one of the other cocktails.

Jackie's gathering her papers like a newsreader and on the verge of launching into organized default mode when Tish falls through the door in a blur of colour and Shakespearean expletives. 'That earth-vexing step gets me every time.' People smile and say hello. Everyone knows Tish. We've been so lucky to have her as a volunteer. All that knowledge and passion, her way of sharing it with the kids and the olds and everyone in between. What a waste. We can't lose her.

She spots us and hurries over. 'Sorry I'm late. I had a run-in with Edgar over a mouse.'

Carol explains to Tom that Edgar is Tish's cat.

'I did wonder,' he says.

'I got you a pint of ale, Tish,' Jackie says. 'That OK?'

'Splendid.' Tish beams and squeezes herself in next to me. She's wearing a hot-pink floaty dress and her long curly hair is piled on her head, tendrils and tufts hanging down artistically. A sea-glass pendant on a silver chain hangs delicately around her elegant neck. The glass changes in the light from green to blue and then back to green. She always wears interesting stuff, has a sense of flair and design that she cherry-picks from history. This one is from the twenties, flapper style. I'd look like a drag queen if I tried it. I'm happier in jeans. But why am I thinking about clothes? I need to be present. In the here and now.

'I can't believe this is happening,' Tish says when

Jackie's given her the low-down. 'I mean, I know the building needs work, quite a lot of work, but he can't just close us down and sell it. It was bequeathed to the town.'

'Actually, it was sold,' Jackie says. 'For a pound. So it does belong to the council, legally, if not morally.'

'Plague sores,' Tish says.

Jackie goes on, giving us the bad news, all of it in one go as if it will be easier to swallow. But it's making me want to spit. Right into Dave Barton's smug, fat face. I can't believe I ever let him kiss me, let alone sleep with me. I can't believe I ever liked the smarmy bastard, that I wasted all those teenage tears over him.

'We need a campaign to fight this,' Tom says. I like how he says 'we', like he's become a part of us without even trying, and we all listen, not because he's a bloke, but because he's someone new to the town, an incomer who appreciates what we do and who has half a notion of how to help. 'Do you have a contact at the *Gazette*?'

'They love us,' Carol says. 'They're always covering events.'

'OK, that's good,' Tom says. 'So maybe divide up the jobs? One of you talk to the *Gazette*. One of you speak to the council. One of you set up the social media. A Facebook page, a Twitter account, etc.'

But what if we can't stop it? What if the sale goes ahead? What will happen to the museum? To those school trips and the memory café and Trampy Kev?

These questions fizz about my head, and no doubt are crashing around the heads of all of us round this table, but no one speaks them out loud. They can't be said. Because they can't be true.

We have to fight this. And we do this now by talking. Fighting talk. After another pint or two we are still talking when Carol stops Tish who's in mid-flow.

'Someone to see you, Jen,' she says.

'Oh?' I can't see anyone. Though there's a nudge on my knee. A slobbering head against my thigh. 'Bob?' Dad must have brought him out for a walk and thought he'd pop in but there's no sign of him. And Bob's not on the lead. And now he's barking. And barking. 'Bob?'

Tom notices the panic on my face because he's up and out of the pew, disentangling himself from Carol, saying, *Let's find Reggie, he'll be around somewhere.* So we leave our drinks, Tom and I, with quick goodbyes and reassurances and a plan to meet up again tomorrow, and we go in search of Dad. But he's nowhere to be seen. Nowhere.

WE EVENTUALLY FIND him at home. In the shed. On the floor. Only it's not a yoga position I recognize and he's not talking to the dog because the dog left him to fetch us. Because the dog is now licking his face and whimpering.

'Dad?'

76

'Sorry, love. I can't seem to get myself up. I must've tripped.'

'You had a fall?'

'No. A trip.'

'Are you OK?'

I'm a bit flappy but Tom's got it. Those years married to a doctor have rubbed off. He's asking Dad all the right questions and checking him over, his pulse, his vision, hunting for signs of broken bones. Concussion. A stroke. A heart attack. Oh, God, no. A heart attack?

'Has he had a heart attack?' I don't mean to shout this quite so loudly.

'No, he hasn't,' Dad says, quite cheerfully like this is a game.

Tom makes a point of looking directly at Dad and speaking to him, not me. 'No heart attack but I think you might have damaged your hip.'

'It's been dodgy for a while.'

'How long?'

'Since 1967. A yoga retreat in the foothills of the Himalayas. I overdid it. Jen's mum was a hard-core fanatic. I was trying to keep up with her. No, hang on. I think it was in Crediton.'

'Crediton?'

'In one of the rooms at the Lamb Inn. I was trying to keep up with her there, too.'

'*Dad.*'

77

'I see there's life in the old dog yet,' Tom says.

Dad laughs but winces in pain so we decide after all it's best to phone for an ambulance.

AFTER A LONG night in Torbay Hospital, the X-ray shows it's not a break or a fracture, just a deep bruise. Though it's enough for me to realize that Dad is actually quite vulnerable so I persuade him to get a medical-alert alarm thing seeing as he's on his own in the shed so much. And a mobile phone.

Yet again Tom's been a huge help, driving me in his car so we could follow the ambulance, keeping me company and topping me up with tea. By the time we're back, it's gone midnight, but we're all hungry so I make us bacon butties, then Tom helps Dad up to bed.

Maybe it's time for Dad to sleep downstairs. We could turn the study into a bedroom. Thank God it wasn't a heart attack or something life-threatening. I couldn't bear to be without him, however frustrating he might be. He's my rock. Without him, I'd be sinking. And though I don't want to think about it, can barely imagine it, I know he won't be around for ever.

I have to make the most of him. And learn the art of floating.

'You all right?' Tom asks, job accomplished. 'You look done in.'

'I'm shattered. Thanks so much for your help. You're making a habit of this.'

'If we're going to be related...'

'Related?'

'The puppies?'

'Oh, the puppies, yeah, of course. When will you know if Betty's up the duff?'

'In a couple of weeks, I think.'

'That soon?'

'They have a short gestation – eight to nine weeks.'

'Blimey, that's quick. Longer than any of Lauren's boyfriends have lasted.'

He laughs, then comes over a bit serious so I wonder what's on his mind.

'Look,' he says. 'Do you want to come round for dinner one night? I mean, we could talk about the museum. I could help you do the social media—'

'Yes, please,' I answer a little too keenly, kick-starting a blush.

'Great.' He smiles, tries to disguise a yawn. 'Friday night suit you?'

'Sounds good. What about the Thirsty Bishop tomorrow?' I check my watch. 'Well, tonight, actually. Can you make that?'

'I'm not sure.' He hesitates, avoids eye contact. 'I might have something on. Text me if I can do anything in the meantime.' And he gives me a sort of pat on the shoulder and stumbles over the doorstep on his way out to the car.

I lock up, switch off the lights, head upstairs with Bob at my heels. 'Time for bed, Bob.'

He doesn't respond. He's a dog. But he's by my side as always, leaping onto the duvet and falling asleep before I've even got into my PJs. Just me and the dog. Which is usually fine though sometimes I wish for a human body to cuddle up to. Only not when I'm having one of these horrendous hot flushes. Must make an appointment to see the doctor.

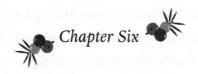

Chapter Six

IT'S 8.30 A.M. and I steel myself to phone the health centre, prepared to beg for an emergency appointment to see one of the women doctors.

'Is this really an emergency?' the receptionist asks once she's demanded to know what I need an appointment for. 'We're already chock-a with sick people.'

'I *am* a sick person. If I don't get help I am likely to murder half the town and injure the other half.'

'Right,' she says. 'In that case I can fit you in at eleven-forty.'

While I'm waiting with coughing children and anxious mothers, I attempt to engage with an ancient magazine full of celebrities who have been completely forgotten about. I have time to think about our conversation last night in the Thirsty Bishop and wonder what was so important that Tom would miss it. Which is ridiculous. He doesn't owe us anything. We can manage without him. Only it's nice to have his experience on hand. And his enthusiasm. It's got nothing to do with his eyes. Or deep voice. Or nice legs. Or caring manner. Or strong sense of justice. Nothing whatsoever.

Tish did make a suggestion during last night's pow-wow, though. Which we all pooh-poohed as it seemed so unlikely and quite frankly impossible. And which I can't stop fantasizing about now. She'd found out from her estate-agent other half, Miranda, that Clatford House is up for auction with a guide price of £1 million.

'How about we raise the funds to buy it?' Tish asked overly casually like she was suggesting a whip-round for a colleague's birthday.

'One million pounds?' spluttered Carol. 'Are you having a laugh?'

'I most certainly am not having a laugh. I have some savings. When I was made redundant from the museum in London, I invested it and it's probably worth a hundred grand or so. Miranda is bound to have a nest egg. And surely the three of you could raise some cash?'

We three – Carol, Jackie and me – looked at each other. I kept quiet knowing that 50p from down the back of the sofa was probably all I could muster.

'I could sell some clothes on eBay?' Carol offered. 'I've got some lovely designer stuff in my wardrobe.'

We ignored that, what with Carol's lovely designer stuff being knock-off and worth no more than £12.50.

'What about your dad?' Tish aimed this question at

me. 'He used to be a scientist. Surely he's got something stashed under the mattress?'

'He worked for the government, so no, I don't think he's got much in the way of savings.'

Tish maintained the Paddington stare into my eyes, trying to fathom if I was hiding anything from her. No way she'd let this go without exhausting all of her ideas. 'What about the house he sold?'

'I can't ask him that.'

'No. Sorry, Jen. Of course you can't. Can you? No.' She slugged back her ale, rebooted her thoughts. 'Who else do we know with money going spare?'

'In this town?' Carol sounded very cynical. And realistic, to be perfectly honest. Dingleton's not a rich-second-home-owner-yellow-welly-brigade kind of place.

'Hmm.' Tish shook her head and more curls escaped her Liberty headband, dressed as she was like an Aubrey Beardsley illustration. 'OK,' she said. 'It's a long shot but we could start fundraising.'

'The auction's in a month,' Jackie reminded us. 'And what if they get an offer beforehand?'

We turned to Jackie who until this point had been very quietly sipping her lime and soda. 'I've got fifty thousand pounds in premium bonds,' she stated. 'And another fifty left by my mother in 1994 in an offshore savings account.'

A moment's silence.

'Let slip the dogs of war.' Tish's earrings fluttered and her bracelets jangled in excitement.

'It's a heck of a lot of money to raise.' Jackie was calm but channelling that determination gained from camping out in the cold, wet mud for weeks on end outside the US army base when she could've been down the youth-club disco with the rest of us, drinking Malibu and acquiring love bites. 'It's not only the purchase we have to consider, but the renovation too. Also, how exactly are we planning to make an income from it? There's nothing to be made from museums. A small entrance fee and a few keyrings won't do it. We need to live.'

And that's when the seed of an idea took root in my brain, though at that point it was barely formed and slippery as a mackerel, and not at all a sensible idea, if it was even an idea at all. 'We'll have to think outside the box,' I told them. 'Diversify. What can we offer that's unique to this area?'

The three of them stared, expecting me to give them an answer, a suggestion, anything, but I had nothing to offer. Not last night. Not today. Maybe soon.

'Jennifer?'

Now I'm back in the waiting room of the health centre with its screechy babies and worn-out carers. The receptionist is clocking me, sideways, warily, probably to see if I have a dagger about my person. I scuttle along the corridor to Dr Morris.

I slump in the chair by her desk and am hopeful she might understand as she has a kind face, surrounded by messy grey hair and stress lines on her forehead. There's a plethora of photographs of teenagers on her desk. Teenagers. I tell her everything. The flushes, the night sweats, the broken sleep, the snappiness, the dry skin. The feeling that I'm not quite myself. She quizzes me on my home life, my work life, my sex life and I give her the briefest of rundowns, making light of my losses, that way we do when we're asked straight out, the British way, and also because I'm pretty sure she's mentally ticking the boxes of the mental-health questionnaire that she's about to slip out from her drawer and wave in my face.

'I'm not depressed. I'm menopausal.'

'Right.' She sounds doubtful. 'When did you have your last period?'

'In 2010 when I had a hysterectomy.'

'Ah, yes, let me see.' She scrolls through my notes. 'And they left your ovaries?'

'They did,' I confirm.

She's quiet, reading and sighing, so I ask her, because my mum always used to say, *If you don't ask, you don't get*, 'What do you think about HRT? Wasn't there some scare?'

'Have you been googling?'

'A bit,' I admit, feeling as guilty and ashamed as if I've been on Tinder.

'Well, then, Jennifer, you'll probably have noticed that opinion is divided.' Dr Morris goes on to say if I asked ten doctors for their opinion on HRT, I would get ten different answers. When I tell her I'm feeling vengeful and violent she decides it best to prescribe it. 'Let's see how you go on a low dose and then we'll take it from there.' She rushes me out of the room and I head straight to the chemist's and swallow a pill as soon as I get home, washing it down with the last of the sloe gin before I have time to think about potential side-effects, knowing that I'd sooner have twenty good years than thirty-plus rubbish ones. Besides, I could get run over by a tractor tomorrow.

I am armed with HRT and ready for battle.

AFTERNOON AND I'VE not achieved much other than acquiring some fake hormones that might or might not improve my quality of life. I can't help but think it's jamming a finger in the dam while Rome burns which I know is mashing my metaphors and historical periods and geographical locations, but my brain's too fogged up to think coherently. But one thing is clear: I love this town. I mean, it's not perfect, it can be a proper pain in the bum, and sometimes I wish I didn't live in a place where everyone knows everyone's business. Where your next-door neighbour's sister-in-law didn't used to bully you at school or your first love didn't have the power to scupper things for you thirty years on. But it's my home.

'Councillor Barton will see you now.' One of the minions, the receptionist at the family construction company, ushers me into his father's office, taken over by Dave since the old man's retirement a few years ago.

He's sitting behind a desk the size of Lincolnshire. Clean, neat and polished to a shine. And the desk.

'Come in. Have a seat, why don't you.'

I've already sat myself down and dumped a pile of papers on his big-boy desk. 'Why do you insist on being called Councillor when you're at work? Surely you're plain old Mister here?'

'I assumed you'd be here on council business, Jennifer.'

'You assumed right, *Dave.*'

He smirks his Dave smirk and I know he'll avoid the discussion I want, as his mind is elsewhere, or he's at least trying to give me that impression. 'Remember when this was Dad's desk?'

I decide vagueness is the best option. 'Was it?'

'Surely you remember, Jennifer? I know it's thirty-plus years ago, but pretty unforgettable, I'd say. We snuck in and you—'

'Don't. Even.' I put up my hands to cover my ears in

a gesture of despair and horror. It's bad enough it happened — I don't need to dwell on it all these years later.

'Honestly, Jennifer, was it actually that bad?'

'You were that bad. You dumped me when someone with a bigger bra came along.'

'I was sixteen years old. It wasn't like we were going to get married.'

'As if I would have married you.'

'My parents would never have approved of the daughter of two eccentric hippies.'

'My parents were the best parents.'

'Yes, Jennifer, I'm sure they were.'

He is doing his damnedest to wind me up and I am like a coiled spring, rusty and likely to give him tetanus. But I can do this. I can tell him what I think about the plans, I can even beg if need be, but I am not going to get upset about a crappy boyfriend from the distant past. 'So what's going on, Dave? Why are you encouraging this sale to a chain that will jeopardize the local pubs and the indie cafés? What good will it do Dingleton? And what about the museum?'

'Firstly, Jennifer, don't get irate.' He does this ridiculous in-and-out breathing exercise to emphasize the fact that he thinks I am getting hysterical and out of control when I am actually simply angry. 'It will be an asset to the town. A meeting place full of countless opportunities.'

'For cheap drinking?'

'For family brunches, Sunday lunches. Where else can you get a meal for a family of five so cheaply round here? Quite frankly, I think you're being a snob.'

'That's outrageous! You're forgetting all the clubs and events we run for the community. All the outreach. It's free.'

'That's also the problem, Jennifer. And my second point. The museum's not bringing in money.'

'It's not supposed to bring in money.'

'In this economic climate, it has to earn its keep.'

He's got an answer for everything.

Think, Jennifer, think.

'All right then. What if we were to bring in more money?'

'You, Jackie, Tish and Carol bring in more money?' he says, astonishment on his big fat gorilla face. 'I hardly think that's likely, do you?'

'It could be.'

'How?' He sighs like I'm a schoolchild and he's the head teacher waiting for me to account for my actions. The bastard. 'Jackie's friends and supporters are penniless crusties. Carol is still living off the legacy of being Dingleton Carnival Queen 1983. And you, Jennifer, are wasted there. Cut your losses. I'll make sure you get a job in the new place. Customer services. That's what you're good at.' He thumps his desk to emphasize his point.

And that's when I lose it, that control I've been clinging on to. The tears start to fall. Which takes him aback. He's never seen me cry. No one ever sees me cry. Because if I have to cry, I make sure I'm hidden away on my own, preferably under my duvet with the curtains shutting out the light, and no audience to witness it. Except for Bob. He knows when I'm upset. He follows me upstairs and lies next to me on the bed, under the duvet, cuddled into the small of my back until he gets too hot and I have to drag him out. He did this every night for six weeks after Mike left. Dave fumbles in his pocket and produces a handkerchief. I shake my head. I don't want his snot rag anywhere near my face. I use my sleeve instead.

After a gigantic sniff, I draw my dignity around me and say very calmly, and slightly too quietly so he has to lean forward to hear, 'This isn't over. In fact, it's just beginning.'

Whatever 'it' is.

Only now the mother of all hot flushes decides to strike me down and I have to leave quickly, embracing the cool outside air as if it were a long-lost friend. Or my children. Or my mother.

I BUMP INTO Tish in the Co-op on the way home, after a brisk walk on the beach and a hundred pebbles chucked into the sea. I've cooled down on the outside but not inside. She can see me taking it out on a bag of spuds and intervenes.

'Someone needs a tonic.'

'As long as it has gin in it.'

'Come on, then. Quick visit to the Bishop.'

I leave the potatoes. I leave all the shopping in my sad basket. The Fray Bentos steak-and-onion pie, the tinned carrots, the Baxter's cock-a-leekie soup. Dad will have to make do with fish and chips from the Chipping Forecast that I'll pick up on the way home. Tish meanwhile has paid for her and Miranda's supper ingredients – Arborio rice, asparagus, parmesan – before frogmarching me to the pub and plonking me down at a corner table. It's quiet as it isn't even four thirty yet. Only the diehard regulars are here. Eileen from the bookie's, George the postie and Trampy Kev who's coddling a half of ale in his usual spot by the gents. He raises his half-glass to me in a kind of salute and I manage a smile. I realize that I'm actually quite fond of him and wonder what his story is, if he's happy. He's always whistling to himself, always doffs his hat, opens doors and uses a hanky (filthy, admittedly) when he sneezes. Do you need money to be happy? Do we always need more than we have? When is enough *enough*?

'Right.' Tish presses a large G and T into my hand. 'Let's have it.'

So I give it to her. The complete low-down of my meeting with Councillor Bastard.

She makes all the right noises and says all the right things including, 'Let's fight to the last gasp,' and somehow I feel a teensy bit better. I'm not alone. I have good friends. Clever friends. Determined, strong and tough friends. I know I'm going to need them. We're going to need each other.

'Right then,' she says. 'I've spoken to Miranda and she's all in. She'll do whatever it takes to help us buy Clatford House.'

'That's fantastic.'

'We can do this.'

'Can we?'

'In the words of the best POTUS, "Yes, we can."'

Later, as I'm walking home clutching a warm parcel of fish and chips, I hope Dad is hungry because I've lost my appetite. Maybe it's the HRT. Or maybe it's the realization that we face a seemingly impossible task. But I won't let a few truant hormones or an uphill slog put me off. Oh, no.

Chapter Seven

IT's FRIDAY EVENING and I've had a bath, washed and dried my hair and changed three times, from jeans to a dress and back to jeans. I've put on lipstick but taken it off again because it made my mouth look old and wrinkly. I found some lip balm in Lauren's room and now all I can taste is cherry so I brush my teeth again and my gums start to bleed.

This is going so well.

I don't know why I'm behaving as though this is a date. I've never been on a date. When I was last single, nearly thirty years ago, you didn't go on dates. Americans went on dates like in *Happy Days* or *Mork and Mindy*. We Dingleton teens just used to 'go out' with each other. This involved a walk along the sea wall followed by a cone of chips and topped off with a fumble under the pier, if you were lucky, or unlucky, depending on who you were with. Anyway, this isn't a date. It's a meeting. Just the two of us. Tom and me.

I check on Dad before I leave. He's in the shed, wobbling on the top rung of his paint-splattered wooden stepladder, searching for a book.

'*Dad*. Get down off there. Have you learnt nothing?'

He wields a tatty old book in triumph as if he's proved a point though I'm not really sure what that point is. 'I'm always learning, Jennifer,' he says. 'That's why I was searching for this and now I've found it. *The Art of Distillation* by John French. It's the earliest book on distillation.'

'How old?' As if this is the question I should be asking now with him so perilously high.

'1651.'

'Right.'

'Distillation is basically alchemy, Jennifer Juniper.'

'OK, Dad, get down now, please, and you can tell me all about it.' I feel like I'm negotiating with a man about to jump to his death rather than one who might just fall to it but at any rate, he does as he's told, obedient for once, handing over the book before descending the half-rotten rungs. Once his feet are on terra firma, balanced and less precarious, I get cross with him.

'What were you doing?'

'I want to experiment with my gin this autumn. I might try something different.' He beams at me, as if he's been waiting a very long time for this eureka moment.

And the book in my hand does feel special, like there's a little magic in it, old and scruffy, not a first edition, obviously, but a vintage one. Like something from *Harry Potter*, a compendium of spells.

'It does look interesting, Dad, I'll give you that.'

'Don't go thinking you can borrow it until I've read it.'

'I can wait.'

'So you do want to read it?'

'I think so.'

'Fancy yourself as a master distiller?'

'I don't know about that.'

'Read the book and then you might know.'

'I thought I had to wait till you'd finished it.'

'All right, Jen. Don't get maudlin on me. You can borrow it over the weekend.'

'Thanks, Dad. Now, please come in the house and put your feet up. I'm off out, remember, and I'll worry if you're not inside. Safely in a chair. Not up a stepladder.'

'I'm not an invalid. I'm simply getting old. Which is no reason for my brain to seize up.'

'I entirely agree, but you can loosen your brain sitting down. Borrow my iPad and do some googling. You know how much you like to google.'

'I do like to google. On a Friday night.'

'Come on, then.'

'You're keen all of a sudden. Do you fancy this Tom? He's a nice enough chap.'

'I reckon he is, yes. But this is just dinner and I want to run some stuff past him.'

'Right.' Dad dismisses thoughts about romantic feelings and moves on to the next. Dogs. 'Ask Tom if Betty's knocked up.'

'I might phrase it more delicately than that.'

Dad shrugs.

I leave him in the sitting room, feet up, resting that hip, iPad and book on his lap, dog nestled against him, his brain-box head bubbling over with thoughts of alchemy, turning base spirits into the perfect gin. Abracadabra.

It's dead easy to find Tom's cottage up on Coast Guards Row because I know exactly where it is. I've passed it enough times over the course of my life. The Row is a terrace of six or seven old fishermen's cottages, some gentrified, others a bit drab, all different colours: yellow, blue, cream, Devon pink. It's a no-through road to cars but there's a steep, narrow lane at the end, just beyond Tom's cottage, wiggling down to the coastal path, and eventually to the beach. When I was a kid, an old trawlerman lived here. He'd sit outside on a bench, mending his nets, singing sea shanties, like he was fresh off *Poldark*. Then, after he'd died, it was rented out for years, summer lets, winter lets, till it got dilapidated and was sold at auction. Tom bought it for a bargain price, which is lucky when you're a teacher and single and have never been on the housing market because of moving around. Though maybe he has money, from his poor wife.

Tom has his work cut out. The small sash windows need attention, stripping right back to the grain – that's if they're not already too far gone with rot. The roof's crying out for repairs. There're weeds growing in the gutters and a constant drip from an overflow pipe. The exterior, which might once upon a time have been crisp white, requires a good sand-down and repainting. But he's installed a new front door, painted a glossy teal colour. And a shiny brass anchor for a door knocker. I give it a firm rat-a-tat-tat.

'Sorry about the mess,' he says, once he's welcomed me inside, into the hallway, standing there before me with a tea towel over one shoulder, a picture of domestication. A rather attractive picture.

I hand over a bottle of wine. 'Didn't know if you like red or white so I went for white because I don't like red as it gives me a headache, not that that should be a prerequisite for gifts, after all, it's a gift and I'm not expecting you to share it with me, though I won't say no if you do.'

'Thanks very much,' he says. 'I like red and white and that's very kind of you and of course I'll share it.' He has a huge grin on his face. Either he's extremely relaxed about all this or he's already made a head start on the booze, whereas I'm clearly a blathering wreck.

I take a look around me, to avoid eye contact and divert attention from my burning cheeks. 'You've been busy.'

The hall has been stripped of its wallpaper. A naked light bulb hangs forlornly from the wood-chipped ceiling, swinging in the draught. The floorboards are bare and stained with years of old paint and grime.

'It's a wreck, I know,' he says. 'It needs boarding out and skimming. The old lath-and-plaster was held together with Anaglypta and once I started peeling... well, you can see for yourself.' He shrugs. 'I always knew it would be a project. I never expected it to be this bad, though. Once you start stripping back, you never know what you'll find.'

'Isn't that the truth?'

Tom does a double-take, is about to say something, but changes his mind, leads me to the kitchen.

He's made an effort in here, I'll give him that. It's tidy and clean and there's a table set for two overlooking a small courtyard with fairy lights. Yes, fairy lights.

Once we've eaten the shepherd's pie he's cooked up, and shared a bottle of Sauvignon, I tell him about the idea to raise funds to buy the museum. He doesn't dismiss it. He doesn't laugh in my face. Instead, he fires up his laptop and, between us, we set up a Facebook page and a Twitter account. '*Save our Museum: Bring Dingleton's Past into the Future.*' We explain what the council want to do, and what we want to do. And that we need to raise £1.5 million. At least a million for the purchase and another half million for renovations. Which is ridiculous when you see it written down in black and white and posted all over social media. Ridiculous and overwhelming and I almost feel like giving up.

'We've not even begun and we've already got three hundred and fifty thousand, just from spreading the word locally.' Tom notices the way I've slumped, my head in my hands. 'We can do this,' he says.

'How?'

'We need more investors.'

'Why would anyone want to invest?'

'Apart from the good old-fashioned philanthropists?'

'Apart from them.'

'There'll be people who want to invest as a business opportunity. To get a share of the profits.'

'The profits of what?'

'Well, yes, there is that.'

We're both quiet for a while.

Then he carries on. 'This is no criticism but...'

Whenever you hear these words you know you're about to be savaged so I get myself into defensive mode. 'But?'

'The museum could be better. I went to Somerset recently, stayed with a friend. She took me to Taunton

Museum, a much bigger outfit in a county town, granted, but it's free entry and it is incredible. We could learn something from it. Our museum needs to reflect the local environment, not just hoard a collection of random old stuff.'

'Is that how you see Dingleton Museum?'

'Er, yes. No offence.'

'None taken, well, not much. I know you're right. There is a lot of stuff that's only tenuously connected to Dingleton.'

'Stuff people have donated over the years when they've been clearing out the loft?'

'Yeah. And it's really interesting, all that social history. How people lived in Dingleton.'

'But some of it is too general. It could be about anywhere in Devon or any semi-rural town. I mean, Appleton have done something special with their heritage centre. They've made the most out of the *Carry On* film shot on location there. In fact, they've milked it for all it's worth. Saucy postcards, seaside kitsch, the lot. But their main focus is on fishing. The fishermen who went to Newfoundland for cod. The women who hauled massive nets of fish up the beach. What's Dingleton got to offer – other than the obvious?'

'The obvious?'

'The amusement arcade and antisocial behaviour.'

'Excuse me?' I feel suddenly protective of my

town. I am allowed to be disparaging, but not a bloody incomer. 'It's a beautiful place with natural features. The red cliffs, the red sand. The rough sea. It's surrounded by Devon's rolling hills and country lanes. And it might have seen better days but people have always had to eke out a living here.'

'And?'

'There's Brunel's railway.'

'Yes. And?'

'Smugglers. And pirates.'

'Yes.'

'And the King who used to come on his holidays here?'

'Right. Trains, illicit booze, royalty. This is what the focus should be.'

'Yes. You're right. That makes sense. But how will we make money?'

'A café?'

'There are so many cafés in town. I'm not sure Dingleton could sustain another one.'

'Vegetarian? Vegan?'

'People don't really go in for that down here.'

'What about a bar? Not a pub or a chain but a cocktail bar?'

'In Dingleton? Are you serious?'

'Why not?'

'Because cocktails are too pricey for our town. Way too pricey. Plus we'd need a licence.'

'A licence shouldn't be a problem. Not if Dave's considering a pub.'

'But he'll do his damnedest to scupper any plans we have.'

'True. OK. Well, let's have another think about what type of joint we want.'

We have a think.

'Somewhere a bit different,' I tell him, more certain now, a plan forming. 'A place women can go and feel safe. Somewhere for a special occasion or for a pre-meal drink. Parties. Celebrations.'

'Now you're talking,' he says.

'Somewhere people will travel to, like a destination. But also somewhere you can drop in on a whim. Somewhere smart but also casual. Friendly. Inclusive.'

'I like it,' he says. 'I like it a lot.'

And what I'm thinking is, I like you. I like you a lot. And just when I'm also thinking I might want to kiss him, I remember this friend he went to stay with in Taunton and tell myself not to be so bloody stupid.

Fortunately Betty saves my dignity by leaping onto my lap and we then of course move on to the subject of puppies. If life was just about puppies, we'd all be happy. We'd never go home alone, teary, like an old teenager who's learnt nothing in life.

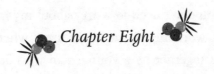

Chapter Eight

DAD, LAUREN AND I are there in good time the next afternoon. Our tour starts at two thirty and we have ten minutes or so to mooch around while we're waiting. It's lovely to see her. She seems to have grown even taller though I know that's not possible. I even check to see if she's wearing heels but they're the same old boots. She witters away about her friends, her tutors, the course, the nightlife, while I ask questions without daring to make suggestions. But Dad remains quiet. He's not unhappy, just in a contemplative mood. You can almost hear the mechanism of his vast brain whirring with inspiration. It worries me sometimes. That he will come up with yet another completely bonkers idea and I'll have to talk him out of it. Like the time he applied to go on *Dragon's Den* with his Marmite chewing gum that would give you your B12 intake for the day.

'Dad? You OK? Is it your hip?'

'Is what my hip?'

'Dad, the hip you bruised. Remember?'

'Oh, I'll live.' He dismisses this concern. 'After all, I could have a rare incurable renal disease for all we know so you don't need to worry about my hip.'

I'm just worrying about his kidneys when the tour is gathered together by a young man who doesn't look old enough to even drink alcohol let alone be an expert on it. But to give him his due, once he starts telling us about the story of gin, about the origins of the Plymouth Distillery, we are hooked. He is really amenable and funny and full of surprising knowledge and we can't help but listen to every single word he utters. He then escorts us into the important room, a vast room that houses the huge Victorian copper still where the distilling takes place. He explains the process. How they start with a 96-per-cent-alcohol grain spirit before adding the juniper and other botanicals, then the Dartmoor water. After the still is turned on and reaches boiling point, the gin turns into vapour and rises up and into the swan neck, then floats down into the condenser. Once it cools, the gin returns to liquid, but now it's far less potent, at 41.2-per-cent proof. Unless it's the Navy Strength in which case it's a whopping 57 per cent, but I suppose if you were at sea for months at a time you'd be in need of a daily stiff one.

Dad's eyes are wide open in wonder; he's taking in every detail for future reference. 'I know someone who had an old copper pot still,' he says. 'I've been meaning to ask her if she's still got it.'

'Who's that, Dad?'

'Old Woman Bates up at Donker Farm.'

'The lady with one tooth?'

'That's her. Used to come into Newton Abbot market and sell her home brews till she got banned. They were lethal. I seem to remember she made her own gin too, back in the eighties, when it was all vodka and Beaujolais and only certain people still drank mother's ruin.'

'Who?'

'Oh, the establishment. The armed forces. Bank managers. The country set. Your mother.'

'But she was a hippy.'

'She was, bless her. But she was also partial to a gin and tonic. She'd visit Old Woman Bates every so often and have a snifter with her. In fact, I've got a feeling she gave your mum some recipes. They must be at home somewhere. Haven't seen them since I moved.'

'We should have a hunt for them.'

'Should we? You fancy having a go at this gin lark? It's not easy, you know.'

'Nothing's easy, Dad.'

'True enough. Even breathing can be tricky. If you've got emphysema or you're drowning.'

'Indeed. Where's Lauren?'

Lauren is talking to the young tour guide, who's actually older than I thought, a graduate from Heriot-Watt, the only university in the UK to offer a degree in brewing and distilling. She's quizzing him on the chemistry side of things, stuff that's beyond me. Forget the art of distillation, I didn't realize how much science goes into gin.

But there's something else nagging me. That seed of an idea I've been wanting to grasp all week, but am too scared to reach out for. Only, before I get the chance to summon it up, this elusive idea, here she is, my daughter, striding towards me, a fired-up gleam in her eye, that intensity she had when she was ten years old and saw a chemistry set in an Argos catalogue and promoted it to the top of her Christmas list. Test tubes, goggles, funnels, pipettes. These became her favourite things. More treasured than her Barbies ever were. More exciting than gymnastics or playing the piano would ever be. Only Mrs Pink has ever been more precious.

'Mum,' she exclaims. 'I know what you should do.'

I don't think she's about to suggest a trip to Topshop. No.

Lauren is grabbing hold of my idea and running with it, gripped tightly in both hands, before I've even had the chance to speak a word.

'You need to open a micro-distillery and start making Dingleton Gin,' she says, breathless with enthusiasm.

'I do?'

'Yes, Mother. And don't stress. I'm going to help you.'

A STIFF ONE is needed and that's exactly what we get in the bar. Lauren, Dad and I cosy up on one of those sofas with our complimentary G and Ts – delicious, divine, delightful – and I can't help but remember being here just a week ago, Tom leaning in, listening intently as I read to him, his smile, the overlapping front tooth with its tiny chip, Betty flopped in a post-coital glow by my feet, and Tom producing these tour tickets. Then the car journey home which passed by in a flash while he told me about his wife, me desperate to touch him which thankfully I didn't, because it wouldn't have been appropriate plus now I'm wondering if maybe he has moved on a bit, what with this woman 'friend' in Somerset.

But why am I having these thoughts now? My daughter has a proposition that could change a lot of lives. Not save them, like Tom's Claire used to. Nothing heroic or dangerous or charitable. But, nevertheless, a prospect that could be a way forward for my friends and my town.

Right then. No more pondering, or grasping, or resisting. 'Cocktail, anyone?'

The dynamic duo nod in sync.

I'm on my feet, ready for action. 'Choose your weapon.'

Dad goes for a Gimlet, Lauren a Little Pink Flower, and I choose a Sloe Gin and Prosecco.

Oh, my giddy aunt, it's good. Very good. One of these and I'll be squiffy. Yippee-doo-dah, thank goodness for Isambard's railway line.

MY HEAD IS buzzing and I can hardly remember the train journey home with Dad. He's quiet, drifting in and out of sleep while I go over and over the conversation we had with Lauren and this dude who took a shine to her. Who is taking her out tomorrow. Who is enthusiastic about the 'Ginaissance'.

'All you have to do is keep your gin juniper-based and give it a certain alcoholic content and then you can be as creative as you want.' His words buzz round my head. Juniper. Alcohol. Creativity.

And Lauren summed it up. 'You should make handcrafted gin in small batches using hand-picked botanicals from Devon hedgerows and seashore.'

This was where Dad's eyes sparked like the sky on Bonfire Night. This was indeed a forager's dream. 'Heather, gorse, elder, honeysuckle, rosehips, crab apples, nettles, blackberries, sloes.' He whispered the words like an incantation. 'Samphire, bladderwrack, sugar kelp, sea pinks.'

'I'm not an imbecile, of course I remember. But that's not really distilling gin, is it? That's just adding a few berries to shop-bought gin.'

'Exactly,' Dad agrees.

'You want to do it from scratch?' She's put down her sandwich and is surveying Dad as if he's a young snip of a thing, which he is in comparison to her.

'Yes,' he says. 'I mean, we'd buy in the grain spirit but then we'd distil it with our own junipers – not sure where we'll source them yet – and add our own botanicals.'

'There was a time you could've picked your own junipers up on the moors. Now you're looking at Italy or India.'

'I was thinking Macedonia or Croatia.'

'That's also true. *Juniperus Communis*?'

'Or *Juniperus Oxycedrus*.'

'You've thought this through.' She takes a bite of her sarney, chews for some time with that one tooth of hers. There's silence in the kitchen apart from the ticking of the school clock on the wall above the Aga. And the sound of her mastication. After a final slurp of coffee she asks, 'How can I help you?'

I'm not entirely sure what Dad is about to ask her though I have a fair idea.

'You gave my wife some gin recipes.'

'Did I now?' She makes out like she's trying to

remember when my guess is she knows exactly what she did or did not give my mother. She's teasing Dad, making him work for whatever it is he wants.

'I wondered if we could use them, if I can find them.'

'If you can find them, you can use them.' She pauses while we wait for the catch. 'As long as I get a bottle off each batch you make.'

'Of course,' Dad says.

'Anything else?' she asks.

'Well, yes, there is one thing.'

'And what might that be?'

'The copper still.'

'Ah,' she says, as if she wasn't expecting this when clearly she was. 'You're after my copper still?'

'Yes, I am. We are.' And he goes on to explain the hoo-ha over the museum, our recently hatched plan.

'That Councillor Barton's a nasty piece of work,' she says. 'You can have the still. It's out in the barn somewhere. Not been used in years. You'd better fetch it before my grandson sees it, though. He doesn't know it's there but once he's got a sniff he'll be wanting to do his own distilling and you'll have competition on your hands. I'll get Luke, the farmhand, to help you shift it.' And she produces an iPhone from her apron pocket and texts like Lauren.

Five minutes later a scruffy man comes in the front door, wearing muddy wellies and an Exeter City beanie hat. I'm expecting it to be Luke, the farmhand, but it's somebody else. Trampy Kev?

'Hello, Ma.' He takes off his boots on the doormat and walks over in his woolly socks to drop a kiss amongst his ma's halo of fuzzy grey curls.

'I'm glad to see 'ee, Kevin,' she says. 'These good people here need a hand and when you've done that, you can have a bath and I'll make you something to eat.'

WE'RE IN THE barn watching Luke uncover the copper still which has been hiding under a hairy blanket and a significant number of cobwebs, tucked away in a forgotten corner behind tortuous-looking farm machinery laid to rest in some kind of junk graveyard. Farmers never get rid of anything, however rusted or tarnished. Every object can have a second, third or fourth use.

'You little beauty.' Dad rubs his hand over the belly of the still. 'Let's get her outside where we can take a proper look.'

Between us, Luke, Kev, Dad and me, we carry the still and its accompanying pipes and tubes, heaving and puffing, out into the daylight. We lay the pieces down and stand in a circle around the collection of seemingly random bits, some of which don't even look like copper.

'It's covered in that green stuff, Dad.'

'Patina,' he confirms. 'It protects the copper.'

'Course,' I say. 'Like Truro Cathedral.'

'And the Statue of Liberty.'

'And the Planetarium.'

Kev and Luke look from one to the other of us in what might be confusion. I'm about to say something to Kev, to acknowledge him, that I see him all the time, that I bought him a pasty and a cuppa, that he's Mrs Bates's son and I never knew, when the woman herself dodders over and, leaning on her stick, lets out a deep sigh that must completely empty her tiny lungs. 'Her 'as a name, you know.'

'Who?' Dad asks.

'The still,' she says, as if it's obvious. 'They always have names. Usually a maid's name.'

'How brilliant,' I say. 'Like a boat.'

'Just like a boat,' she agrees.

'But it carries booze, not fish,' Dad says. 'What's she called?'

'Violet,' Mrs Bates says, again as if we should know this. 'After my dear old mother who I was named for.'

'Charming,' Dad says. 'A proper Devon name.'

'Dingleton was famous for its violets,' she muses. 'Before the war, all the farms around these parts grew 'em. Even here. Carpets of blue everywhere and a scent straight from heaven.' Her misty eyes gaze backwards to a time gone by. A time before holiday parks and wi-fi and Ant and Dec. 'I was Dingleton Violet Queen one year.'

'Like Carnival Queen?' An image of Carol as a teen busting out of her princess dress flits through my head.

'Like that, yes. There was an annual Violet Ball where I was chosen and then we led the procession through town. I wore a pretty frock made by my gran and I sat on a float that was decorated with violets. The crowds could smell us before they could see us.' She nods at Kev, her son. 'Just like some I could mention. Help shift this lot into this young lady's car and then get your bath.'

This young lady pulls down the back seats of the Polo and somehow, between us, we squeeze in Violet and her accessories. Dad and I say our thanks to Old Woman Bates and take our leave, with a promise to keep her up to date on progress. Just before I get in the driver's seat, she gives me her mobile number, written with a neat schoolgirl's hand on a scrap of paper. The back of a betting slip. 'Call me any time,' she says. 'Whatever time I've got left, you're welcome to it.' Then, as an afterthought, 'Your mum was a lovely lady. You must miss her.'

'I do, Mrs Bates. Very much.'

'I won't lie and say you'll get over it. I still miss my dear ma. But the loss'll ease.' Her eyes are kind and mine well up. 'How's your father?'

I look at my father, who's talking to a hen.

'He's all right. He misses her too.'

'Well, them was married a long time.'

'Nearly fifty years.'

'He's lucky to have you, my lover,' she says. 'Not every child can manage to live with a parent.'

I know she means Kev. It must be hard for her to watch him live the life he does, dipping in and out, neither here nor there.

She pats my cheek with her tiny hand and makes her way back across the farmyard, skirting the milk churns and plastic crates, stopping to share a few words with my father before disappearing indoors.

Dad opens the gate for me once again to drive through, then forces it shut behind him. We bump off back down the track, the car lower than before with its new cargo on board. At the middle of one of the larger puddles, the car slows and I rev the engine, really rev it, Dad telling me to put my pedal to the metal but this doesn't help. We're stuck in the mud in the middle of nowhere with a massive copper still called Violet for company.

'I'll get out and push,' he says.

'No, you won't. I will.'

Dad doesn't object. We both get out and assess the situation. He makes the noise that mechanics and plumbers make when they evaluate a job. A sort of whistle-sigh that strikes fear into me. He thinks I have no chance. Well, I'll prove him wrong. I have superhuman strength when required. I indicate the driver's seat and he gets in obediently and starts up the engine. I put my shoulder to the boot and proper push with all my might. The wheels spin and the engine cuts out.

But help is at hand. Here come Kev and Luke. Kev hands me a bottle of his mother's gin. 'Ma wanted you to have this. Don't drink it on an empty stomach.'

I thank him profusely and pop it in the boot and then, without saying a word, the two men position themselves one on each side of me and, on my count of three, we push. Within moments, the car is out and free and Dad is off with a whoop and a yee-hah. I think he might've forgotten about me and it's a pig of a long walk home so I yell a thanks and leg it, squelchily, after my father.

'DAD!'

FOUR O'CLOCK AND I've showered, changed into clean clothes, and readied the tea things on the kitchen table. The kettle's filled, the pot warmed, and Dad's fruit cake sliced and arranged on one of Mum's seventies Hornsea pottery plates, the ones that could probably survive a nuclear fallout. It's silly getting sentimental over a plate but the familiar groovy pattern always transports me back to childhood, when I had nothing to worry about other than making sure I didn't miss *Grange Hill* and that I had enough Hubba Bubba to get me through the weekend.

First to arrive is Jackie, punctual as ever, which is comforting and reassuring in a life-goes-on kind of way. Next up is Tish, wearing a gauzy shift like she's Josephine Bonaparte, her wild hair tamed into a chignon. The dress is completely inappropriate for autumn except she has a fur stole around her shoulders. 'Vintage,' she says, noticing Jackie eyeing it up suspiciously. 'It doesn't count.' She sits down with a dismissive gesture of her hand as if we can completely ignore the dead fox at the table, its cold hard eye staring at Bob and making him retreat to the safety of his basket.

Then Tom turns up, clutching a bunch of carnations.

'You managed to get away from school OK?'

'I went in extra early this morning to sort out tomorrow's lessons.'

'How very organized.'

'You have to be one step ahead of that lot,' he says, pretending to wipe away the sweat from his brow. 'These are for you.'

We're in the kitchen now and he hands me the carnations, which makes me blush, especially when I see the raised-eyebrow exchange between Jackie and Tish.

'A little something to cheer you up,' he says.

'Cheer me up?' I query.

'You know, what with the museum situation.'

'Right,' I say, awkward but touched. 'Thank you.'

'*Lulled in these flowers with dances and delight.*' Tish sniffs one of the flowers, shuts her eyes dreamily.

There's a moment when we contemplate these words but then the doorbell goes again and Dad shepherds in Carol who allows him to disengage her from the snugly fitting denim jacket that she's wearing, before sitting herself down on the chair next to Tom's, which was actually supposed to be my seat but she wasn't to know that.

While I have the chance, I give the assembled guests the update on Dale and Harry. They make the right replies, not one of them in the slightest bit surprised, so I know I can summon my son and his lover and all will be good.

Once I've sat down myself, every chair around the table is taken: Jackie, Tish, Carol. Dale, Harry, Tom. Dad and me. I wonder if we should appoint a chairperson like an official meeting but I don't have to wonder for long as Jackie is setting up a PowerPoint presentation and distributing handouts. Nobody objects. In fact, everyone's relieved to dodge this onerous task, especially as we know how much Jackie thrives on it. Not that she's bossy. She's just the type of person who gets excited if she so much as steps inside a Ryman's. A stationery fetishist if ever there was one. Tish also has a notebook, leather bound and beautiful and I almost expect her to brandish a quill. But she manages with a fountain pen. The rest of us have to make do with the stack of Dad's football coupons and stolen biros arranged in one of Lauren's pencil-pot holders she made at primary school. A ragu jar papier-mâchéd with cut-out Teletubbies. I miss her. But no time for day-dreaming. Introductions are needed, then it's down to business. We have quite an agenda to work through.

1. Auction
2. Finances
3. Fundraising/grant applications
4. Setting up a co-operative
5. Social media campaign
6. AOB

TWO HOURS AFTER we have discussed points 1 to 5, having consumed three pots of tea, two packets of Hob-nobs, and a half-ton of Kettle Chips, we have a plan of action. But now that we've reached Any Other Business, and the sun is past the yardarm, I feel the need to produce the bottle of Bates's gin which miraculously survived the bumpy journey home from Donker Farm.

'I suggest we take a comfort break and then I have a proposition for you,' I tell them.

All eyes turn to me but I'm giving away nothing. Not just yet.

'Five minutes?'

They agree and there's the sound of chair legs scraping against my floor tiles. Tish pops outside with Bob for some 'fresh air'. Dad is red in the face and I suggest he removes his jumper which Carol volunteers to help him with. Dale and Harry talk to Tom about Canada. Jackie goes to the loo. I gather eight tumblers which I fill with ice, Sicilian lemonade tonic, and a shot of Old Woman Bates's magic. If nothing else persuades them, this will.

'Blistering barnacles,' Tish exclaims.

'Not bad at all.' Dale has another sip.

'That'll put hairs on your chest.' Dad hiccups.

'Proper job.' Carol gives a thumbs-up.

'Impressive.' Jackie makes notes.

'Awesome.' Harry does a fist-pump.

'Very, very, very nice.' Tom smiles the twinkliest of twinkly smiles.

ONCE THE GLASSES have been drained and I've asked them to guess what botanicals they think Mrs Bates has used – it seems Carol has a nose – I pitch my idea of us starting up a small-batch handcrafted micro-distillery and opening a gin bar in Clatford House. They look bemused for a moment, like they're wondering who I am and if the real Jennifer has been kidnapped and replaced with a clone, or possibly a clown. But when I tell them what Dad and I have discovered, about the Plymouth Distillery, and Old Woman Bates, and the wealth of knowledge we can draw on, that this isn't a mad punt, it's surprisingly easy. Especially when the wild-card Canadian chips in.

'Harry told you I'm a mixologist, right?'

Carol asks what that is.

'It's kind of like a glorified bartender, but with some differences,' Dale explains in his mild Canadian manner, carries on when he sees our expectant faces. 'A mixologist designs seasonal cocktails, makes recipes. This might mean preparing house-made syrups, tinctures, bitters, infusions, every ingredient you need behind the bar, and then the bartender would use these to make drinks for the customer, which is where his or her job begins.'

'I'm just a humble bartender,' Harry says.

'So a mixologist is like the puppet-master?' Dad asks. 'Or the man behind the curtains?'

'Kind of.' Dale considers this. 'But the roles can get blurred. I do my work behind the scenes before the bar opens, but when the customers arrive I become a bartender. Anyways, I've been training up Harry.'

I look at my son and see the admiration and love in his eyes. He's not my little lad any more.

'What Dale didn't mention,' he says, oblivious to his

mother's bleeding heart, 'is that his parents own not only the bar where we worked, but a whole chain of them across British Columbia.'

'Like a certain pub chain that Dave Barton wants to lure to the town?' Tish asks.

'Nothing like it.' Harry shakes his head. 'Dale's bars have an individual feel, so you'd never know that they were connected, other than that they're the place to get the best drink.'

'Have you always worked for your parents?' Jackie asks.

'Always. Since I was a kid when I'd help run errands. And full time since I left college.'

'What did you do at college?'

'Business studies.'

Dad beams.

'I'd be happy to help, is all I'm saying,' Dale goes on. 'In any way I can.'

And I take my chance here, listening to this man who seems to very much know where he's going in life. I need to see where Harry figures in all this. 'Are you planning on sticking around?'

'With Harry?'

I know I'm blushing and I know I'm pissing off Harry. I also realize there's a better time and place for this question but I power on through. 'I actually meant are you planning on staying for a while in the UK? Do

143

you have visas and everything? And right, OK, now you mention it, I did wonder if Harry was part of this move or whether it was something you always wanted to do?'

'*Mum.*'

Dale puts his hand on Harry's hand. 'A bit of both, I guess,' he says, a small shrug to his broad shoulders. 'It would be awesome to spend some time in the UK. My family emigrated from the West Country in the fifties so it would be nice to get to know my heritage a little.'

'You never know what you might find,' Tish says. 'There could be all sorts your family wanted to escape from.' She winks at him.

'Incest and sheep rustling?'

'So you do know it down here then?'

I ignore my father's attempt at humour and seize the day. 'Right, then. Thoughts, everyone? Is this a hare-brained idea?'

'The best ideas are hare-brained,' Carol says.

'But what about the museum?' Jackie asks. I knew she'd be concerned, being the most measured of our group, but she's also the one whose opinion I respect most, whose judgement should be listened to.

'That all comes back to Clatford House and our chances of buying it,' I go on. 'What if we could combine it all, the museum, the distillery and the bar?'

'How would we fit all that under one roof?' Jackie's brain is whirring overtime.

'I'm not talking about producing as much gin as Gordon's or Plymouth so there'd be the space in Clatford House. The distillery could be in one room. We could do tours, even. And the bar in another room. And the rest could be for the museum.'

'But there's renovations. There's no way we could do all that.'

'Maybe not at first. We could use Dad's shed for the gin to start with, couldn't we, Dad?'

He nods enthusiastically.

'So we'd concentrate on the bar for now and obviously the museum. But we'd have to make it very specific to Dingleton, concentrate on what's made the town the place it is.'

'And what is that?' Dale asks.

'Smugglers, pirates, royalty, Isambard Kingdom Brunel.'

'Who's he?' Dale asks.

'The second-greatest Briton as voted for by the public in 2002 on the Beeb,' Dad says. 'As championed by Jeremy Clarkson.'

'Who's he?'

'A rude, sexist, spoilt pig.' Carol's never been a fan of grease monkeys.

'So why did he make it to second position?' Dale's

very confused and I can see the gulf in our cultures is wider than first imagined.

'No, not Clarkson,' Dad says. 'IKB was a genius. He revolutionized public transport and modern engineering – he built railways and bridges and steamships. The world would be a different place without him. And Dingleton wouldn't even be on the map.'

'We're going a tad off piste now,' says Jackie. 'This endeavour should be far more than keeping a museum open for people to walk around and point at stuff. We've always tried to make it about the community we live in. I'm adamant that's not going to change. We need to get everyone involved, especially the ones on the edge.'

'Exactly,' Tom agrees.

'So where does the gin fit into this?' Jackie asks. 'Surely the museum is for families?'

'It'll be another string to our bow,' I tell her. 'A way to generate money, to employ locals. Something for Dingleton to be proud of.'

'Booze needn't be about getting drunk,' Dad chips in.

'Granddad's right,' says Harry. 'We can encourage a healthy attitude to drinking.' This is astonishing for a twenty-year-old, especially one who grew up in a seaside town. I have a violent urge to applaud but I've embarrassed him enough as it is. I'm just grateful he's enthusiastic about getting involved.

'Shall we have a top-up?' Dad suggests. 'After all, low

to moderate alcohol consumption can have some health benefits. It may reduce the risk of strokes, heart disease and diabetes.'

THAT EVENING, MUCH later, once the others have gone home in a daze and a fug, Tom stays on for supper, rustled up by Dad with Carol's help. Corned beef hash, Dad's signature dish, with runner beans and carrots, a working supper of comfort food while we update Facebook and Twitter to get the public behind the drive to keep the museum open.

'You should start a blog, Mum,' Harry suggests. 'The Adventures of a Menopausal Gin Lover or something.'

'Blimey, Harry. You know how to make a woman feel special. Just as well you're gay.'

'Don't worry, Jenny,' Dale says. 'He's rude to me too. Keeps reminding me how old I am.'

'Which is?' Carol puts down her fork, stares at him, waiting for an exact response, including star sign and position of moon as he was heading down his mother's birth canal.

'Thirty-two,' he says.

There's a moment's hesitation. I slug my wine in an attempt to unclench my toes.

'Age is just a number.' Carol's a fan of motivational quotes plucked off the internet.

Soon after this, we drift away from the table. Harry and Dale go for a late-evening walk to get some air. Carol goes with Dad down to the shed so he can show her Violet. That leaves Tom helping me wash up.

'You should head home,' I tell him once we're done. 'It's a school night.'

'Trying to get rid of me?'

'Not at all but I was thinking about lighting the log burner and having a nightcap.'

'I'll join you. Just for one.'

'You're not driving?'

'Nope. I like to walk as much as I can.'

'Great.' I grab two glasses and the bottle and lead the way to the front room. He lights the fire and soon there's a good heat coming out.

We sit side by side on the sofa, a gin apiece, awkward until Bob skitters in, leaping up, settling himself between us.

'So,' Tom says. 'Can I ask you something?'

'Sure...'

'It's a bit personal. I mean, you've told me some of it, but what happened between you and your ex? I know there was another person involved but they say there's usually something wrong with a relationship for that to happen.'

'Oh.'

'Don't they?'

'I suppose.'

'Sorry, I don't know why I'm asking. Forget it. It's none of my business.'

'No, no, it's fine. I haven't really thought about the reasons why. I've been too busy dealing with the fallout. Which I know isn't healthy.'

'Do you want to talk about it?'

'I'm not sure what to say really. I thought we had a happy enough marriage. Not that I ever thought explicitly about it. You just sort of get on with your life, don't you, and when kids come into the picture it's like a treadmill that you never get off. You lurch from one drama to another and all the while there's a monotonous backdrop of dirty socks and packed lunches and music practice.'

'Maybe I didn't miss out on having kids?' he teases me.

'Oh, no, don't get me wrong. I wouldn't change anything. And I'm sorry it never got to happen for you and your wife. I guess my life didn't turn out the way I planned it, like it didn't for you. We both made marriage vows and both our marriages ended. Only I'm half to blame for the break-up, if what you're saying is right. And none of it was your fault. Cancer bloody sucks.'

'Yes, it is a right old shitter.'

He fills up my glass. Then his own. We're drinking it straight and it's warm and comforting only now the room is spinning ever so slightly so I tell him I need to get some air. I also need to check up on Dad and Carol.

'I'll come with you,' he says and as we move into the hallway, Bob gets tangled up in our feet and I'm pushed against Tom, close enough so I can feel the warmth of him, and smell that man smell – not the bad one but the lovely one. I almost make a grab for him but before I do, he takes me in his arms and gives me a hug. Which is a surprise. A nice surprise. Only just as I reckon we might be about to kiss, he says he has to go.

'You do?'

'It's a school night,' he confirms. So organized. So prepared. So... annoying.

But, actually, I don't buy it. I'm not asking him to sleep over. I'm just wanting him to kiss me. Which would take two minutes of his time. But he shrugs his shoulders and says a reluctant goodnight. And I do nothing to stop him because I don't want to make a fool of myself. So I let him go.

And he does. He goes.

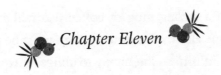

Chapter Eleven

ANOTHER THURSDAY MORNING without work, though that doesn't mean I don't have a whole bunch of stuff to do. First up is going with Tish and Jackie to the bank to see if we can raise a mortgage as, so far, we are half a million gazongers short of the guide price for Clatford House. *Halfamillion*. If I say it fast enough it doesn't sound quite so daunting though I know it really is. It really, really is. What are yokels like us doing, thinking we can buy such a huge place? How in the heck will we compete against the big guns?

Still, there's a ray of hope. Just as I'm putting on some make-up, squinting into the hall mirror, having already dressed in the smartest outfit I could cobble together, Dale asks if he can have a quick word. They've been away for a couple of days, exploring, but now they are back they want to help, he says.

'That's kind. We need all the help we can get.'

'More specifically, I want to help financially.'

'What do you mean?'

'With money,' he says.

'Ye-s... but how?'

'I've got a proposition.' He sits me down at the kitchen table with a strong mug of coffee. He makes it better than anyone else in this house which must be the North American in him so I'm happy to oblige, curious to hear what he has to say.

'You know Harry told you my parents own this chain of bars?'

'Yes. They've done very well for themselves.'

'They have. But they had some help off of my grandparents to get started, else I don't think they would have made it this far.'

'We all need a helping hand off our parents, if we're lucky enough to have them. And then we try to pass that help on to our kids.'

'Uh-huh. But it can work the other way.'

'What do you mean?'

'Look, I know I'm not your son or anything. I'm your son's boyfriend – and while we're on the subject, I know you're concerned about the age gap but I want you to know I love Harry very much and I'm never going to do anything to hurt him.'

Maybe I don't appear to be convinced because he carries on.

'I appreciate he's young. He still has his twenties to live through. It's an important decade to find yourself.

I won't do anything to hold him back. I don't want to cramp his style.'

'I wasn't aware that Harry had much style.'

'I know,' Dale says. 'He needs to chuck that Adidas jacket in the trash. Slavic chic doesn't quite work on him.' He laughs, understanding that my poor attempt at humour is my way of saying I appreciate his words and sentiments and knowing that if he reciprocates, then we have an agreement. We both want the best for Harry.

I check my watch. I don't have much time but this is important and I don't want to scupper my chances of finding out as much as I can about Dale and Harry. Though I can't help but think that every decade you live through is important in finding yourself. I mean, look how lost I've become. But this gentle man seems to have it sussed.

'Harry aside,' Dale goes on. 'I've been talking to my parents.'

'Oh?'

'They're always expanding their portfolio in the hospitality industry, and they want to invest in your project.'

'Excuse me?'

'They want to invest a considerable amount in your venture to enable you to purchase the property. They'd be back-seat investors, wouldn't get involved in the nitty gritty, but they'd be there for support and expertise when required.'

'Wait. What?'

'I appreciate this is short notice but, well, what do you reckon?'

'What do I reckon?' I sip the coffee, feel the buzz of it in my brain. 'Why would they want to invest in a mad enterprise, in an uncertain Britain, with four crazy ladies?'

'For those very reasons.'

I can't help myself then. I get up and I hug him and tell him he's a miracle. A big whopping bloody miracle.

So it transpires that Dale's parents are willing and able to commit half a million pounds to this project. That means we have the guide price amount but no certainty of a purchase as we will no doubt have at least one competing bidder, otherwise known as Bastard Barton. I ask Jackie, Tish and Carol to meet me at the jetty, pronto, despite the blusteriness of the day. They turn up, wrapped against the wind, and I shepherd them halfway along the concrete wall and then we are able to look back at the town. The place we know inside out and yet it always surprises me when I see it from this perspective. This is how the smugglers would have approached Dingleton. Captain Clatford would've been watching from his observatory, telescope at the ready. The telescope that's been wrapped up in storage because we've never had the money to repair it and display it properly. The observatory itself, up on that loose-tiled roof, is unsafe. All that could change.

Waves crash below us, roaring and angry. All my bad thoughts about Mike and Dave Barton, all my confused thoughts about Tom, are swept aside by the news from Canada, as if the wind itself has emptied my head of nonsense and worry and made one thing perfectly clear.

We have to go all out now and purchase this place.

I spill the beans to my friends as calmly as I can, which is tricky with the elements going haywire. I tell them what's happened and they are delighted. Amazed and flipping delighted.

'Zounds!' Tish exclaims.

'Marvellous,' Jackie adds.

'Shitting fantastic!' Carol screams, so loudly a flock of seagulls disperses into the distance.

Then there's a silence that holds all our thoughts and dreams, just the wind rushing into our backs, pushing us back to shore.

'Coffee?' Jackie suggests. 'Before we head to the bank?'

We nod and trail after her, aiming for dry land and the nearest café.

THE BANK MANAGER is Tracey Hillman who was in our year at school. I didn't realize it was the same Tracey as she has a married name now but I recognize her as soon as she ushers us in to sit down, like schoolgirls summoned to the head to account for their misdemeanours. I have to remind myself that we are a team of strong women with a plethora of experience between us and quite a sum of money. Surely she will at least consider the possibility of the bank allowing us to have a mortgage?

We let Jackie take the lead. Tish, Carol and I sit quietly and sedately, nodding and making reassuring noises, as Jackie lays out our plan. She has handouts and spreadsheets for Tracey, fortunately not a PowerPoint this time as I'm not sure that would be entirely appropriate.

After an hour of discussion, we leave the bank, feeling that we actually have someone on our side. Tracey was receptive and keen to help.

'I remember you lot from school,' she said. 'You were always nice to me. Especially you, Jen. A lot of kids weren't.'

I remember that too. She was picked on. She might be a svelte, well-dressed businesswoman now but then she was on the large side. She hated PE. Must've been torture for her, all the lads making snarky comments. Once she and I were lagging behind on a cross-country race up on the moors and she was in tears. I sat with her behind a rock and we shared a Mars Bar and after a bit she stopped crying. Then we managed to get a lift off Mr Mole, the butcher, who was a friend of Dad's. He dropped us off round the back of school and we sneaked past the science labs and were first back in the gym. Mrs Rowland almost fainted when she saw the pair of us.

'And I love gin.' Tracey shook our hands one after the other, like she was the Governor of the Bank of England rather than manager of a remote local branch struggling to stay open. 'About time Dingleton had something new to offer and God forbid that Dave Barton gets his way.' She had this knowing look. 'I'll ring you later, Jackie.'

Maybe things just might go our way?

'Is it too early to celebrate?' I ask the team.

'Course it is,' Jackie says. 'But that's not going to stop us.'

WE'RE WAITING IN the Bishop, drinking G and Ts and talking about the future which might not be our future but we're too excited to avoid the subject.

'So what's our top bid?' Carol asks.

We all turn to Jackie.

'Don't let's get ahead of ourselves,' Jackie says. 'Tracey could still say no.'

'Hypothetically then?' Carol won't let this go. 'Come on, don't be a spoilsport.'

'Oh, I don't know.'

'You don't know?' Tish says. 'Poppycock, Jackie. We rely on you to always know.'

Jackie sighs, exasperation not far out of reach. 'Funnily enough,' she says, 'I used to manage a small provincial museum. Never have I ever part-owned a distillery slash cutting-edge museum in what appears to be the most unexpected co-operative in history.' She downs the rest of her gin like an old sop. 'Let's take one step at a time, shall we? How about that?'

We sit there quietly, reprimanded and remorseful, muttering apologies until Tish chips in her two penn'orth. 'I'm sorry,' she says, which you know means the opposite. 'But enough already of this platitudinous verbiage. We just want this to work so badly that we can't help but think ahead.' She crosses her arms, jangling her bangles like she's Mike Oldfield's percussionist and then that sets me in mind of *The Exorcist* that Carol, Mike and I watched together when we were sixteen and I couldn't sleep properly for six months without having to check under the bed and in the wardrobe.

I nearly jump out of my skin when Jackie's phone vibrates on the table, so dramatically that it leaps off the end and is heading towards its doom when a hairy dirty hand appears out of nowhere and deftly catches it with the reactions of a first-class cricketer.

'Here you go.' Trampy Kev hands it over to Jackie

before shambling to the gents.

In all the kerfuffle the phone is still vibrating and Jackie only just remembers to answer it in time.

'Tracey, hi. Thanks for getting back to us so soon.' She heads out of the pub so she can hear and presumably so that it doesn't sound like we're all piss tanks.

We shuffle after her and huddle around while she listens intently, nodding and uh-huh-ing, spare hand covering her other ear to block out the wind. If only she'd put it on speakerphone but she won't know how to do that and she won't want anyone else eavesdropping so I practise patience. Try to work out her body language, the muffled words of Tracey who holds our future in the palm of her hand. After five agonizing minutes, Jackie says 'Goodbye' and 'Thanks'.

We're hopeful, though the expression on her face suggests we are quite possibly wrong. Her eyes are watery and she fans herself with her hand at which point Tish withdraws a lacy fan from her Mary Poppins carpetbag and elegantly wafts Jackie's face for her.

I take a deep, deep breath. 'Well? Put us out of our misery.'

'Tracey from the bank... she says – Yes!' Jackie chucks her phone recklessly in the air, forgetting she's not got the best eye–hand coordination but help is close by again in the form of a flying Kev who catches it one-handed but knocks out a tooth in the process as he falls to the ground, a rough patch of tarmac, so that all thoughts of gin palaces fly away and we gather around this man who isn't what we thought he was. Who can teach us all not to judge.

BACK IN TORBAY hospital. Kev, Carol and me. We get some strange looks, two power-dressed women and a beat-up, bleeding hobo. Luckily, Mondays are convenient for an accident or emergency and he's seen pretty quickly. But then we have to hang around for someone to come down from maxillofacial. In the meantime Kev, who has a row of chairs to himself, spreads himself out and nods off. A nurse suggests the League of Friends café to Carol and so we head there and order tea and Chelsea buns.

'So you reckon we can do this thing?' Carol asks, icing stuck to her lipstick.

'It won't be easy but I reckon we can, yes. People are making their own gin all over the country so there's no reason why we can't have a go.'

'But combining it with the museum? Has anyone done that?'

'I don't know. Museums often have cafés, so why not a gin bar?'

'Well, when you put it like that...' She shovels the rest of her bun in her mouth.

I'm glad I sound convinced, because I don't particularly feel it but we spend the next hour or so pitching ideas to each other, talking them through, and I can see the light in Carol's eyes, brighter than it's been in a long time, confirming that we must give this our very best shot, for all of our sakes.

We've not long returned to the waiting room, when a patched-up Kev is delivered to us, clutching a prescription and a letter. The nurse takes me discreetly to one side.

'Is Mr Clatford related to you?' he asks.

'No.' I shake my head.

'But you know him?'

'Sort of. Well, yes, I do know him. He lives in our town. Everyone knows him, actually. But no one really does. Except his mother.' Even to my own ears I sound like I'm talking in riddles but the nurse doesn't question it. He'll have seen and heard all sorts in here.

'He needs to get his prescription from the pharmacy. Are you able to go with him?'

'Of course.'

'And can you get him home or do I need to call someone? I'm trying not to judge him by his appearance, but he is in pain. Not enough to keep him in overnight, though.'

'What happens now, then?'

'He's got an appointment with the consultant as a follow-up. He says he doesn't have a dentist.'

'That doesn't surprise me.'

I look over at Kev. He smiles at me and then winces and holds his hand to his cheek. I realize that his missing tooth, top front left, is the exact same as the only one left in his mother's mouth.

'We'll take him back to his mum. I know where she lives.'

'Thanks,' he says, clearly relieved.

'No. Thank *you*.'

As we make our way to the pharmacy, I glance back and see the nurse dispense a gallon of anti-bac onto his hands before spraying some Lynx around the waiting room.

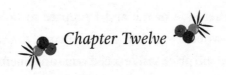

Chapter Twelve

THE BIG DAY is here. We've been preparing for it by watching *Homes Under the Hammer* and *Flog It!* so we now know the value of a damp 1920s terraced house in Sheffield and a pewter tankard from Ipswich. Armed with this knowledge and the information gleaned from the estate agent, the legal pack and the internet, the five of us go together to the auction house in Newton Abbot but on arrival we spread out, dotting ourselves across the room as we don't want to make it too obvious. It just seems better to play it low key.

Tish finds it difficult to play it low key. Today she is dressed like the Queen circa 1955 in a powder-blue woollen suit with matching pillbox hat, navy court shoes and handbag, and white gloves. Yes, white gloves. The rest of us are wearing our bank outfits, because that's pretty much it as far as our business-dress collection goes.

Jackie is feeling sick, blaming it on the dodgy prawns she ate last night, but I can see through her. It's nerves.

She's so overcome she has to sit to the side near the door in case she has to make a swift exit. So needs must. I step up and offer to do the bidding. Carol and Tom sit one on either side of me and I prepare to hold up my catalogue, wondering if I'll get the chance to brandish it or whether the price will exceed our funds before we've even got going.

The room is full. There's a hum of anticipation, people peeling off coats, delving into handbags, hunting for specs. It's like we're at the theatre only I've got to perform in some way I've never done before. Not counting that school play when I was one of the four-and-twenty blackbirds baked in a pie. When I really should have been Jenny Wren but that role went to Char Bannister because she was failing to thrive.

'You all right?' Carol is looking at me, concern in her eyes.

'What, now? Or in general?'

'Both, I suppose. But especially now.'

'You'll be fine,' Tom replies, which is a bit annoying seeing as it was my question to answer but also nice because it shows he has confidence in me and I'm really beginning to think he just might be interested, like *interested* interested, but I must dash those thoughts now and concentrate because the auctioneer's appeared like the MC of a variety show in a bright-coloured stripy blazer and those pink chinos that only certain men of a certain age and background can get away with. And even that's debatable.

'Ladies and Gentlemen,' he begins after a thorough clearing of his throat. He then gives us a brief run-through of events and rules and we're under starter's orders.

First up is a cottage on the moors that looks like it hasn't been lived in since the Black Death killed off its inhabitants. But some property developer could turn it into a money spinner so it's soon sold for what might seem like a crazy price for a pile of granite stones but actually when you consider it's in a National Park with views that are priceless, it's a good buy for someone.

Next is a plot of land on the edge of Appleton which an impoverished farmer is selling off. It's already got outline planning permission and no doubt some coun-cillor will help steer it through and then the fields will be gone for ever. I know there's a housing shortage, I know my kids will need to live somewhere when they are ready to settle, but it's sad all the same, watching the familiar landscape change and disappear.

'Jen? You sure you're OK? You're actually twitching.'

Carol's right. I must focus.

Next up is Clatford House. Carol clutches my arm and Tom sits upright. I glance over at Jackie who is a whiter shade of pale and at the Queen, on the other side of the room, sitting demurely next to a ruddy-faced wideboy who is barking up the wrong tree.

The one person I can't see is Dave Barton. Where is he? I thought he'd be here, prepared to gloat. Twonk. And yes, here he comes, striding in now with smugness plastered on his fat face, the grand entrance, secretary in tow, flanked by two pinstriped men, a flipping entourage. They'll have to stand at the back as all the chairs are taken but no, of course someone is keeping his chair warm, three seats away from me. Dave shuffles down the row, apologizing charmingly to the people who have to squash their legs aside to let him through. As he squeezes past me, he looks down. Unfortunately, at that moment his crotch is at eye level and although I immediately turn my head to avert my gaze, he laughs that laugh that makes me want to deck him. 'Excuse me, Jennifer,' he says, making it sound sarcastic, as if I've encroached on his personal space when it's him waggling his willy in my face.

'Get knotted,' I whisper in a shouty way.

'Lot three,' the auctioneer announces. 'Clatford House, currently the museum in Dingleton, a fine Regency property, in need of some restoration. We'll start at one million pounds.'

Onemillionpounds.

There's a moment when I wonder if no one is going to make an opening bid and that the price might be lowered. But that's soon scuppered as I catch Dave out of the corner of my eye, more specifically the woman who has saved him a seat. She gives a curt nod of her head.

'Thank you, madam. Do I have one million and ten?' The auctioneer acknowledges someone at the back, a man on the phone

'Thank you, sir. Do I have one million and twenty?'

The woman puts up her hand again before I get the chance to do the same and I wonder if I'm going to miss out and I wish someone else had the responsibility. I feel sick to the stomach and out of my depth. Who is this woman? And how does she know Dave?

Before I can move my hand or head or anything because I seem to have suffered some kind of paralysis, there's another bid from the man on the phone – is he acting on behalf of the brewery? – and then straight back to the woman so now the price is hovering at one million and forty. But it's soon up to one million and fifty and then someone else chips in, a young couple no doubt down from London with cash aplenty. So we're at one million and sixty and Carol nudges me and this causes me to shoot up my hand like I'm back at school with the answer to a question when really right now my head is full of nothing. I'm not even sure I can recollect my name or address or who's the current prime minister – it could be Harold Wilson for all I know. And now she's nudging me again because the couple have upped their bid so I do the same, shove my hand in the air like a loon and I think we might have it for one million and eighty and that's not too bad, we can make this work, we've come this far, but no, it's back to the London couple. Then the man on the phone. Then the London couple. And Dave's woman is leaning forward in her seat, hand up high, and there he goes again, the man on the phone, back in the game after some frenzied dialogue with the puppet-master who won't be able to see the desperation of his hand gestures and when I glance to my left I see Dave mumbling something to the woman and she folds her arms and shakes her head at the auctioneer.

One million, one hundred and thirty.

The room is hushed.

The London couple are hesitating. She looks eager. He shakes his head. She pouts. He grimaces. They're out.

I want to be sick on the carpet.

I'm going to keel over.

But I feel something on my leg. A hand. Carol's hand. She gives me a squeeze and my hand shoots up.

One million, one hundred and forty.

'Thank you, madam.'

Then: 'It's against you, sir.' More hesitation. 'How about one million, one hundred and forty-five?'

The man on the phone nods. I want to punch him but I can barely stay upright. I can also feel the beady eyes of Dave on me like he's laughing at my idiocy, that I should ever think I could be part of an innovative project that could put Dingleton on the map the way his family have never been able to because they've only been concerned about themselves over the people who make up this town. People like my dad and my mum. Like Trampy Kev and his one-toothed mother. Like my kids and my friends. My best friend, Carol. And even Mike. I'm doing this for them. And for me because it's OK to think about myself too. It actually is.

My hand goes up, deliberately and firmly.

'One million, one hundred and fifty pounds, madam. Back against you, sir.'

Silence.

'First time then,' the auctioneer says. 'At one million, one hundred and fifty thousand pounds. Second time— Ah? Do we have another bidder?'

Everyone turns round. I'm expecting to see the man on the phone but it's my bloody father. *Dad!*

'Are you bidding, sir?'

'What? Me?'

'Yes, sir.'

'No, I was swatting a fly. Bloody nuisance.'

There's a collective groan. Carol sniggers. I put my head in my hands.

'Third and final time.'

And the sweetest, scariest sound I've ever heard is the fall of the hammer.

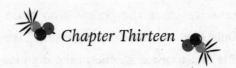

Chapter Thirteen

WHEN THE KIDS were little, before they started school, I used to worry about Hallowe'en. I thought they'd be scared of the witches and ghosts and I wanted to protect them from all that. But Mike pointed out that sometimes you need to be scared of something so that you understand what it's like to feel safe. And then they started school and once that happens you get the slow drip-feed of peer pressure and before you know it you're taking them trick-or-treating dressed up as the bride of Frankenstein.

And now, even though my kids are adults, they still get excited at the prospect of a burning pumpkin. I've already seen Lauren's Instagram. She's got up as a black cat in ripped fishnet tights because of course you always see cats wearing fishnet tights. But she's having fun, out with her mates in Plymouth. And here's Harry with his boyfriend who, being North American, knows how to do Hallowe'en. He's scooped out the pumpkin in super-fast time and put it on the doorstep, only instead of sculpting a wicked face, he's carved a heart. This is so sweet I get a lump in my throat and take the logical decision to seek comfort in the lethal punch Dad has concocted. Which, it has to be said, is impressive. He has an old baby bath filled with green liquid and smouldering, swirling dry ice.

I've dressed up as Cruella De Vil and have shoehorned a humiliated Bob into a Dalmatian costume. He looks very cute which makes me think of puppies. Tom's invited so if he turns up I'll ask him. I could send him a text to see if he's coming?

Can you make it tonight? Jen x

          Got someone staying soz x

You can bring them too if you want?

          Ok, might well do that, ta x

Don't forget it's fancy dress.

It's only six o'clock and my ridiculous make-up is already slipping off my face. I can hear a gaggle of kids and parents coming up the road, door to door. Dad, dressed as a zombie Albert Einstein, is on treat duty with a basket of Haribo.

'When are you putting on your costume, Granddad?' Harry asks.

'Very witty, Harry. Very witty. But I think you'll find

'there's nothing funny about quantum theory.'

'No, Granddad. It's serious stuff.' Harry says this deadpan, dressed as Robin to Dale's Batman.

By seven, after a face-repair job and a couple of glasses of Dad's punch, the party is in full swing. The team are all here. Tish as a tattered, dusty Miss Havisham with her partner Miranda as a mono-browed Frida Kahlo. Jackie as a bloodied serial-killer librarian. Carol as an unlikely Rosa Klebb. I'm hoping Tom will turn up. Perhaps that's why I keep checking my face in the mirror and disappearing to the loo. Or that could be the inroads I'm making on Dad's cocktail.

Just as I'm thinking he probably won't come, there he is in my hallway with his 'friend', a stunningly beautiful curvaceous woman got up as a vampish Fenella Fielding in *Carry On Screaming*. A mass of black hair, pale skin and blood-red lippy.

'This is Sarah, aka Valeria,' Tom says. Tom is dressed up as Kenneth Williams's Dr Watt. 'She's involved with museums and I thought you could pick her brains.'

I was hoping she wouldn't have brains as well as looks but obviously she does and I've been asked to pick them. I don't want to pick them. I want to bar her from the house. I know I'm feeling this anger towards her – yes, it is actually anger – because I'm pretty sure she and Tom have got something going on. And I realize now, seeing him laugh with Sarah, that I really do like him. A lot. But it seems I missed the boat. If there was even a boat to catch.

To make matters worse, Sarah is charming and sweet and incredibly helpful and tucks into the punch like a pro and gets on with everybody and I can't work this out because I want to like her but how can I if she's Tom's girlfriend? I'll just have to accept that he's not interested in me like that. But I thought that he was, I really did, so that's confusing. And a big pile of pants.

But right now, I'm wondering about Dad who's abandoned his sentry post as the kids have gone home. Where is he?

I head down to the shed, with difficulty as I'm wearing ridiculous killer heels. Inside I find Bob has been relieved of his shameful costume and is curled up in his bed. Dad's Einstein moustache has gone wonky so he's even more the mad professor, especially as he's cleaning Violet, the still, rubbing in salt with half a lemon and buffing with a pair of old St Michael's Y-fronts.

It's working, though. The blue-green is gradually coming off and I reckon Violet will be stunning after her facelift.

'Nice job, Dad.'

'I'm quite pleased with it.' He sits back on his heels and his knees crick-crack. 'I've had these underpants since Margaret Thatcher was prime minister.'

'Glad to see you're putting them to good use.'

Tom turns up at this point and my stomach jellifies. 'This is where you're hiding. Figured you'd both be out here. How's Violet coming along?'

'She's having a thorough rub-down,' Dad says. 'Then she'll be good to go.'

'You're cracking on with the distilling?'

'That's the plan,' I tell him. 'While we wait on planning permission and a distilling licence.'

'Fingers crossed for that. And the campaigning. Anything I can do?'

'I reckon we've got it under control, thanks.'

'Oh. Right. Well, that's good. Let me know if you need any help. Any time.'

I mutter a pathetic thank-you and this is followed by an awkward minute while we watch Dad continue to work his magic.

And then Tom makes me jump when he says, 'Oh, yes! I almost forgot! I came here to deliver some news.'

'About the gin business?'

'No. Actually for that chap over there.' He points at Bob. 'He's going to be a father.'

'Oh, really?' I hear myself getting all emotional. Even Dad has to wipe at his eye.

'It's puppies all round for Christmas. Though of course dogs are for life and all that.'

'And we really get pick of the litter?' Dad asks.

'Course.'

'But I haven't said yes, Dad.'

'No, Jennifer Juniper, you haven't. But you will.'

Next in the shed is Carol with Sarah in tow. They seem to have hit it off and I'm even more annoyed now.

'Did you know Sarah works in a museum?' Carol asks me.

'Yes,' I reply. 'Isn't that a coincidence?'

'Much bigger than ours,' Carol blunders on.

I slink over to the corner and give Bob a cuddle, try to focus on puppies because that's much happier than thinking about Sarah and her perfect life.

While she charms my father and Carol, Tom sidles over to my side and asks quietly, 'You all right, Jen?'

'I'm fine, thanks. How are you?'

'I'm fine too. You seem a bit, well, agitated?'

'Do I? It's a busy time. I'm keen to get started on this gin to see if it's something we can actually do. I mean, we have this massive property and we can't do anything till we have planning permission and sometimes I don't know if it's completely mad.'

'You'll be fine. Between you lot, you've got it all covered.'

We watch the others who are huddled around Violet. Dad is telling Sarah and Carol about the Hague Convention for the Protection of Cultural Property in the Event of Armed Conflict of 1954. Carol's completely used to this rambling but Sarah, a newcomer, is also taking it in her stride. And now Sarah and Carol have left the shed to take Dad up to the house for a cuppa as it's a school night and people are heading off.

'So... what about Sarah?' I do my very best to look Tom in the eye which is slightly tricky because his make-up makes me want to laugh and I'm trying to be serious.

'What about Sarah?' He looks straight back at me.

'Is she... I mean, how do you know her?'

'She's my sister-in-law.'

'Your sister-in-law?'

'She's Claire's sister.'

'Oh. Right. I didn't realize.'

'I thought I told you she was my sister-in-law.'

'You said she was a friend.'

'She's that as well. I've known her for years. She was the one that introduced me to Claire.'

'Right.'

'It's been hard for her too, losing her sister.'

'I bet. I mean, I wouldn't know because I'm an only child but I know Lauren and Harry would be devastated to lose each other.'

Now I'm thinking about the death of my children, making it all about me again. Which is stupid. I should just tell him.

'I was a bit jealous.'

'Jealous?'

'Do I have to spell it out?'

'I think maybe you do.'

'Right.' I take a lungful of air. Two lungfuls. 'This is the thing. I seem to quite like you. And I thought maybe you liked me. You asked me round for dinner and we had a lovely time and there were fairy lights and everything and I thought about kissing you but I didn't know if you were interested. Then there was the other night when you hugged me in the hall and I thought you might kiss me but you didn't though I hoped there would come a time when we might actually manage it and of course I know you're still grieving so I don't mind being patient. But then tonight you brought Sarah round and I thought she was your girlfriend and so yes, I felt jealous. Only now I feel stupid. So there. I've said it.'

I'm waiting for Tom to leg it out of here but he stays put. He's on his haunches stroking Bob's belly and I can't help but think how much I wish he would do that to my tummy, despite the stretch marks and all. He smiles at me now, eyes twinkling the way they did when I first met him, and my stomach curdles. That punch was a bad idea, though I've been pretty sober this evening all things considered but not enough to stop my hand from shaking when he gets to his feet and says, 'I like you too, Jen. But I'm not in the habit of, you know, being with a woman.'

'Being with a woman?'

'Er, feeling something like I used to feel for Claire, only different obviously because she was different.' He shakes his head. 'You see, I can't even put words in the right order.'

'Claire must've been an amazing woman. I'm just a local girl struggling to keep it all together. We're different.'

I look at Tom, in his *Carry On* outfit. Against the white of his make-up, his eyes are dark, silent pools of emotion.

'Life is precious, Tom.'

'It is.'

Then I do it again. I lean in towards him and go to kiss his lips with mine but he stops me, a gentle hand to my shoulder.

'Wait,' he says.

'What is it? Have I got this wrong?'

'No, there's a spider in your hair.' He moves to take it but I'm already swatting at my head, making the ridiculous noise of the arachnophobe in contact with an eight-legged monster. It flies to the floor where Bob proceeds to eat it.

'Your dog adores you.'

'At least someone does.'

'Lots of people do, Jen,' he says. 'Now come here.' He reaches out to me and I move towards him, taking him in my arms and giving him a big, fat kiss because let's be clear about this, if you want something you have to bloody well go out and get it. After all, you're a long time dead.

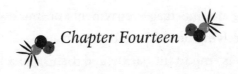 *Chapter Fourteen*

WHEN I WOKE up the morning after the party, All Hallows Day, a soft grey light was creeping in through the gaps of the curtains, and I imagined Tom lying next to me in my bed. But of course he wasn't there. After a rather lovely kiss in the shed he'd made his excuses, saying he needed to go home and let Betty out. And although I knew he had to do this, I felt a pang of jealousy. Which was stupid. Feeling jealous of a dog, especially one needing extra care due to her belly being full of Bob's puppies.

I'm hankering after some TLC myself – particularly as a week has passed since that kiss and I haven't heard from Tom. Not a dickie bird. Not that I've tried to contact him either. I've been flat out and no doubt Tom too what with Bonfire Night and the run-up to Christmas which has probably already started at school. And now I'm wondering whether I read too much into the whole thing. Maybe it was just a slip of the tongue.

And I'm worried. I keep dreaming about my house

being destroyed. In a storm. In a fire. In a mysterious alien home abduction. I know enough to realize it's a manifestation of my anxiety over money. Whether I can make my mortgage repayments on my dwindling savings, relying on Dad as a backup plan.

Today is important. Jackie and Tish have a meeting with the conservation officer from the council. We need listed-building consent before we can do any alterations or renovations to Clatford House. It's crucial we're given the go-ahead because otherwise our plans are dashed before we've even passed Go. Meanwhile I've agreed to get together an application to the Heritage Lottery Fund. The most adventurous I've been in the past is applying for a credit card and that was bad enough. But there's someone who could help. Someone who knows exactly how to do a funding bid. Who knows what the powers that be need to hear. All those key words like 'engage', 'community', 'added value' etc. Someone who understands and empathizes with the importance of preserving the house, its unique setting, its special features, what it means to Dingleton, to our heritage, our community, our future.

So I text Tom.

He texts back.

I change three times, put on make-up, take it off again. Style my hair, then put on a hat. Then I go to meet him.

THE LUNCHTIME CAFÉ is steamed up with dog breath and wet coats.

'It should tell the story of Dingleton,' Tom says, stirring his tea frantically as he only has a half-hour before afternoon registration. 'The museum must give a voice to those who've gone before and it should breathe new life into the town.'

He's tucking into egg and chips while I scribble down his words, wishing I knew how to record him with my phone or be competent at shorthand. But it's been a long time since the Pitman's course I did in evening class the year after leaving school. Which is how I got out of the amusement arcade and into office work.

'Jen?'

'Hmm?'

'You're drawing a picture of a dog. A very fat little dog. Are you OK?'

'Oh, blimey, sorry. I zoned out for a while there. I'll be all right once I've drunk this coffee.'

'So this is basically what we need to say,' Tom continues, eyeing me sideways, a whiff of concern about his handsome face. Yes, handsome. Drop-dead gorgeous in a silver-fox way. In any way. 'We want to include an education element, an outreach programme, get in volunteers from excluded groups. The disabled. The unemployed. Pensioners with too much time on their hands. The homeless.'

'Like Kev?'

'From what you say he's not technically homeless. He's got a home up at the farm.'

'I know. But he's disengaged from society. From everything. Spends his days hanging around town, only going back to the farm for a bath and some food and a bed every few days. It's people like Kev we should be including.'

'Maybe we could get him to help us with the application?'

'Really? Do you think he would?'

'You won't know unless you ask him.' Tom smiles that ridiculously twinkly smile and I have to restrain myself from running my hands through his hair.

'Me?'

'I think so.'

'Right. OK. When?'

'No time like the present.' He points outside.

There is Kev himself, slouched on a bench down by the Brook, snoozing in the autumn sun.

'I'd better go now,' Tom says. 'Can't be late for those Year Sixes. There'll be anarchy and it won't be pretty.'

We get ourselves ready to leave, making plans to meet up to do this thing.

'How's Betty, by the way?' I ask. 'Not long now?'

'About four weeks.' He shrugs on his jacket and retrieves my hat from where it's fallen on the floor and puts it on my head. Which is quite erotic. 'Do you think you want one?'

'Excuse me?'

'A puppy, Jen. Do you think you want a puppy?'

'Yes. Yes, I think I do.'

I APPROACH KEV carefully so as not to surprise him. He's had trouble in the past with drunken scumbags duffing him up, jumping him, and yet he still stays out here. When he has a home to go to. What happened?

'Wotcha,' he says. 'You wanna know what happened?'

'Did I say that out loud?'

'You did. Siddown.'

I sit down.

'Sorry, Kev. I didn't mean to be rude.'

'S'all right.'

There's a pause while we watch a couple of black swans sunning themselves, making the most of this late, unexpected warmth. Then he speaks, out of the blue and from the heart.

'I used to have a wife.'

And straight away I think, oh, he's a widow like Tom, but—

'She left me.'

'Oh. Right. I'm sorry.'

'Only that's not the worst part.'

And he tells me it all, what he can. Cuts open his vein and lets the blood pool on the floor by our feet. He tells me how they were childhood sweethearts, him and his wife, and I can't help but think of me and Mike. He tells me how they got married and had a little boy and that they lived up at the farm with his ma and pa and they had a good life. Only something bad happened. Ripped his world apart. His little boy, David, four years old, was crushed by some sort of farm machinery, while he was on Kev's watch. His wife never forgave him and, within a year, she'd left him too. And that's when he lost his way. Started drinking too heavily. Not eating. Taking painkillers. Giving up the farm work. Dropping out of life. So his brother moved in, bringing his own family, and now his nephew has stepped up.

By the time Kev's recounted all this I'm crying, full-on snot-nosed crying and then he starts crying too and I actually give him a hug because I am so consumed with this grief. To lose a child. A little boy. Nothing, but nothing can be worse than that. So why the hell do I get so hacked off with life when I have not only my kids but also hope in the future?

'Thank you for telling me this.' I take out a clump of scrunched-up tissues from my bag and share them out so we can wipe our noses at the very least. Then after a while, as the swans slip into the water one after the other and head downstream, I know this is the chance to reach out. 'I need your help with something, Kev.'

'Help?'

'Yes. With the museum.'

'Not sure how I'd be of help but I'll be glad to try. 'Bout time I stopped mucking about.'

He smiles and I notice his new shiny white tooth. So new it makes the rest of his gnashers look even more yellow.

WHEN I GET home, Dad is absorbed with something in the kitchen sink.

'What you doing, Dad?'

'Washing up.'

He starts humming 'Ten Green Bottles'.

'Are you making a start on the gin?'

'Yes, indeed I am. Harry and Dale are in the shed with Violet so I thought I'd sort these out.'

'Where did you get them from?'

'Oh, you know. The usual.'

'Hanging around the bottle bank at the Co-op? You used to tell me off when I hung around the Co-op car park.'

'That's because you were usually smoking. Or chatting up boys.'

'True.' I blink away an image of me and Dave Barton, his hand up my jumper, dirty bastard.

'I'll pop down and see Harry and Dale.'

'Make sure you knock first.'

'Noted.'

I make a brew and tread carefully down the garden with the Silver Jubilee tray laden with mugs of tea and a plate of the chocolate digestives that Dale has become addicted to. He's putting on weight. As is Harry. Being in love can do that to you. I lost a stone when Mike left. If it wasn't for Dad and Lauren, I think I'd have stayed in bed for ever, just Bob for company. I'd torture myself wondering what Mike and Melanie were doing. Were they in bed? Were they out for dinner? In the pub? Sitting on the sofa in front of the telly with him massaging her tiny, slender feet? And I'd compare myself to her. I'd even write down lists. Was she good at sex? Could she cook? Did she trump at inappropriate moments? What was her pelvic floor like?

One day Dad caught me out. He came in with a bowl of Heinz tomato soup and a plate of soldiers and he wrestled one of these lists from my hand, ripped it into shreds and set fire to it in the garden, ordering me to come out and watch. Which I did. And it was cathartic. I cried and I laughed and then I got exceedingly drunk and he and Lolly had to put me to bed with a sick bowl beside me.

After that, each day got a little bit better and I did a little bit more. I stopped the self-destruction and I began to build a new life. And now Dave Barton's had to come along and scupper things.

But I will not let him win.

We have Clatford House. We have planning under way, a grant being applied for, Violet is up and working, we've got Kev on board, the campaign is building up and now Harry and Dale are making the first attempts at the gin. This could all come together. Or it could all go down the swanny. But you've only got one life and you have to give it your very best shot.

And because I'm dreaming I forget to knock on the shed door and what I see is not good for a menopausal mother.

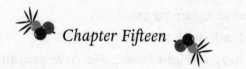

Chapter Fifteen

DECEMBER HAS BROUGHT with it a northerly chill and drawn-in evenings. Half four and it's dark. The time of life for advent calendars has passed but I suppose that will come again. If I have grandchildren. I don't know why I'm thinking about grandchildren. Is it because I miss holding a baby in my arms? The bedtime stories, the cuddles, the sheer love for and of a child?

I'm standing at the kitchen sink now, a stew in the slow cooker, jacket potatoes in the oven, clearing up after the latest batch of gin. There's quite a team been working on it these last few weeks. Dale, Harry and Dad. And Carol, who really does have a nose for it. Between the four of them they've come up with various concoctions. Some better than others but none quite right yet. Dad assures me we'll get there. He found Mum's recipes that came from Old Woman Bates. They were pressed in the pages of an old copy of Fanny and Johnnie Cradock's *Cooking with Bon Viveur*. One of them had a mysterious ingredient called bullum. Dad explained that it was like a cross between a plum and a sloe, found round these parts, if you knew where to look. But we've not got to that yet. We're still on the basics.

We decided not to distil from scratch as making our own alcohol from mash would need a distiller's licence from HM Revenue and Customs, tricky to get. So we're using duty-paid grain-neutral spirit and turning it into gin by re-distilling it with juniper berries and a mixture of other botanicals. For this we need a rectifier's licence, which Dad already has. Who knows, in the future we could make it completely from scratch, but this seems to be the way forward for now.

The shed is the still room. I can see it from here, lit up like a spacecraft in the shadow of the naked pear tree. Heads bob up and down and this way and that. Inside they'll be beavering away amongst the gleaming copper pipes and vessels, all giving their input. I hope this batch is better than the last. That one was bad. Far too much juniper so that was all you could taste. Too piny and peppery. Too resinous. Like the antiseptic smell of a school hall. But the one before that was disastrous. There was so much going on it was overwhelming. It hurt your head. Literally. Our gin needs more subtlety. This is where Carol comes in. Which is ironic as she's never been subtle in her whole life. But she has a gift. She can tell the difference between cinnamon and cardamom, coriander and cassia whereas I only know if I like it or not.

Right now all I can smell is the delicious aroma of beef casserole. Time to get the workers.

BY TEN O'CLOCK we've eaten, cleared up, and the team has returned to the shed. I'm taking the opportunity to put up my feet and watch crap telly in front of the log burner. And now my phone is vibrating. Tom.

'Can you come over? Betty's in labour and I'm panicky if the truth be known.'

'I'm on my way.'

I grab my coat, leave a message on the kitchen table and scarper, heart beating fast but full of excitement.

Halfway there, I spot Kev walking along the road towards the seafront. I take the decision to stop, wind down the window and call out his name. He does a double-take and then smiles.

'Any good at delivering puppies?' I ask him.

'I've seen a fair few born,' he says.

'Can you come with me? Betty's about to have her litter.'

He gets in, no questions asked, and I put my foot down so that in minutes we're parking up at the end of Coast Guards Row.

'In here, come on.'

He follows meekly, going with the flow, his calmness what I need right now.

Tom opens his front door before I even have the chance to knock. He ushers us in, barely acknowledging Kev, whispering in an almost frantic way, leading the way to the front room where Betty is in her basket, heaving and panting. She glances up at me, sad doggy eyes, perplexed and scared, and I hunker down next to her, soothing her with my voice, telling her what a good girl she is.

'How long's she been like this?' I ask Tom.

'She's been restless all day but only like this for a while. Look at her belly. Those are contractions, aren't they?'

'They are,' Kev confirms.

Just as he says this, Betty strains and lets out a whimper and a little doggy head appears. After a minute or so, nothing more has happened and Tom's clearly agitated.

'Shouldn't it be out by now? Is it stillborn?'

'Give her longer,' Kev says. 'This her first litter?'

'Yes.'

'The first pup of the first litter don't always make it but we've still got time.' Kev puts his hand on Betty's tightened belly and talks gently to her.

Then the puppy slips out like a water rat and Betty licks it vigorously to break the sack so it can breathe. Only it's not breathing.

In a swift, practised movement, Kev takes the poor

little mite in his big hands and gives it one hard shake and I have to restrain myself from shouting at him to be careful but I hold back because gloopy stuff flies out of its mouth and there's huge relief when we hear a whine. It's alive!

Kev hands the puppy over to Tom who wraps it carefully in a towel, cradling it like a baby. Which it is. Betty's baby. Bob's baby.

'Keep it warm,' Kev says. 'Rub his back.'

'It's a boy?' Tom says.

'No doubt about that,' Kev confirms.

He's back with Betty now, and within minutes the next one plops out no problem and now that the initial shock is over and her instincts kick in, Betty knows what to do, licking her pup with gusto. This one's like a guinea pig, shiny and compact, eyes tight shut.

Kev carries on with his dog whispering and over the next hour another three pups are born. Five puppies. Another boy and three girls.

Only then Betty starts panting again and a sixth one appears, bigger than the rest, a right bruiser. A boy. Three of each.

'Well done, Betty. You're so clever,' I tell her.

Betty is busy washing them, one by one, and soon they are sniffing out her teats and latching on, pushing at her with paddling paws.

I make us all a well-earned cuppa.

Two o'clock in the morning and Kev has long gone. Despite offers of lifts or the sofa to sleep on, he said he was sorted and left, a big smile on his face.

I've stayed on and watched Betty and her pups, now safely moved and settled into her whelping box. All of them are feeding and she looks worn out but content.

Tom and I have eaten beans on toast and are currently having a nightcap. He's on single malt, me on hot chocolate. We sit side by side on the sofa, gazing in awe and wonder at Betty and her litter.

'We should be drinking gin really,' he says. 'But I don't have any in.'

'Not long and you should be able to taste the Dingleton Gin.'

'Dingleton Gin?' Tom says, after a while, breaking the companionable silence. 'That has a good ring to it, you know.'

'Dingleton Gin? Hmm. Yes, it does. I like it. Simple. True. Effective. I'll suggest it to the others. We've not got as far as thinking of the name yet.' I finish the last of my drink and am about to call it a night when another thought strikes me. 'What are you going to call the pups?'

'Oh, yeah, the pups. I suppose we should give them temporary names.'

'How about gin-related ones?'

'Like...?'

'Well, the obvious one is Juniper.'

'Good, yes. That could be a boy or a girl, I suppose.'

'Yep. How about Olive?' I suggest. 'So many gin cocktails go with an olive garnish.'

'Brilliant,' he says. 'And on that note how about Martin? As in Martini?'

'Oh yes, definitely Martin.'

'What about Denis? As in Thatcher?'

'He loved his gin.'

'OK, so we're still two names short. Who else likes gin?'

'The Queen?'

'Queenie then.' He counts on his fingers. Five down. One to go.

'How about Quincy?'

'Quincy?'

'After the quinine in tonic water.'

'Of course.'

'That's it then. Six names. Now we just have to divvy them out.'

We talk about this for a moment. He makes a note of the dogs, their distinguishing features. They're a mixture of mainly white with brown or black markings. The bruiser has a black splodge over his eye like a pirate patch. Tom even weighs them, with my assistance, placing them carefully one at a time on some digital kitchen scales.

'Most importantly you have to decide which one you want,' he says, sitting next to me on the sofa again.

'How am I supposed to choose when they're all so cute?' I protest.

'First things first. Do you want a dog or a bitch?'

'A dog, I think. Though I'm tempted to get Bob done after this, and the little chap too.'

Tom crosses his legs. 'Any idea which one? I mean, you don't have to decide just yet. You can get to know them first.'

'I guess. Though I sort of have a feeling I might go for the bruiser. Can he be Denis?'

'Course.'

Denis and Bob. A new double act. I beam at the prospect.

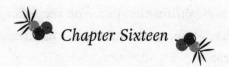 *Chapter Sixteen*

THE END OF term and Lauren is coming home later today for three whole weeks of holiday. It'll be a full house. She'll be wanting her room back so I'll do the decent thing and offer mine up to Harry and Dale. I can go on the sofa bed in the office. No need for a double bed just for me and Bob.

The puppies are thriving at nearly two weeks old. Tom gives me daily pup-dates by text, with weight gains and any exciting developments. He signed off with a wide-eyed emoji the day they opened their eyes earlier this week. I have to admit I was excited at the news and popped in for half an hour once he was back from school. There they were, six pairs of eyes peering up at me when I leaned in to say hello.

I offered to take Betty out for a quick walk to give her some space from the constant clamouring of six babies. Tom was really grateful, as was Betty. We went onto the beach and she ran around in the dusk embracing her freedom and barking at the waves. After twenty minutes, it was too dark so we headed back to the cottage and on our approach I could see Tom through the window as he was yet to draw the curtains.

He was asleep on the sofa, sprawled heavily, surrounded by marking, vulnerable yet untroubled, and I felt the urge to kiss him. But instead I crept in like a thief in the night, deposited Betty back in the whelping box where the puppies instantly woke up as if an alarm had gone off.

I stayed a while longer, Tom snoring gently, and once they'd finished feeding and dropped back off into their baby sleep, I scooped up Denis and gave him a cuddle, stroking his pixie, velvet ears, thinking of Mrs Pink and longing to see Lolly.

And today she'll be home. Mike has partially redeemed himself by volunteering to pick her up in his van so I've made the most of this offer and instructed him to get a Christmas tree on the way back. Lolly can choose it and that way Mike will pay, as I really don't have enough cash to splash around this year. Meanwhile I have shopping to do, beds to make, food to cook.

LAST CHRISTMAS WAS the worst on record. Mum gone. Harry in Canada. Mike with Melanie. A dismantled, scattered family. Dad, Lauren and I had been asked round to various people's homes, all genuine invites, but none of us could face doing someone else's Christmas. You have your own traditions and even though so much had changed since the previous year, we wanted to keep what precious little we had left. So we bought a real tree from a farm, somehow squashing it into my car, and Lauren retrieved the decorations from the attic – the snowmen, the angels, the baubles, the tinsel, all the tacky pieces collected over the years. And we did Christmas in honour of our family, toasting them with Dad's sloe gin after the Queen's speech. But the turkey was too dry, Mum's pudding overcooked, the brandy butter curdled. We all had indigestion and went to bed after three hours of *Downton Abbey*.

This year will be different. Carol will be with us for a start. She usually goes to her mum's in Bristol but Stella has a new boyfriend who's whizzing her off on a cruise. Carol's actually excited to be spending Christmas with us. She's here already, ten days ahead of time, waiting for the return of the student because not only is she Lauren's godmother, but she's also desperate for her opinion on the latest batch of gin. She can't work out why this last one, for all its improvement in flavour, is cloudy. Dad suspects it's the essential oils from the juniper berries.

As I'm putting away the first of the Christmas shops, having used up this year's Co-op dividends, the door clatters open and in she comes, my Pippi Longstocking.

She has rainbow hair and a nose ring. And goodness knows what else. But I'm so happy to see her, here where she belongs, that I don't moan or nag, I just give in to the hug, inhaling the winter cold coming off her freckled cheeks.

'Hello, stranger.'

'Sorry I've not been back before, Mum. I've been like, so busy.'

'That's OK. I'm glad you've been all right after the initial hiccup.'

'Yeah, soz and all that. I've laid off the Jägerbombs.'

'Good decision.'

She gazes around the kitchen, taking it all in, brushing her fingertips along the table, opening the fridge door, smiling, taking out a black cherry yoghurt, shutting the door again. Then she sniffs, like Bob on a scent, and peers through the glass oven door. 'Mince pies?'

'Granddad's finest. With a secret ingredient.'

'Oh?' She sniffs again. 'Not gin?'

'Yes, gin.'

She squeals and rushes off to the shed, yoghurt still in hand, where she knows she'll find Dad and Bob. She'll be climbing the walls when she hears about Denis.

And then there's Mike. Standing by the kitchen door like a desolate spectre at the feast so I cave in.

'Cup of tea?'

'Thought you'd never ask.'

He sits down at the table while I make a brew. I can sense his eyes taking everything in, like his daughter just now, though nothing like his daughter. She's filled with happiness and nostalgia and gladness to be home. He's filled with loss and regrets. What used to be his kitchen. His home. His wife. He gave all of that up the day he left.

'Is it true?' I asked him one rainy morning last year, right here, at this table, over cornflakes he'd been chasing round his bowl.

And to give him his due, he realized what I was asking him and he answered with a simple 'Yes'. To which I said, 'Oh.'

Twenty-eight years of marriage and 'Oh' was all I could come up with. All the questions I could've asked, all the accusations I could've thrown at him, and 'Oh' was my response.

'Jen?' he asks now, his hands wrapped round his mug of tea.

'What?' I'm busying myself extracting Dad's mince pies from the oven and sliding them onto the cooling rack. Every object is loaded with emotion and memory. Every smell, every taste, every last Christmas motif.

'You OK?'

'I'm fine, thank you, Mike.' *It's none of your goddam business, Mike,* is what I want to say but I manoeuvre the subject away from me. 'Did you get the tree?'

'We did. Lolly chose it. Seven-foot Norway spruce. It's on the driveway. I'll fetch it in and trim it. Do you need me to get the stand out of the loft?'

'Dale's already done it, along with all the decs and lights. He's a marvel.'

'A marvel?'

'Yes, a marvel.'

'Well, then, that's good.'

'Yes, it is good. Very good.'

He looks bereft. Left out.

Sympathy kicks in. I sit down at the table across from him. 'You need to get to know Dale. You need to spend time with Harry. Invite them round for tea or something.'

'I suppose, yeah. Sometime over Christmas. In fact, what are you doing for Christmas?'

'Oh, you know, the usual,' I tell him nonchalantly. 'Only with the added bonus of Dale and Carol.' And now of course I have to ask him. 'You?'

'Melanie's parents.' He sighs. A deep-down sigh.

'Melanie's parents? So she's taken you back?'

'Yes,' he says.

'And you wanted to go back to her?'

He thinks about this for a moment, wrong-footed by the question, comes up with a defensive answer. 'Well, you didn't want me, did you?'

I'm about to shout rude things at him, angry that I have been feeling pity just now, that he is trying to put this on me, when he makes a grab for my hand which I pull away and hide in my lap.

'Sorry,' he says.

'Sorry?'

'Yes,' he says. 'I'm sorry. About everything. And yes, I did.'

'You did what?'

'I did want to go back to Melanie.'

'Right.' So I do what any abandoned wife would do to her estranged husband. I offer him a mince pie which he accepts with a thank-you before taking a bite that nearly blasts his head off.

'Sorry, I should've said. They're still hot.' I pour him a glass of water and he sticks his tongue in it.

He recovers pretty well and continues eating the mince pie in that slightly shocked way you do when something is flailing the skin off the roof of your mouth. Then he adds, with a subtle bit of his own nonchalance, 'And the other Bartons.'

'The other Bartons?'

'Melanie's grandparents.'

'Good luck with that.'

'And her uncle.'

'Her uncle? You mean you're spending Christmas Day with Dave Barton?'

He shrugs and says, 'How did it come to this? I bloody hate Dave Barton too.'

And I want to scream at him, *Because you've been a bloody idiot!* But I don't. Because right now, despite the stress of Christmas looming, despite the lack of a job, and despite trying to launch a terrifyingly new venture off the ground, it dawns on me that this weird mix-up of anger and sympathy is morphing into something quite different.

'Can I pop round at some point to see the kids?' he asks.

And that's it. What I'm feeling is sadness. Sadness at what we've lost.

'You're still their dad,' I tell him.

Dead on cue, in troop Harry and Lauren from the shed, chattering like baby birds.

'I've sorted it, Mum.' Lauren's excited. 'You need vapour infusion for the botanicals, rather than maceration.'

'In English?'

'You need to put the juniper berries into a gin basket in the arm of the still so that the ethanol vapour passes through it during the distillation. That way the juniper oil won't make the gin cloudy and the flavour should be softer.'

'Right, OK, I'm with you.'

'You see, Mum, ethanol draws the oils out of the cells of juniper berries, which are mainly monoterpenes and also some sesquiterpenes.'

'Right.'

'You know, like alpha-pinene. That gives a piny flavour.'

'I see.'

'And sabinene is spicy. As is caryophyllene. And limonene is citrusy, obvs. And camphene is woody. As is cadinene. And terpinene. Beta-myrcene is sort of balsamic and musty, cineole is minty.' She takes stock of her mother, knowing full well I'm clueless as to what the heck my daughter's talking about.

'This is impressive, Lauren,' I tell her, rustling up what enthusiasm I have. 'I wish I could tell you I understand or that I'll remember any of it. But I get the basket-infusion bit.'

'It's not just the way juniper is made up, Mum. It'll be slightly different depending on what other botanicals you mix in.'

'How do you know all this?'

'The guide from the distillery. We've been out a few times.'

'Oh, that's nice.'

'It is nice. It's really nice. But we're just friends, to be clear.'

'OK, all clear.'

Lauren is sitting at the table next to her father, a cuppa in hand, helping herself to a mince pie. 'Carol's pretty good at all this, you know.'

'She is?'

'She really is.'

'I am doing my bit too, you know. I'm more than a washer-upper.'

'I know that, Mother,' she says. 'Don't get your knickers in a twist. You're the one who's got everyone on board. None of this would be happening without you.' She's up on her feet again, hugging me. Then she swipes a second mince pie before bounding up to her room, Bob nipping at her heels.

'That told you,' Mike says. 'And she's right, you know. You're doing really well.'

Once upon a time I'd have lapped up appreciation from him, but now it's empty praise that I just don't want. Luckily I don't have to respond because Mike disappears to sort the tree.

And now Lauren's familiar 'music' is thumping. I switch on the radio in a vain attempt to drown out DJ Nobber with 'Once in Royal David's City'.

David.

An annoying image of Dave Barton floats into view. I swipe it away with the tea towel and think about Tom. A much nicer thought. But still confusing.

I need to take matters in hand so I text Tom to ask him round for supper. One more mouth to feed won't make any difference now, will it? He says he's already eaten and my heart sinks. But then it lifts again when he says he'll pop round anyway for a cuppa.

BY THE TIME Mike has lugged in the tree, sawn off the end, pruned the lower branches, got it to stay upright in the stand, tested and positioned the lights, it's supper time. Vegetable chilli and rice, something to warm the cockles. I cave in yet again and ask him if he wants to stay as there's enough to go round, and he says yes, but I haven't really thought this through because just as we're on to the rhubarb crumble which makes Dale pull a face as he's never tasted such a tart flavour, there's a knock at the front door and I realize that it's Tom.

I leave the table quickly before anyone else bothers and let Tom in.

'Can't stay long,' he says. 'Don't like to leave Betty. Thanks for going round to see her earlier, by the way. Between you and Morag next door, it seems to be working OK.'

I lead him through to the kitchen, conscious that it might be a bit overwhelming, faced with all the family including Mike, who looks up, surprised to see a man in what used to be his kitchen, but I will not get wound up any more by his reactions, so I ignore him and pass Tom a bowl of crumble, the custard jug and a spoon. He sits down in Carol's vacated chair as she's headed back out with Dale to check on Violet's progress.

The chat round the table, after a brief stutter, flows

again. Dad fills our glasses with wine and we're back on the subject of gin.

'The second key ingredient is coriander seeds,' Lauren announces. 'Two parts coriander to one part juniper.'

Back and forth we chat, chipping in with ideas for the botanicals, with ideas for the future, until suddenly I realize that Mike has gone. I excuse myself discreetly in order to look for him. I can't hear him in the loo. He's not in the office. I try the front room. He's not there either. But the tree is standing proud, twinkling softly and waiting for the decorations, in its usual place in the bay window, its lights reflected in the glass.

There is one decoration already in situ. The silver tinsel star at the top. That was always Mike's job, putting on the star. I feel a wave of annoyance that he should do it without us, this tradition of ours, on his own. What's he playing at? And when I check out the window, seeing the space on the driveway where his van was, sadness bubbles up again. That he felt he had to leave without even saying goodbye.

I hurry back to the kitchen and join the warm hum of chatter and food and friendship.

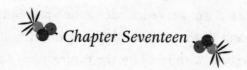 *Chapter Seventeen*

CHRISTMAS DAY AND for the second year on the trot I wake up to Bob licking my nose, my stocking unfilled. All those Christmases hoping and praying the kids would make it past six o'clock, and here I am at seven, a dog breathing on me in the dark, in the office downstairs.

He growls quietly and I listen out. I can hear water pipes clanking and the boiler firing up. Dad most probably.

I heave myself out from the warmth of my duvet, whip on my dressing gown and slippers and head to the source of the noise, Bob ahead of me, my mini protector.

'Lolly? You're up early.'

'I came down to see if Father Christmas had been.'

'Of course he has. Have you checked under the tree?'

'I did. It looks amazing though I'm not sure how he afforded it this year.'

'A little helper called eBay.'

'Praise the Lord for eBay.' She gives me a kiss. 'Happy Christmas, Mother.'

'Happy Christmas, Daughter. Are you making a brew?'

'Go back to bed and I'll bring it in.'

'But the turkey...'

'It's already in the oven, as per the instructions you left for yourself last night. What time did you get to bed?'

'Um, well, quite late, I suppose.'

She raises her eyebrows.

'About half one?'

'Half one? Blimey, Mother. What were you doing?'

'Oh, you know, the usual Christmas Eve stuff a parent does.'

'Go back to bed then. About time someone helped out around here.'

I don't mention the extra washing I've been doing since she came home, or the trail of empty mugs around the house, or the odd socks discarded into corners and under chairs. Instead I head back to the sofa bed and within minutes I'm asleep.

Two hours later I'm woken up by Dad who brings me a cuppa and takes away the cold one left by Lauren.

'All under control,' he says. 'Take your time.'

Which is all well and good but if we want a proper Christmas dinner today, someone will have to direct proceedings. The spuds need peeling, the table needs laying, Mum's final Christmas pud needs boiling. And on and on.

Dad's shuffled back to the kitchen, leaving my door wide open so I can hear him going out to the garden. Even on Christmas Day, he needs his shed.

My next visitor is Harry, bleary-eyed, a reminder that some things are constant. Harry and mornings have never mixed particularly well.

'Happy Christmas, Mum.'

'Happy Christmas, Harry.'

'You all right down here? I feel bad tipping you out of your room.'

'I don't mind. It's just lovely to have you home.'

'And you're OK with Dale being here?'

'Absolutely. Let's show him a right old British Christmas. Starting with a Buck's Fizz while you two sort the sprouts. And carrots. And swede.'

'All right, all right...' He leaves the room before I can finish reciting his list of jobs.

THREE HOURS LATER and we're on track. We've also finished the third bottle of Buck's Fizz and are now on to gin. Not one of ours as it's not there yet but we're hopeful it's not far off. Lauren was right about the infusion basket which Dad rigged up and with Carol's newly discovered talent we're pretty much there with a smooth-tasting gin. We just need to give it that Devon twist. The magic ingredient that will make Dingleton Gin unique.

AN HOUR AFTER that, dead on time, we sit down together at the kitchen table, which is all pimped up, glitzed out and candlelit. Arms linked, we pull our crackers simultaneously and the smell of sulphur competes with the crazy array of food: turkey, bread sauce, stuffing, pigs in blankets, roast potatoes, parsnips, sprouts, carrots, swede, cauliflower cheese, gravy.

'Put your hat on, Dale,' Lauren orders. 'Otherwise no food for you.'

He does as he's told, a little sheepish in that Canadian way. 'Don't you say grace?'

The rest of us chorus, 'Grace!' and Dale shakes his head, a wry smile on his face.

'The old ones are the best,' Dad says. 'But I take your point, Dale.'

I'm wondering if Dad has suddenly come over all religious but no. He chinks his glass with his knife and says he'd like to make a toast.

I groan inwardly.

'In Japan eating Christmas dinner at KFC is so popular you have to queue for two hours in some places. And if we were in Greenland we could be eating fermented birds, kiviak, that have been kept in a seal carcass for seven months.'

'Is this going somewhere, Dad?'

'Does it have to go anywhere?'

'We don't want dinner to get cold.'

'True. Sprouts need to be warm.' He coughs dramatically. 'I just wanted to say a big welcome to Dale on his first Christmas here. And of course to Carol too.'

They both murmur thank-yous.

'And welcome home to my grandchildren.'

They both look slightly horrified.

'And lastly I'd like to make a toast to my daughter, Jennifer Juniper. For being a top banana.'

'A top banana?'

'That's what I said. To Jennifer Juniper.' And he raises his glass of fizz and we all follow suit, apart from me because that would be weird, toasting myself, the top banana, so I just drink.

The mood is happy, jolly, easy and it's not till we get to the pudding that I think about Mum. This is the last pudding from the final lot she made. It will have the usual sixpences that she'd kept from the old days. And I think of Mike because that was his job, setting fire to it with brandy, making the kids go all quiet in awe.

But now Lauren steps up. 'I'll do it, Mum,' she says, reaching in the larder cupboard for the Aldi brandy and a box of matches. I watch her do the honours while Dad uncorks the sloe gin.

'Come on, then,' he says. 'Other room. Queen's speech.' He's on his feet, so nimble you'd never think he'd recently had a fall – or even a 'trip' as he still refers to it. 'We can't miss it. Who knows how many more she has in her?'

'She's getting on,' Carol agrees.

'Don't worry,' Dad says. 'There's an Indonesian man who claims to be one hundred and forty-five years old. She could have loads left.'

'I haven't watched it since about 1978.'

'Wash your mouth out, Carol.' Dad's only half-joking. 'She's your queen and sovereign. Or to use her full title: Elizabeth the Second, by the Grace of God, of the United Kingdom of Great Britain and Northern Ireland and of Her other Realms and Territories Queen, Head of the Commonwealth, Defender of the Faith.'

By now we are squeezed together in the front room, Dad in his armchair, Dale in the other armchair, Harry on a big cushion at his feet, Carol, me and Lauren on the sofa, Bob sprawled in front of the log fire. The tree's pretty in the soft afternoon light. The pile of presents has been decimated, with only half a ton of needles piled up in their place.

We eat the pudding with lashings of brandy butter and its perfect accompaniment of sloe gin. Which of course makes me think of the afternoon we picked the berries. The afternoon Bob fathered a litter. The evening Tom and I spent in Plymouth.

Tom.

He'll be at his sister-in-law's in Taunton now. Said he'd just go for a few hours because he didn't want to leave Betty or the puppies for long. I might pop in and see how they're getting on. Besides, Bob needs a walk. He's eaten twice his body weight in giblets.

'Anyone fancy some fresh air?'

No response apart from a few sleepy murmurs and a massive snore from Dad.

'I won't be long.'

BOB AND I have a brisk walk to Coast Guards Row and it's only as I reach Tom's place that I wonder if it's a good idea, bringing Bob with me. I'm not sure what he'll make of the puppies or what Betty's reaction will be to seeing him again. I'm about to retrieve the key from under the flowerpot when the door mysteriously opens.

'Tom?'

'Happy Christmas, Jen. Come in.'

I pick up Bob like a rugby ball and step into the warmth of the hallway which looks tattier than ever.

'I thought you were in Taunton.'

'Decided not to go in the end.' He shrugs.

'Worried about leaving them?'

'Yeah—' He stops, like he was about to say something else but decided against.

'And...?'

'Well, as much as I love Claire's family, I couldn't face being there. Without her. You know.'

'I'm sorry. Are you OK?'

'I've been better,' he says. 'But this lot are keeping me busy.'

'Can I see them? I was just coming round to check everything was all right. But I'm not so sure about Bob now.'

Bob is wriggling under my arm, desperate to get down and investigate the smells beyond the closed door.

'I'm sure he'll be fine. Betty might have other ideas.'

Betty does have other ideas. As soon as Tom shows us into the living room, she growls ferociously at Bob and I'm not sure if it's because of their previous encounter or because she's protecting her young. Tom tells her not to worry and she seems to understand. Bob's a coward anyway, hiding behind my legs and then hurling himself onto the sofa when he spies the pups. The gorgeous pups, on the move, one after the other, scaling the whelping-box walls and dropping over the side onto the floorboards, like they're escaping Alcatraz. They're here, there and everywhere, the little ankle biters – or 'angle twichers' as Kev calls them – Tom trailing around the room wiping up puddles of pee and poo.

'They've started on solids then?'

'Oh yes, they have indeedy. It gets quite messy.'

'I can see that.'

He's on his hands and knees, cleaning up after Queenie. Or is it Olive?

'Shall I put the kettle on?'

He nods apologetically and Bob skitters after me into the kitchen, which is remarkably clean. No sign of a Christmas lunch. I make us some tea, looking in his cupboards, wondering if Claire chose the Orla Kiely tea caddy, an echo of Mum's Poole pottery. The seventies. That was the time to be a kid at Christmas. Everyone watching *Morecambe and Wise*, the one day a year you were allowed to pig out on a selection box. The one day you weren't left feeling a little bit hungry at the end of a meal.

But still. The whole Operation Yewtree scenario kind of blighted some of our best memories.

Tom interrupts me while I'm adding milk to the mugs.

'Look at this little fella.'

'Oh. Is that Denis?'

Tom nods. Denis has that fetching black patch over his eye and a mischievous glare. 'He won't leave his poor mother alone. Thought you might want a hug while the others get their share?'

'I'd love to. Hand him over.' I sit at the table and notice the fairy lights in the courtyard and remember how that night ended, on the date that wasn't a date, with me running home like a love-struck teenager.

Now Tom plonks Denis on my lap and Bob edges closer to see what the heck is going on. He sniffs and sniffs and then flops down by my feet, either in a mood, or in exhaustion. Meanwhile pandemonium breaks out. Tom forgot to shut the living-room door and there's a stampede of puppies, running amok all over the kitchen, in and out of our feet, harassing Bob who lies there in submission, even when they try to latch on to him. We spend the next five minutes herding them back to their box. Two minutes later, they're all sparko, including Betty, while Bob waits by the front door, staring hopefully at the handle as if by the power of psychic manipulation he will be able to open it and escape from this craziness.

'Someone wants you to go.'

'Yep.'

'I'd like you to stay.'

'Oh. Well. I'd like that too...'

'But?'

'I should be getting back. I've been gone long enough.'

'Oh.' He sounds deflated. Knackered. But is gracious. 'Course. It's Christmas.'

'Talking of Christmas, have you eaten today?'

'Boiled egg and soldiers,' he says.

This paints such a piteous picture I want to hug him and take care of him but also do things to him that are quite filthy. But I must pull myself together. 'No turkey?'

'Not so much as a whiff of Paxo.'

'Right, then. Have you drunk anything?'

'Nope. Just several pints of tea. Why? Would you like a lift home?'

'That would be lovely. But really I was thinking you could grab a bite to eat with us?'

He looks doubtful. 'Not sure I'd be the best company...'

'At least let me plate you something up and you can warm it in the microwave and eat it in front of *Call the Midwife*.'

And now I feel bad, in case that reminds him of his own doctor wife but he's smiling.

'That's kind of you,' he says. 'I'd like that.' And he grabs his car keys from a hook in the hall and I put Bob back on the lead.

The town is deserted. The amusement arcade in darkness. The Co-op shuttered. The streets and pavements empty of cars and people. No sign of Kev who I hope is enjoying Christmas in the comfort of his home up at Donker Farm.

When we turn into the road, my heart sinks. Mike's van is on the drive.

'You all right?' Tom asks.

'It's Mike. Come to see the kids.'

'Ah.'

'Christmas makes you realize what you've lost.'

'It does.'

'I'm sorry, Tom. That was naff of me.'

'You've had a loss too. It's not a competition.'

'I know. But still. You coming in?'

'Do you mind if I wait here?'

'Course not. I'll be as quick as poss.'

So I leave the poor man in his car while I let myself in. It's all quiet. Either everyone is still asleep or watching telly. God knows where Mike is. Bob makes a beeline for his basket and curls up. I follow him into the kitchen and start making up a plate of food, surprised and relieved that someone has tidied up. Whoever it was has wiped down the sides, put cling film over the veg and shrouded the turkey with a tea towel. Carol, I suspect. Carol. I'd forgotten she was even here.

'Jennifer? Where've you been?'

'Dad! You made me jump.'

'I'm after a turkey sandwich.'

'Already?'

'Why not? Are you helping yourself to a second dinner?'

'It's for Tom.'

'Where is he?' He scouts the kitchen as if Tom might be lurking in the shadows.

'He's in the car.'

'Right.' And with an astonishing lack of questioning, Dad constructs his sandwich with doorstop hunks of bread, slabs of turkey and lashings of cranberry sauce before heading back to the living room. 'Mike's here,' he says as an afterthought.

I'm tiptoeing out with the plate of food, wrapped tightly in foil with a small jug of gravy, when Mike opens the living-room door and appears in the hall. My hall.

'What are you up to?' he asks.

I feel myself blush and am cross that that's the reaction I come up with. It's not as if I'm doing anything wrong. I'm giving a lonely widower Christmas dinner, that's all.

'None of your beeswax.'

'I wasn't interrogating you.' He throws his arms up in surrender. 'I was trying to be friendly, that's all.'

'Oh.'

'Happy Christmas, Jen.'

'Are you being facetious?'

'No, I mean it. Happy Christmas.'

'Oh. Thanks. It's been all right actually.'

'Good. That's good.' He smiles half-heartedly. 'Mine's been miserable.'

'Spending the day with the Bartons? Miserable? Surely not.'

'They weren't too bad. Considering.'

'Considering?'

'Considering they're the Bartons. I missed the kids, though.'

'I really don't know what you want me to say to that, Mike. I mean, I know exactly what I *want* to say but you won't like it.'

'Try me.'

Of course, in the spirit of Yuletide I should button it, keep those thoughts to myself but I can't, I really can't.

'You've only yourself to blame. You've made your bed. You reap what you sow. Will that do?'

He's speechless, his eyes glistening. I probably shouldn't have rammed that home quite so hard but I won't let him make me feel bad. Not any more. He does only have himself to blame. But now he's puffing out his chest, about to come up with a retort. 'Maybe I wouldn't have left you if you were kinder,' he says. 'Maybe I'd have stayed if you gave me more respect. If you weren't always running around after other people.'

It's like a slap. A cold hard slap in the face. Only it's not my face that's getting slapped. It's Mike's.

'Happy Christmas, you pillock.'

And with that, I leave him holding his cheek, disbelief on his face, while I flounce off to the kitchen, shove a portion of Christmas pud into a takeaway container and then storm out of the house and into the cold, crisp evening.

Tom is ready and waiting with the engine running.

'Drive, Tom. Just drive.'

And he does. He puts his foot down and he drives,

me balancing a full Christmas dinner on my lap, my face burning, my heart raging. So much for not getting wound up.

TOM HAS HIS dinner in the kitchen while I have a boiled egg with soldiers, calmer now in the safe haven of Coast Guards Row. We drink tea and we talk about Christmases past. We toast absent friends and we share a few laughs and even a few tears and suddenly it's twenty past nine and Lauren is texting me.

Where r u, Mum. U ok?

I'm at Tom's. A bit sozzled tbh.

Go, Mother!! How are you getting
home? Or are you staying there?!
Everything fine here.

Would you mind if I stayed?

Granddad's gone to bed, Carol's
passed out on yours, me and the boys
playing whist. It's all good.

Thnx Lol xxx

Happy Xmas Mama xxx

I switch off the phone.
Tom's still eating his pudding.
'Can I stay over?'

He pauses, spoon midway to his mouth. 'Course,' he says. 'If you want to. Do you want to? I can make up the spare bed?'

'Tom.' I can't help laughing at his confused reaction. 'That's not really what I had in mind.'

'Oh? Oh. I see.' He carries on eating his pudding but then he starts coughing. Like really coughing. Choking actually. He's choking. Ohmygod he is actually really choking.

I rush over to him and somehow wrestle him to his feet, then, relying on the first-aid course we recently did at the museum, I do the Heimlich manoeuvre.

'Ueugh!!!'

Something flies through the air and hits the kitchen window before bouncing to the floor. What was it?

I stop worrying about Tom who has recovered and is now drinking water and I check on the floor where something small and silver is glinting in the glow of the fairy lights.

One of Mum's sixpences.

I pick it up and show it to Tom. 'It seems my mother tried to kill you.'

He looks up, heavenwards. Then he looks at me, takes a step and as I hold my breath, I feel his arms close around me and hold me tight and I am just where I want to be. Happy Christmas.

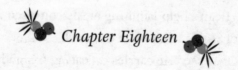

Chapter Eighteen

CHRISTMAS HAS BEEN and gone in a flash and blur of food, washing, low-grade bickering, telly, card games, dog walks and gin. Today is a new year and I'm feeling almost upbeat. I've seen Tom a couple of times over the last week. I didn't stay the whole of that Christmas night as I thought that was a bit much so I crept home in the early hours like a dirty stop-out, which technically I was, and had to share the sofa bed with a sizzled, snoring Carol.

The puppies are coming along nicely. Lauren and Dad went for a visit and decided Denis was definitely the one for us. So in a couple of weeks we'll have a new addition to the family. Lauren's annoyed she'll be back in Plymouth by then, but no doubt she'll come home more often this term. Denis will be hashtagged relentlessly.

As for Tom. He's spent the holidays running with his pack. School returns on Thursday so I've said I'll pupsit while he's at work. He's more than happy with this arrangement. As am I. Though it would be nicer if he were with me too instead of with a bunch of maniacal ten-year-olds.

But today is the annual walk on Dartmoor. We always take a trip to Hay Tor on New Year. A picnic in the car, a walk up the hill, a climb to the top of the tor, whether it's windy or foggy. And it's usually one or both of these, though sometimes you're rewarded with one of those sharp, bright, clear freezing stunners. But not today.

Right now I'm making up the big flask of coffee, compiling sandwiches, and assembling the tail ends of the Christmas shop. When we return from Dartmoor, that's it. Yuletide over. No waiting till Twelfth Night. The tree's on its last legs and the very sight of tinsel makes me want to garrotte myself.

Everyone is up now, tired-eyed and husky-voiced after the previous night's fairly tame celebrations. The young ones went to the pubs in town, fancy dress as is the custom here, a bemused Dale going along with it, dressed as an ice-hockey player. Dad and I stayed in, grazing on dates and figs and sugared jellies while watching *Gladiator*. Seeing the New Year in with some full-on Roman death wasn't the jolliest, but it's a good film and I cry every time. Last night was no exception. Russell Crowe grieving for his dead wife made me think of Tom. And Dad too, of course, who I noticed surreptitiously wiping his eye. So I sat next to him on the sofa, Bob between us, and held his hand. Sometimes no words are needed.

This morning Dad is on breakfast duties. He can somehow rustle up a decent eggs Benedict even when he's not mentally present. His mind might be roaming all over the universe but he can still poach an egg to perfection and make a hollandaise sauce that Delia would be proud of.

As we sit together round the table, Lauren pipes up with the words I dread: 'What are your New Year resolutions?' She's addressing everyone. But, game as ever, she goes first. 'Mine's to go to all my lectures. Even the one on Fridays at nine a.m.'

'How many have you missed?'

'That's not the point, Mother. I'm stating my resolutions so I can be accountable for going to all the rest of them.'

She's good at this.

Dale says, 'I want to find out more about my family heritage. Just to check that Harry's not my second cousin or something creepy.'

I'm tempted to say he wouldn't want any of Mike's genes. Actually I do say it, to which Harry replies, 'Dale only wears Levi's. Dad buys his from the market.'

There's a groan round the table and then I do the decent thing and have my go.

'I intend to stop saying negative stuff about your father. I mean, he can be a right twonk but he's your dad and I should respect that.'

Harry and Lauren look at each other, surprised.

'I'm not that bad. Am I?'

'Nothing he doesn't deserve,' Lauren says. 'He is a right twonk. But he's my dad and I love him.'

Harry is quiet. Dale gives him a gentle nudge. 'I think you've done brilliantly without him, Mum. And if you want to call him a twonk, you do it.' He smiles. 'And I intend to pay off my overdraft this year.'

'Overdraft?'

'It's a tiny one. I'm just stating my resolutions so I can be accountable.'

'Right.'

Lauren sniggers into her tea, pulls herself together and turns her attention to her grandfather. 'What about you, Granddad?'

Deep breath.

'I'll do my bit to help get this gin business up and running.'

'That's nice, Dad.'

'Nice? It's gintastic.' And Dad laughs helplessly as if this is the funniest thing anyone in the history of the world has ever ever said.

Two hours later, with an excited Bob on Lauren's lap, we pull into the car park at Hay Tor, along with half of Devon. The other half must still be nursing hangovers.

As predicted it's foggy so we decide to eat our picnic first. It's a squeeze in my car and Dale looks at us like we're mad. He checks the other cars and sees their inhabitants doing the same.

'I suppose you have drive-through Tim Hortons in your National Parks,' Dad asks.

'Every kilometre,' Dale responds.

'There's a kiosk over there if you want some proper coffee,' Harry says.

'I might just do that. Anyone else?'

'Can you get me an ice cream?' Lauren asks.

'Seriously?'

'Seriously. Strawberry, please.'

Dale heads out into damp fog, shoulders hunched, hood up.

'How does he survive the Canadian winters?' Dad wonders aloud.

'Canadian winters are nothing like British ones,' Harry says. 'He says he's spent his time here permanently damp.'

'Maybe I should put the heating up a notch.'

We discuss the merits of Britain versus Canada while we eat. Dale gets back in and declines my offer of a hard-boiled egg, saying he's all 'egged-out'.

'You'll never make a bodybuilding chess player,' Dad says.

We wait for Dad to continue but no clarification follows. He gets out of the car and starts putting on his anorak. And overtrousers. And hiking boots.

'I suppose we're going now then,' Lauren says, clipping on Bob's lead to his new Christmas collar.

IT'S BRACING AT the top of the tor and the fog has miraculously lifted for us to see the dizzying views. I point out Dingleton in the far distance. Dale says it's awesome. Dad explains how the tor was formed. That it was a combination of freeze-thaw weathering and hydrolysis.

'Hydrolysis?'

'The decomposition of a chemical compound when it reacts with water,' Lauren chips in.

'That's... interesting,' Dale says.

I realize we've reached the stage where Dale might be happier finding a cosy pub so I suggest we head on to Widecombe.

Everyone's happy with this idea so we set off back down the hill. Only by now the fog is back, thicker than ever. Suddenly I'm on my own but my feet know their way back to the car park. Just follow the well-trodden path downhill. What could possibly go wrong?

A face appears, followed by a body. It's unnerving. Like a ghost.

'Jennifer. Fancy seeing you here.'

That's all I need. Dave Barton. Here. Now.

'Happy New Year,' he says.

I nod and mumble about getting back to the car. But he ignores me and carries on like the windbag he is.

'Out with the family?'

'We're just going.'

'Run along then.'

Could he be any more annoying?

'I'll see you at the meeting on Wednesday, I presume?'

'The meeting?'

'The public meeting.'

'What public meeting?'

'The public meeting to discuss the impact of your proposal for a gin palace in one of our most treasured buildings.'

'Hang on, you were proposing a budget pub.'

'I'm not the owner of Clatford House. I have to listen to my constituents' concerns.'

He disappears then, melts back into the fog. Of course he can be more annoying. He can always be more annoying. How the hell didn't we know about this meeting?

I ELECT HARRY to drive because I want a pint. Despite the crush of bodies in the Rugglestone Inn, we find a table. Unfortunately it's outside and Dale once again fails to hide the astonishment on his face. Honestly, I don't know how he manages to play ice hockey if he can't manage a pub garden in January. It's not as if it's raining.

I feel a raindrop on my nose. Then another. Dale has doleful eyes.

'All right, let's get home.' We down our drinks and pile back into the car, steaming it up so that Harry has to put the heating on full blast.

ON OUR RETURN, Dale gets the log burner going for Bob to hog. The rest of us do our own thing. Napping, telly-watching, tea-making, reading. I'm just wondering what to do about this public meeting when I get a text.

> How R U today? Fancy coming over?
>
> Yes, I do. When?
>
> Whenever you like. I'm not going anywhere.

I'm not sure if this means Tom is bored and in need of company or if he actually really wants me to come over. Either way, I'm going. I need to ask him about this meeting, apart from anything else. Anything else will be a bonus.

I'M GREETED BY mayhem. Tom's frazzled, hair dishevelled and cheeks flushed like an alky. There are puppies everywhere.

'Thank God you're here,' he says. 'I need help.'

Mixed messages again. He wants me? Or my canine assistance? Or medication?

'I've got some aspirin in my bag. And a bottle of the latest batch.'

'I'll take both. Now help me gather the pack.'

We spend the next however long gathering the pack. The whelping box is now defunct as they just climb over the sides but he's made a sort of pen that he puts them in at night. We get five inside it. Betty's already in there, asleep in the basket. Her offspring join her. But there is one missing.

Denis.

A mad panic to find Denis. We hunt downstairs for him. Under sofas, behind sofas, behind sofa cushions. In kitchen cupboards.

'Can he go upstairs?'

'Er...'

I go upstairs and try the bathroom first. Steamy. Tom must've had a shower. Then the spare room. Neat, tidy. Nowhere for a dog to hide. So that leaves Tom's bedroom. The door's ajar and I push it open with a creak. Clean laundry is piled on the bed. And on top of the clean laundry lies a naughty Denis. How the heck did he manage to clamber up there with those little legs?

'You rascal. Come here.' Denis gazes at me with to-die-for eyes and I scoop him up and hold him close, breathe in that puppy smell, absorb his warmth. I'm in love.

'Are you?'

'Did I say that out loud?'

'You did,' Tom says, standing in the doorway. 'I'm assuming you mean Denis the Menace?'

'Who else could I mean?'

He smiles. But says nothing more. This is really getting to be hard work. Is he just out of practice? I know I am.

'Um, so are they all asleep downstairs?'

'Feeding. This little fella had probably better join them or he'll miss out.'

I hand him over, reluctantly. Tom smiles at me again and says, 'Come on.'

So I follow him back downstairs where he's made two mugs of tea.

'You take sugar, don't you?'

'One, please.' He remembered. 'Then I'd better be getting home.'

'Do you have to go?'

'Um...'

'I mean, you could stay for supper.'

'Oh, right. That'd be nice, yeah, thanks.'

'Will omelette do?'

'Lovely.'

I'll be a bodybuilding chess player yet.

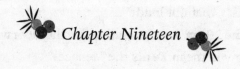

Chapter Nineteen

Day of Public Meeting

08.00: Woken up by Pippi Longstocking, asking me if I'll proofread her assignment. Tell her I'd rather have a cup of tea.

08.20: Am brought a cup of tea only the tide's out. 'Soz, Mum. I tripped over Dale's shoes. They're massive. And before you say anything, don't worry, I've cleared it up.' Assignment is left on my bed.

08.30: Try to have shower but impossibly large queue so I make do with wet wipes.

08.45: Smoke alarm goes off as someone has the audacity to make toast. Headache follows.

09.00: Have a banana.

09.05: Carol arrives. With shoulder pads.

09.15: Jackie arrives. With box file of papers.

09.30: Tish arrives, like the Queen of Sheba.

09.32: Dad leaves for shed.

09.40: Business meeting convenes at the kitchen table. Wish I'd suggested meeting at one of the others' houses but they always come here for some reason.

09.42: Open packet of Jammie Dodgers.

09.43: The vultures appear.

09.44: The vultures disperse.

09.45: Throw empty Jammie Dodger pack in the bin.

09.50: After five minutes faffing, we begin. Discussion about tonight's public meeting. Turns into rant as we all call Dave Barton rude names. How did none of us know about the meeting? Apparently neighbours had leaflets pushed through their letterboxes but none of us. And then Christmas got in the way. Hope that no one will turn up tonight. Or at least, just the friendly ones.

11.00: We have plan of action. Jackie will speak on our behalf and the rest of us will be backup. That's it.

11.30: They leave, after more rude name-calling.

11.35: Put out recycling. Find leaflet about public meeting in the paper box.

11.40: Go back to bed. Find Lauren's assignment. Start to read.

11.42: Fall asleep.

13.10: Woken by Lauren asking if I want a sandwich and if I've read her assignment yet. Tell her I've nearly finished it.

13.15: Lauren brings me a limp ham sandwich and a mug of tea.

13.20: Attempt to read assignment.

13.25: Fall asleep.

13.55: Wake up with a start when Bob barks at the front door. Tom is here.

14.00: Meeting in the shed: Dad, Lauren, Harry, Dale, Tom, me. Still lacking that elusive botanical that will turn our gin from good gin into great gin.

15.00: Tom goes home to finish planning for new term which starts tomorrow. Will see him at meeting later.

15.10: Sneak back to bed to read Lauren's assignment. Don't understand much of it but impressed nevertheless. Don't even fall asleep.

16.05: Take Bob for walk. Cold nip in the air. Forget poo bags so have to pick up deposit with handful of leaves. Squirt masses of anti-bac on hands.

17.00: Dad has tea on the table. Spag bol. Crusty bread. We are all in state of nervous excitement about meeting. Surely people will be happy with our proposals?

17.45: Leave house to set off for town hall where meeting is taking place.

18.00: Help put out chairs. Tish is wearing demure, elegant Queen Elizabeth outfit again. Jackie, Carol and I are back in business suits.

18.15: Dave Barton turns up with woman who bid on Clatford House. Who is she?

18.30: Meeting starts. Chaired by town clerk. Agendas on chairs. Dave Barton and Jackie on panel. Dave Barton first up to speak against proposals. Says museum needs bottomless funding and will become damp squib if run by new owners. Stares pointedly at yours truly. Also says the 'gin palace' – as he insists on calling it – will have negative effect on existing local businesses, that it will become eyesore in prime location when it should be focal point of town. This from the man who wanted it to be cheap family boozer. Insists idea of combining it with museum won't work and that project is doomed to failure.

18.40: Tom stops me from getting to my feet to shout obscenities at Dave Barton.

18.42: Jackie speaks on our behalf. Cool, calm, collected. Using all the right words but something missing. Mood in the room hard to gauge.

18.50: Jackie sits down, deflated.

18.55: Q&A. Panel asked a series of questions by people obviously planted by Dave Barton. Concerns raised about alcohol abuse and antisocial behaviour. Jackie replies calmly that the gin joint is not about getting drunk, it's a social experience and will enable us to run the museum. The alternative was a cheap boozer which would be far more likely to encourage irresponsible drinking. Back and forth it goes and it seems even stevens. Just as the Chair is on verge of calling time, an angel steps in.

19.20: Old Woman Bates stands up. For one so small and stooped, she has a foghorn of a voice, especially when handed microphone. She tells us we need Dingleton put on map. That our town was built on smuggling and that this will bring back tourists and day-trippers. She says museum must stay open at all costs. It's the only place that reaches out to community. It's our heritage. And our future. Suspect Kev may have primed her. After all, who'd listen to him?

19.25: Rapturous applause which turns into standing ovation. Sometimes a wise old woman is the only person for the job. Usually. Actually, always.

19.30: While packing up chairs, notice Old Woman Bates leaving. Have a word. Then a hug, gently so don't crush her. Then realize what that magic ingredient should be. When I tell her she says, 'You took your time working it out.'

19.35: Spot Dave Barton smoking outside as we head to Thirsty Bishop. If looks could kill, I'd be pushing up daisies come spring.

20.50: Arrive home.

21.30: In bed, head whirling with chemical symbols and fabulous botanicals. Is this what it's like to be my father? Or my daughter?

21.40: Father knocks on door. Tell him to enter. He stands in doorway. 'Well done, Jennifer Juniper. I never doubted you,' he says doubtfully.

21.45: Sleep.

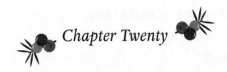

Chapter Twenty

THIS IS A time of ups and downs. Good news, bad news. Hurrahs and boos.

The first half of January has all been about getting Lauren back to uni, gin, puppies, keeping busy so as not to worry about the future. I've also done a load of eBaying, selling old tat that's been hanging around for far too long, including all my First Day Covers, my collection of *Smash Hits* magazines and an eighties bling gold bracelet Mike gave me when we got married. Dad keeps assuring me he's got it covered, but it's not fair to deplete him of his small nest-egg and pension.

Two and a half weeks after the public meeting, on a dreary Saturday morning, a letter arrives from the planning department. I can't open it, not on my own. So I call the others. They pelt round, arriving within minutes of each other, breathless and scruffy. Though Tish manages to make scruffy into a stylish art form, dressed today like a member of Bananarama.

We sit around the table, the letter in the middle, unopened. It's like a seance. We hope to conjure up good news. It could be good news. Or it could be catastrophic. There's only one way to find out.

'Open it, Jen,' says Carol.

'Why me?'

'It's got your name on the envelope.'

'And "Associates".'

The front door bangs and a few seconds later Lauren walks in.

'Lolly? What are you doing here?'

'I'm up to date on my work so I thought I'd catch up with my homies.' She drops her backpack on the floor and empties the contents of a bin bag into the washing machine. 'So what are you lot up to?'

'One of us is opening a letter from the council.'

'Who is?'

'Your mother,' says Carol. 'Only she isn't doing it.'

'Why aren't you doing it, Mum?'

'You do it, Lauren.'

She doesn't have to be asked twice. She picks it up and tears it open, starts to read.

We look at her.

She smiles. A huge smile. Her rainbow hair and her nose ring and her Pippi plaits might make her young and studenty, but she is one tough cookie. 'Right,' she says. 'As long as we comply with the conservation officer, we have Listed Building Consent so we can go ahead and do the repairs and renovations to the museum.'

There's a loud chorus of screeches.

But then a reality check from Jackie. 'What about change of use?'

'That's still being considered,' Lauren says, handing over the letter to her.

All eyes on Jackie as she takes her time reading the letter. Then she removes her glasses and inhales. 'We still need permission for change of use and for a licence. Let's not count our chickens and all that.'

The mood sinks somewhat.

'How does it work then?' Lauren asks.

'We applied for the licence at the same time as the planning,' Jackie explains, 'hoping the process would be quicker if the planning officers talked to the licensing officers to agree mutually acceptable opening hours and everything. But the two departments have different criteria for approval and they don't always agree.'

'Right...' Lauren puts her head to one side, thinking it through. 'What you're saying is... this could be a risky strategy.'

'Exactly,' Jackie says. 'I have a feeling a certain bastard councillor will make representations against the licensing application whereas if we had planning permission in place, he'd be less likely to do so.'

'Representations?'

'A nicer word for "complaints". "Representations" can be positive as well as negative.'

'So what happens if they get representations?'

'It goes to the licensing subcommittee and there's a hearing. And to be honest, Dave Barton's just as likely to make representations to the planning department over change of use.'

'Which would mean a separate subcommittee and hearing,' Lauren says.

'Hairy arses,' Tish says.

'What can we do?' Carol asks. 'We must be able to do something, Jackie? What can people object to over the change of use? Right now the museum's closed. Surely people will support us if we can find a way to keep it going?'

'One would hope.' Jackie shrugs. 'Planning looks at the impact on the surrounding area – neighbours, parking, highways etc.'

'We have that on our side then,' I chip in. 'There aren't any close neighbours, there's parking, and there's also the train station and bus stop right at hand.'

'Exactly.' Jackie is on fire now. 'Plus it's in the council's mission statement to recognize the value of tourism to Dingleton. They want to promote well-managed premises. But it also has to take account of the needs of its residents. And I quote, "who have the fundamental human right to the peaceful enjoyment of their property and possessions".'

'But if there's no one living close by, then it's not a problem, surely?' Lauren is now handing out tea. She's sloughing off the inertia of her teenage years. 'Isn't that down to licensing?'

'Well, yes.' Jackie nods. 'Licensing deals with four things: prevention of crime and disorder, public safety, prevention of public nuisance and protection of children from harm.'

'What's public nuisance?' Lauren sounds bemused. I suppose if you live in student halls in Plymouth you might have a different view of what constitutes public nuisance.

'Noise, basically,' Jackie confirms.

'But we're not having music,' Tish says. 'And we're not having rowdy drunks because we're not selling cheap booze. We're selling classy cocktails. It's a relaxed evening out, pre- or post-food. Not a piss-up. And it's not like we're applying for a late licence.'

'Light pollution?' Jackie adds.

'A bit of mood lighting in a gin bar is nothing compared to the coloured light bulbs strung all the way along the seafront,' Carol says, getting riled.

'Noxious smells?' Jackie continues. She'd make a brilliant prosecutor.

'No food.' Lauren's on it. 'No chips, no burgers. Just a

few packets of crisps and maybe some olives.'

'Always olives, darling,' Tish says and an image of Noël Coward comes to my mind. And as if she's telepathic, she quotes him. 'A perfect Martini should be made by filling a glass with gin, then waving it in the general direction of Italy.'

'Litter?' Jackie ignores this theatricality, continues to focus on possible issues.

Now it's my turn. 'The only litter we'll get is what the bloody seagulls leave behind because the council never empties the bloomin' bins. And we won't be adding to that because there's no packaging or take-aways or anything.'

'All right, Mum, calm down.' Lauren pats me on the shoulder, offers me a custard cream which I shovel into my mouth, barely tasting or chewing. I'm left with a tacky taste so I wash it away with tea but I feel a bit sick.

'So what can we do?' Carol asks again.

'Wait and see if there're any representations, I suppose,' Jackie says. 'If there are, the council have to inform us. And if they're negative, then we have to get some nice people to make positive ones.'

Thank goodness for Jackie. Everybody needs a Jackie on their team.

Two days later, I open a group text from Jackie.

There's a representation. Says we've
not addressed prevention of crime or
antisocial behaviour. Time to be
very antisocial and fight back.

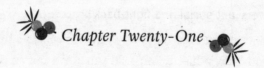

Chapter Twenty-One

SINCE LAUREN'S RETURN to Plymouth last Sunday, we've had a week teeming with relentless, soul-destroying rain. Harry and I have taken it in turns to walk Bob. Bob isn't bothered by the rain. He just wants to sniff for rabbits and roll in poo. Dale is not on dog-walking duties because he has been struck down by a cold much like the bubonic plague. I try to reassure him that there hasn't been a case of the Black Death in Dingleton since 1666. He says, 'You guys have so much history.' As for Dad, I'm not letting him roam in this weather; he gets as drenched and muddy as Bob and I don't fancy another case of man flu.

Much excitement in the house as we prepare for our new arrival at the weekend. Denis the menace! The place needs to be puppy-proofed, a bed needs to be found, newspaper needs to be gathered. I'm secretly relieved Lauren's at uni because her excited anticipation would be a lot to handle. Plus I wouldn't get a look-in on the cuddle front. And right now I need some cuddles.

Meanwhile, I've met up with an old school friend and arranged to meet up with another – the first is a genuine friend, the second more of a dirty sod.

On Tuesday, I asked Tracey round for supper. We spent a lovely evening together, just her and me, as thankfully Dale and Harry had taken Dad out for a curry. We ate pasta, drank wine, and slagged off Dave Barton who was one of those snarky lads who was always mean to her at school. She reminded me that once Dave threw a tennis ball at her head and I'd had a proper go at him.

The big surprise was finding out that as well as being a bank manager, Tracey's also a magistrate. So she's all clued up on petty crime and antisocial behaviour. Not only that but she genuinely loved the latest batch of gin, which we sampled at the end of the meal. In fact, she was dead impressed.

Today, I've arranged to visit Councillor Twonk. I texted him and asked him to meet me for a coffee at the café on the seafront. He texted straight back and said he could squeeze me in. Hmm.

Off I go, taking the car and parking on the seafront. Because of the rain. And so I can make a quick getaway if need be. I'm there early, find a table in the corner, unsure if I want to be seen fraternizing with the enemy, though ridiculously hopeful of some sort of peace treaty.

As soon as he turns up, I can see he's in one of his most obnoxious, patronizing and aggravating moods. He acknowledges me with a curt nod of his fat head and says my name. Jennifer.

The waitress comes up to the table and he winks at her. Actually winks, despite being old enough to be her father.

'Two Americanos, please,' he says, no reference to me or what I might want. But an Americano is what I actually want so I don't bother to correct him. Pick your battles, that's what Mum always said.

'Right, then, Jennifer. What's this "meeting" all about?'

'You know what this is all about.'

'Mother's ruin?'

'Why do people insist on calling it that?'

'People? What people?'

'People who think they're funny when they're really not.'

He smiles at me. I can't work out if it's a real smile or a fake one. 'You used to find me funny, Jennifer.'

'That's because I was a naive, impressionable schoolgirl.'

'Look, we were sixteen. We went out for a few weeks. We fooled around a bit, granted, but it was consensual. You never told me to stop.'

'I know that. I wanted it too. But that's not what I'm upset about.'

'Tell me, Jennifer. What are you so upset about? I mean, we weren't Romeo and Juliet.'

'You had sex with me which was a big deal and then, shortly after, you dumped me. You broke my heart.'

'I didn't realize I meant that much to you, Jennifer. You need to put that to bed. If you'll pardon the pun.'

'You *didn't* mean that much to me, not you, yourself. It was the dumping bit that was so hard. Being chucked away like a disposable bottle.'

The waitress brings our coffee and he gives her that look. That look I want to forget but can't.

'You're infuriating.'

'Me? *Pourquoi?*'

'You think you're God's gift.'

'I can't help it if women fall at my feet.'

'You're not all that.'

'You used to think so.'

'When I was sixteen. Then I grew up and knew better.'

He slurps his coffee. Stares out of the window, exaggeratedly, then turns back and looks at me, straight in the eye. I force myself to hold his gaze, like in one of those daft competitions you do when you're a kid.

He looks away first, under the pretence of checking his cufflink.

I win.

'Why aren't you more supportive of this venture? We want to keep the museum open. We want to make it better, more relevant, more accessible to everyone, and a gin bar will be something new for the town. It's not going to be a place to get rat-arsed but somewhere to go out for a nice time.'

'I'm sorry, Jennifer.' He shakes his head. 'I can't support you. It'll never work. The people of this town like a cheap drink. My plan would've been perfect.' He drains his coffee. 'It's not too late to sell it on.'

'Hang on a minute. Back up. You're telling everyone that the gin bar will be a den of iniquity, that mothers will be lying drunk in the street as if it were Gin Lane. That it will be a pustule on the face of Dingleton. And yet you'd happily buy Clatford House off us and sell it to the brewery? You're telling me that all your arguments against our plans suddenly won't apply to yours?'

'Don't be naive, Jennifer. This is politics.'

'This is about you taking a backhander.'

'You can't say things like that.' He appears to be affronted but it's all smoke and mirrors. 'It's slander.'

'Oh, for goodness' sake, I can't talk to you. You're an ignorant idiot.'

I get up, push my chair back so that it grates across the tiled floor and so that all the pensioners and builders stop eating their cakes and burgers and stare at the pair of us, wondering if it's a lover's tiff when that is the furthest thing from the truth. So I drop a fiver on the table and storm off, out of the café, the bell ringing like an alarm, right out into the pouring rain. And I don't have an umbrella. But I need the air. Oh, blimey, do I need it. I need to breathe, breathe, because right now I'm about to explode and send little parts of me, all my molecules, all my atoms, all my bits of Jennifer Juniper, right across the bay so that they float off into the English Channel, off to the Atlantic and disperse to feed the fish and seals, and dolphins and all marine life including plankton. And it's at this point that I wonder if I really am more like my father than I ever knew and of course I must be, there's the science gene rooted in there somewhere, cast in our DNA, because it got passed on to Lolly, my Pippi Long-stocking, doing her chemistry degree, doing her stuff.

Trouble is, I'm in such a rage I know I can't drive and so I keep on walking, across the green, the grass squelchy and boggy, all that rain, all that Devon frigging rain, towards the brook that runs down to the sea, not caring about the drenching, just needing to put some distance between me and Dave Barton. Bloody Dave bloody Barton. And actually it's welcome after being stuck inside with that pig. The cool dampness is reviving, invigorating, refreshing, the clinginess of my clothes to my body reminds me that I am Jennifer Juniper, with a will of my own, and with absolutely nothing at all to do with some man who once had me in his thrall when I was a maid of sixteen.

But soon, suddenly, unexpectedly, shockingly, I feel someone take my arm and hold it firmly in their grip.

I'm about to karate chop this attacker when I realize it's Dave. Bastard Dave Bastard Councillor Bastard Barton.

The dull, grey rain has gone, replaced with bright red, orange and golden sparks of hatred.

'What the bloody hell are you doing?' I'm shouting so loud it hurts my throat. It takes the breath from me and throws it up to the elements.

He's bending over double, panting, holding up one of his hands as if to halt me in my tracks but there's no stopping me now. No chance. No, no, no. He gathers enough breath and voice to grunt, 'I was trying to catch up with you.'

'Leave me alone.' This time I know I'm quieter because the force of my words doesn't hurt so much. Because I can only just make out the spat sentence. *Leave me alone.* Something I should have said a long, long time ago.

'You forgot something,' he says. And to my ears he sounds like a little boy. Not the adolescent who thought he was Morrissey, who thought he was the bee's knees, who took my heart and squeezed it till there was nothing left but a shattered teenage dream.

'What? What did I forget?' I'm whispering now, the life gone out of me, the fight buggered off. 'Did I forget to tell you I actually hate you?'

'This,' he says. 'You forgot this.' And he hands me my bag. My handbag with my purse and my phone and my address book and everything that is personal to me.

'Oh. Right. Thanks.'

'Are you all right, Jennifer? You look flushed.' He reaches out, slowly, touches my forehead, gently, and there's a fleeting notion that he might actually be concerned for me, that there might be a residual element of care, only then he goes and ruins it.

'I've always fancied you,' he says, eyes dark and steamy. He gives me that Dave Barton smile, which was cute when he was a young lad, yes, it was bloody cute and to die for, but now it's not. I don't know what it is but it's certainly not cute. 'I'm sorry I treated you badly back in the day. I really am.' He lays his hand on my arm, touchy-feely as ever. A tingle shoots through my veins. I have no idea what that's all about.

Before I can decide, another man appears.

'Tom?'

'Jen?' He's clocked Dave's hand which is still resting on my arm. I snatch my arm away, shove my hand in my pocket. 'Are you all right?'

'She's fine,' Dave says. 'I've got it.'

I'm speechless.

But Tom speaks for me. 'It? You've got it?'

'It's a manner of speaking,' Dave says. 'A phrase.'

'Words are important, mate.'

'So are actions. Mate.'

'What, like this?' And Tom makes a swing for Dave, only he slips on the grass and misses. By which time

Dave is ready to have a pop. I've never seen two more unlikely men to have a fight. It's so ridiculous I can't think straight. I want to laugh but I also want to shout at them. Both of them. But they're not listening. Now they're on the muddy ground, rolling around like idiots, scrapping like toddlers on ice, sending ducks squawking and flapping, edging towards the edge of the brook. A nearby swan has a vicious glint in his eye.

And I am equally angry. How dare they speak for me? How dare they fight over me? Just as they topple into the water and splash around like they need arm bands, I turn away and stomp off. It's not like they're going to drown. The water is knee deep. But that swan does look murderous.

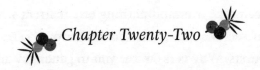

Chapter Twenty-Two

TODAY'S THE DAY we get our puppy. Much excitement only tainted by the prospect of having to see Tom. I'm still angry with him and I'm angry with myself for being angry with him and that makes me even angrier. I don't know if this is all worth it, all these disturbing, agitating emotions whipped up by another man, an unknown quantity. I almost miss Mike. I knew where I was with Mike. Only I didn't, though, did I? And now I'm annoyed because I'm already breaking my resolution of not getting cross with Mike.

I'm going to find Dad and see if he'll come with me to Tom's. I can't face any kind of chat. I just want to bring home Bob's puppy.

Dad's in the shed. 'You're looking glum, Jennifer Juniper. What's the matter?'

I tell him about the idiotic fight between Tom and Dave.

Dad coughs, a poor attempt to suppress the urge to laugh. 'Boys will be boys,' he says.

'No, Dad. That theory doesn't wash. They're men and they should behave like men. Proper men.'

'We all make mistakes, Jen. In the heat of the moment. Anger can take over and nothing else matters when all you can see is a fuzz. You should know. You're prone to outbursts. Why is it OK for you to get angry and not them?'

'I didn't ask them to get angry. I didn't ask for them to get involved.'

'But they are.'

'So what should I do? Will you come round with me to get Denis?'

'You're a grown woman, Jennifer Juniper. You can do that on your own.'

'Oh, Dad. Why do you have to be so... so...'

'Clever?'

'I was going to say annoying. But unfortunately I think you're probably right.'

Dad sits at his desk and opens his diary, starts writing.

'What are you doing, Dad? I'm trying to have a conversation with you.'

'I just need to make a note before I forget. This is an historic day. My daughter admitting I am not only clever but probably right.'

'*Dad.*'

TEN MINUTES LATER, I turn up at Coast Guards Row, alone, because Dad's so annoying I didn't want him to come in the end – which, thinking about it, was probably his plan.

Tom takes his time answering the door, long enough for me to turn and walk away but—

'Jen. Come in. Please.'

Tom looks tired, worn out, so I go inside, hauling the travel crate to transport Denis home with me.

'He's asleep right now,' Tom says. 'They all are.'

He shows me into the front room. The pups are scattered across the wooden floorboards in various soporific states.

'I got rid of the carpet,' he says.

'Probably for the best.'

'Cup of tea?'

I say yes, because it's polite, the civilized thing to do, and I sit down on the sofa, next to Betty who has clearly had enough of being a mother to so many. Her ears are soft like Mrs Pink's and I wish Lolly was with me now. Betty sighs and rests her chin on my leg. She's warm and solid and I realize that she and I, we're in the same boat. Empty-nesters. Though Tom's keeping Juniper so she'll not be rid of all her offspring. Having said that, I have Harry back home and Dale for good measure. Maybe your kids never actually leave. If you're lucky.

Tom returns with the tea. He smiles, hesitant,

awkward, and I notice again that vulnerable chip in his front tooth.

'I'm sorry,' he says. 'About that stupid fight. I don't know what came over me.'

'Don't you?'

'OK, yes, I do.'

'What? Tell me.'

He hesitates again, opens his mouth, shuts it, opens it again. 'I don't like seeing you upset.' A pause. 'Because you mean a lot to me.'

'I do?'

'Surely you know that?'

'Well, no, not really. I mean, I'm not really sure what to think.'

'OK, then, right, well,' he says, not so eloquent today. 'Er... Is it enough for me to say, for now, I really, really like you?'

'It's a start, I suppose.' I give him what I hope is an encouraging smile.

'Right then,' he says, clapping his hands, teacher mode, like he's sorted out a squabble. 'Drink your tea and we'll get Denis into his crate.'

'And?'

'And what?'

'Is that the end of this conversation?'

'No. It's just on pause.' He scoops up Denis, who is snuggled next to Martin and my heart lurches at the thought of separating the siblings but this is the way it has to be. 'Have a hold of the bruiser.'

I have a hold of the bruiser. Betty lifts her head from my leg and sniffs Denis's bottom. Satisfied with that, she curls up and goes back to sleep. I can feel a tear creep into my eye and so I busy myself putting Denis in his crate. Tom pops a small blanket in there.

'It smells of his mum. Just till he settles. Don't worry. He'll be fine. He's a lucky boy. He'll be living with his dad and he'll be seeing Betty all the time.'

And with these words of reassurance, I reach up to Tom and plant a kiss on his lips. 'I really, really like you too,' I tell him.

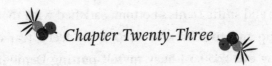

Chapter Twenty-Three

AFTER A FEW sleep-disturbed nights, I give in and let Denis sleep in the sofa bed with me, much like I did with Harry as a baby. He snuggles into my feet while Bob takes up his place curled into my back. I don't know why I bothered trying to sleep-train Denis as this was inevitable.

Bob was very sniffy when I brought Denis home. He kept eyeing him, askance, probably hoping I'd take him away again. But he's slowly getting used to him. I've even caught him letting Denis into his basket which is alongside his in the kitchen.

Anyway, much coffee is needed this morning as today is the licensing hearing. And I'm hoping that Dave will have met his match with our secret weapon. Sometimes living in a small town has tremendous benefits. Who knew that a cross-country run in the early eighties and a shared Mars Bar could lead to a potential breakthrough in my career thirty years on?

THE HEARING IS at 11 a.m. in the council offices. There are three councillors on the subcommittee plus a reserve. Two of them are middle-aged, paunchy know-it-alls, and the reserve is an old duffer, who's been on the council since the Jurassic Period. But the fourth one is a youngish woman whom I recognize. She used to work in the bakery. Helped run the Brownies. She's proper local, proper Devon and she knows what this town needs. And I reckon she'll put those needs over and above her own wants.

The others attending include the various officers who've been involved in the process, the council solicitor, and the woman who was with Dave that day at the auction, who bid on Clatford House on his behalf. Turns out she's an accountant. Well, well, well, of course she is. But we have a magistrate speaking on our behalf because sitting alongside Jackie, Tish, Carol and me is Tracey, our agreed speaker. I hope she has a tennis ball in her pocket and that she's improved her aim since school.

Game on.

First on the agenda is to elect a Chair. Paunch 1 is voted in and opens proceedings, asking for confirmation that there are no Members with disclosable pecuniary and non-pecuniary interests that relate to the business on the agenda. I look pointedly at Dave, a Member with a capital M, who gazes nonchalantly ahead at the Chair.

The Chair, easily satisfied, reads through the basics

263

of the application, informing us that there are no representations from the Responsible Authorities. I can tell already that he's biased, that he completely supports Dave's claims that we intend to open a gin palace and that crime and disorder will ensue, plunging Dingleton into a gin-soaked no-go zone.

Then he invites the woman, Miss Jones, to speak. She is dressed like Melania Trump, trying to look classy, but there's a certain fakeness lurking behind the foundation and the kohl-rimmed eyes. She talks about how we haven't addressed the issue of antisocial behaviour, Dave nodding along. Dave who displayed and continues to display the most antisocial behaviour I have ever known. And then, unbelievably, she talks about the bloody bins. How the seagulls are out of control and that the museum has not helped with this. How opening a bar would exacerbate the problem. Bloody cheek of it.

Next up is Tracey. She addresses these points head on.

'This is not about gin palaces, Gin Lane or Mother's Ruin. This is not the slippery slope. This is going to be an artisan endeavour. These local women are making small batches of craft-distilled gin using locally foraged ingredients. This is about Dingleton. The gin will tie into the museum – there will be links to our smuggling past, to the engineering of Isambard Kingdom Brunel and the science behind his atmospheric railway, to the violets that used to be sent by train to London. In fact, violet will be a key botanical in our gin. We could reinstate the Violet Fair which would both unite our town and bring in the tourists and day-trippers who've fallen away in recent years.

'As for crime and disorder, there will be CCTV. There won't be a late licence. There are no issues with parking, or noise, or light pollution. Most importantly, the gin bar will raise revenue which will enable the museum to reopen, and be bigger and better, more relevant and a beacon of outreach to all, including the disadvantaged and the excluded. All in all, I heartily support this new business venture.'

I want to leap to my feet, shout and stamp, but I just aim the biggest smile at Tracey for being our champion. I'd buy her a multi-pack of Mars Bars only that might be considered a bribe and we must remain squeaky clean.

In the end, it's a close-run thing and we owe something to the Jurassic councillor who votes in our favour.

'My wife and I used to enjoy a gin and tonic before supper,' he says. 'It saw us through the good times and the bad times. As Churchill said, "The gin and tonic has saved more Englishmen's lives, and minds, than all the doctors in the Empire."'

By *gin*-go. He's got it.

And we have a licence.

THAT EVENING, AFTER supper and under the ginfluence, I text Tom to thank him for his support.

He pings straight back.

How's Denis?

Denis on my bed. On my pillow.

Sleep training going well then?

Couldn't be better. Can u meet us at museum tomorrow? After school?

Yep, can do. What about?

Ideas. We need ideas.

I'll be there.

Maybe after we can go for a drink?

Steady on. Next you'll be proposing.

I'm still married.

Maybe you need to do something about that?

Maybe I do.

Yes, maybe I really do need to do something about that. Must arrange to meet up with Mike and discuss. After all, this is a week for doing business. I'm on a roll.

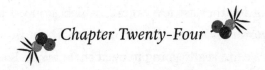

Chapter Twenty-Four

WE ARE SITTING on the window seat in the library of Clatford House, extra chairs gathered round, drinking coffee. It's a stormy February morning and we watch the waves wash up and over the sea wall and onto the railway track below us. The Paddington train chugs along slowly and there's a sense this could be the last train out of here. We really need this line. It attaches us to the rest of the country and, as much as we all love Dingleton, we need it to stay open so we know we're a part of the world beyond. We all need ambition and dreams. If we're lucky enough to be able to stay here, make a life here, then good, that's great. But some of us want to head off into the big wide world. Stay, leave, return, all of us are connected in some way to the landscape, to the slightly scuzzy town that has so much potential.

Tom has congratulated us all on our triumph – we have not only a licence but also change of use – because one would be useless without the other. We are all still beaming. 'Let's hope the grant comes through from the Heritage Lottery Fund,' he says.

And the butterflies in my stomach that have been flapping for the last few weeks, which stopped briefly after yesterday's news, start up with their fluttering again. We are really going to need that money. So much for all the ridiculous beaming.

'What's the plan today, Jackie?' Carol asks.

'I thought we should have a tour of the building, generate some ideas, construct some sort of plan of action. I know nothing's certain at this point, but we need to be looking ahead.' Jackie has her clipboard and means business.

Tish, dressed in a sixties miniskirt and boots, hair in a band and big hooped earrings, is languishing on the window seat, like she's posing for David Bailey. 'I know we're supposed to have an eye to the future, but obviously being a historian, and working in a museum, I can't help but glance back over my shoulder. And yesterday is a day I want to remember for the rest of my life. I only wish I had a photograph of the expression on that gouty-legged ninnycock's face.' She reaches into her hippy bag and pulls out a vape. 'And now, if you'll excuse me, I'm popping outside for five minutes.'

'You're vaping now?' Carol asks.

'I told Miranda that if we got the licence I'd give up the cigs. This vile contraption is a step towards that goal.' And she swaggers off, leaving a trail of *Je Reviens* in her wake.

We spend the next hour thrashing out ideas for the museum, building on what we wrote in the funding application, Jackie making notes. These are the items agreed:

- A callout in the local paper and on social media for people to search in their attic for objects of historical interest. Stuff connected to their grandparents etc. that shed light on how life was lived in Dingleton.
- Making our collections more accessible through digitization and by getting the community involved in creative, fun ways.
- Improve visitor access and facilities (new lavs, a lift and a ramp).
- An education programme.
- An outreach programme.
- Recruiting volunteers who may be long-term unemployed, socially isolated, or living with mental-health challenges.
- Creating and maintaining a strong sense of community and place. Giving our town a focus.

'Time for a comfort break.' Jackie stretches and I notice for the first time how tired she looks. Tired but that glint is still there. 'Then we'll wander round the building, wrestle with how we want this vision to be.'

'Where's Tish?' Carol asks. 'She never came back.'

'Maybe she went to buy fags?' I suggest.

'Have you seen it out there?' Tom nods towards the window that's rattling in the wind, fat rain splashing off it so we can barely make out the angry sea below.

'A hurricane wouldn't stop Tish getting fags,' I point out.

'I'll text her,' Jackie says but it's unlikely she'll get any response as Tish, not being one for new-fangled contraptions, will either have left the phone on her kitchen table or it'll be out of battery.

By the time we've had our comfort break, she's still not returned.

'Right,' Jackie says. 'While we're waiting for Tish, let's carry on. She's probably sheltering from the rain somewhere.'

So we do the tour of the museum. We visit each room in turn downstairs, the smaller rooms currently used for archives and exhibits, the less salubrious rooms in the old servants' quarters which lead off dark, dank corridors. Then the library, with its old books, some of which could be sold seeing as they're not connected directly to Dingleton and could raise extra funds. Then the Captain's Parlour which we're all agreed is the obvious place for the gin bar. Not only does it have access from the street but it also has French windows leading onto the terrace with its stunning view of the bay. A lovely room, with grand proportions, but needing a ton of work. It's all going to be a ton of work and it's completely and utterly terrifying. But it's also exciting and energizing and hopeful.

Then upstairs. As we reach the large airy landing, the light is mysterious, a storm flickering on the horizon. From the window of the master bedroom, where Captain Clatford no doubt woke of a morning and could look out to sea while having his first grog of the day, we can see how angry the Channel is, in turmoil, waves arching over the railway line which surely now must be closed. But over and above this roar we can make out an unmistakable drip-drip. A leak. The bloody roof. There's a puddle in one of the corners so we hunt for a bucket to put under it and towels to soak up the water. We check the other rooms too. More leaks. More puddles. And a rattling window in the maid's room that you can feel the wind rush through.

'Time to batten down the hatches,' Jackie says, biting her lip. Then she turns to me. 'I didn't want to ask you this but is there any way Mike could come down and help us?'

I'm thinking about the prospect of asking Mike to come down and help us when we hear footsteps clonk up the stairs and an out-of-breath and sodden Tish announces, 'The storm is up, and all is on the hazard.' She gasps. 'Sorry I've been so long.'

We ask what happened and she goes into a lengthy

speech worthy of Dame Judi Dench. 'I went to buy some cigarettes – I know, I know but that vape is most vexatious. Anyway...' She inhales a lungful of air. 'I decided to drive to the newsagent's and that was when I saw Kev walking along, drenched, heading out of town and the fates were urging me to follow him and ask if he needed a lift somewhere. "I must get home," he said. "Ma's not well." He'd been out to buy her flowers but the wretched bouquet was awfully sad and bedraggled by this point, as was he, more so than usual. I ordered him to get in the car, which he did, and then I drove up the back lanes to the farm. It wasn't easy. I had the wipers on full, the car was buffeted by the wind and at one instant I thought we were likely to get stuck up that cursed track but my car's as strong as a tank so by the power of Grayskull we made it and I followed him into the farmhouse to see if there was anything I could do.'

She stops for a moment, gathers her thoughts. Steadies herself.

'You're soaked, Tish. You should go home and get changed,' Jackie urges.

'I'll be fine. I have the constitution of a block of iron. But Old Woman Bates is in a bad way. Kev's nephew was on the phone to the doctor when we arrived. The doctor called for an ambulance. I left them to it then as it seemed an intrusion to remain. But I do feel something bad in my bones.'

Tish's bones are legendary. They feel the weather coming. They feel bad news.

'It's terrible outside,' she goes on, as if she needs to underline this when we're surrounded by drips and buckets. 'The rain is lashing so hard it hurts what exposed skin I had— Oh.' Finally she spots the immediate problem.

I'm really hoping Tish is exaggerating how sick poor old Violet is because I can't think too much about her now, not when we've got to focus on the problem of a very expensive house falling down around us. And I know Violet would be urging me to do something so I swallow my pride and phone Mike, who's a builder after all. He's actually very accommodating and says he'll be with us in half an hour. Which gives us enough time to go up to the observatory and see the state of it – broken panes of glass shattered over the floor. Rotten window frames. A hole in the roof where tiles have slipped and through which you can see the black clouds unleashing their vengeance. And the four of us for the first time really, really understand that this could be an impossible challenge.

But it's Carol who comes out with a statement, not from Facebook or a tattoo, that makes me realize how much I underestimate her.

'"I am not afraid of storms for I am learning how to sail my ship."' And even she is surprised when she adds, 'Louisa May Alcott.'

She really is my best friend in the whole wide world.

MIKE, WEATHER-BEATEN, IN a water-logged hoody, examines the damage and makes that builder noise that yet again strikes terror into my heart. But he knows me well enough to realize this won't help matters and so he turns all businesslike and says he'll call in some favours and get the place secured so it doesn't suffer too much more as the storm's still raging.

Over the next couple of hours we have a chippy, a spark and a roofer. Between them and Mike they board up the observatory and patch the roof from the inside as it's far too hazardous to get out. They do what little else they can to the most vulnerable rooms but I can tell from how they're talking to each other in low voices that they think we're mad to have taken on a project like this.

'You get off,' I suggest to the others. 'I'll stay and see the lads out. They shouldn't be long now.' They're all so tired they don't argue but Carol gives me a hug and says she'll text later.

Not long after, I let the builders out with much thanks and appreciation and then it's just me and Mike.

'Can we have a chat?' he asks, a bit shifty so I'm wondering if he knows more than the others were letting on. 'It's about the kids.' A smattering of panic while I wonder which of the children is in trouble or maimed but that's daft because he'd have mentioned it earlier.

'Tell me then.'

'Not here. I need a pint. The Bishop?'

SOMETIMES IT WOULD be useful to be a dog because you could just shake the rain off. Instead I have to make do with shivering on the pub doormat and drip-drying. It's fairly quiet inside but with enough body mass to make the windows steamy. Mike nabs a table for two near the wood burner, tells me to sit while he goes to the bar.

I peel off my coat and hang it like a sealskin on the back of the chair, sit down and wait, watch him wave a twenty-pound note at June. I know he knows I'm watching him; I can tell by his familiar body language. He tells June to keep the change, Flash Harry, and joins me at the table, plonking down the tray which holds four pints.

'Is someone else joining us?'

'Nope.' He hands me one of the pints, takes one for himself. 'Cheers,' he says, uncheerfully.

'Cheers.' I chink his glass, afflicted still with hard-dying habits. 'We're not celebrating, are we?'

'Not exactly, no.' He downs his pint in one go and makes inroads on the next.

'What is it, Mike? You're worrying me.'

'We need to talk about our marriage.'

'Mike, no. You can't come back.'

'That's not what I'm saying.'

'Oh? You've definitely gone off the idea then?'

'It was wrong of me to put you in that position. I know it's over, you and me. I was unhappy and wanted our old life back but it's a different life now.'

'You can say that again.'

'I'm sorry I was such a tosser.'

'You were a mega tosser but what's done is done. I'm ready to lay the past to rest.'

'I've not died.'

'Our marriage has died.' A wave of sadness licks about my ankles. Thankfully, before the tide rises and swamps me with salty grief, something occurs to me and I know I have to share this little gem with Mike. 'It's like gin distilling,' I tell him.

'You what?'

'In gin distilling, we've discovered there's a fair amount of waste involved and our Lolly's suggested we put it into an effluent tank and take it to a local anaerobic digestion plant to be turned into bio gas.'

'Hang on, where are you going with this? Are you suggesting we recycle our marriage into bio gas?' Mike's confused, but worse than that, he's playing confused. It's deflection, an old habit that he's obviously not shifted. 'What are you saying, Jen?'

'Let me speak.'

'Sorry, only I did want to chat to you for a reason.'

'Never mind that, you can tell me in a minute. My point is that the cuttings at the beginning and the end of the distillation process are waste because they have impurities and can't be drunk. They're called the heads and tails.'

'Where's this going?'

'My God, you've got the patience of a child on Christmas Eve.'

'Sorry. Go on.'

'Right. Well. What we're left with, once the waste has gone, is the good bit, the drinkable section. And guess what that's called?'

'Not a clue.'

'It's called the hearts.'

'Right.'

'Don't you see? Our marriage was distilled and we've got rid of the waste. And what we're left with is our kids. They're our hearts.'

'That's a nice way of looking at it.' He smiles. Takes another gulp of his pint, sighs, then starts drumming his fingertips on the beer mat in front of him.

'What is it, Mike?'

'That's sort of why I'm here.'

'Right.'

He says nothing, flips his beer mat with the back of his fingers and catches it. Does it again. And a third time.

'So why are you here?' I ease the mat from his clasp. 'Tell me.'

'Melanie wanted me to talk to you.' He shifts on his chair. 'I mean, I want to talk to you as well, it's just that she was keen for it to happen right away, so you see, I've been sent here to tell you that... well... there's another little heart.'

'Pardon?'

'Melanie's pregnant.'

HE FETCHES ME a gin and tonic, a double by the taste of it, while I digest this latest information. Mike is going to be a father again, at the grand old age of fifty. I manage to mumble half-hearted congratulations though I'm not sure if this is the right etiquette, or if he even feels like congratulations are in order. But at least he does attempt to answer my questions.

Melanie is fine. Melanie has had her twelve-week scan. Melanie is almost over the morning sickness. Melanie is delighted. Melanie wants a bigger place.

But there's a final question and he's avoiding it so there's only one thing for it. I shall take control of the situation.

'Shall we get a divorce, Mike?' I'm asking this of the man across the table from me, a man I've loved nearly all my life. To my ears, it sounds so ridiculous, like asking him if he wants a cup of tea or something from the chippie, and I never expected it all to end like this but now it has, it's OK. It's actually OK.

'Yes, please,' he says.

So that is that. Our marriage will cease to exist but we'll be left with the hearts. Three hearts and who knows how many in the future?

'Right then,' he says. 'Just because we're divorcing doesn't mean I can't still help you out. I'll do whatever I can at Clatford House but it's a big job.'

'Too big?'

'Too big for me alone. But there's someone who might be prepared to help.'

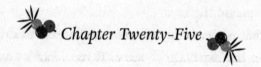

Chapter Twenty-Five

I WAS UP for most of the night what with yesterday's events tumbleweeding through my mind and the noise of the hoolie blowing outdoors. At one point there was a lightning bolt directly overhead. The room lit up and I could see two small dogs snuggled up to each other at the end of my bed. And a couple of seconds later there came an almighty crack of thunder that seemed to shake the very foundations of the house. It sounded seawards, hopefully far enough out and away from poor old Clatford House hanging on by its bitten fingernails.

I lay there, waiting for the next one, and the next. And I thought about the new baby in our lives, because this new baby, Mike's baby, *will* be in our lives, a sibling for Harry and Lolly. And I thought about death too, because a baby goes hand in hand with it. My mother used to tell me that. Out with the old and in with the new. And yes, she was an unashamed hippy, but she'd grown up with the old country ways.

All's calm and still now. Like the morning after a

riotous party. Everyone is pale and tired, shuffling around in dressing gowns, clutching mugs of tea. Dad's doing the dishes, a bowl full to the brim with bubbles. He calls me over to survey the garden. 'Lucky there's no leaves on that pear tree.' He points his sudsy washing-up brush in the direction of the bald tree, like he intends to conduct a magic spell or maybe a re-run of the 'Ride of the Valkyries'. 'The whole thing could've come down. Imagine if it fell onto my shed?' And he slaps his forehead as he remembers. 'Any news on Clatford House?'

'Not great. Jackie texted to say more windows have blown and more tiles have fallen.'

'I'll peel the spuds then.' The obvious answer.

'Spuds?'

'Potatoes. *Capsicum annuum. Solanum tuberosum.* For the roast dinner.'

'Are we having a roast dinner?'

'Of course we are. It's a Sunday.'

'We don't have any meat.'

'There's half a lamb in the freezer. I got it off Kev.'

'What? When?'

'I saw him at the hospital yesterday when I visited his mother.'

'When did you go there?'

'When you were out with Mike.'

'Oh.'

'I passed the Bishop on my way home and saw you

walking in together. Why were you out with Mike? Does he still want to come back?'

So I recount yesterday's conversation. The divorce. The baby. And he listens, makes no comment, probably thinking about genetics and DNA and what-have-you, but still, he takes it well, even pours us both a sherry.

'How are you going to defrost half a lamb?'

'Don't worry about that. Kev cut it up and I've kept out a piece. It's in the shed. I'll fetch it now, sprinkle on some rosemary, rub in olive oil and garlic, season, pop in the oven. You watch the dogs. I'm not sure Denis is up to raw sheep just yet.'

'I'm going to check on Clatford House. See the damage for myself.'

'On your own?'

'No, Dad. I'm never on my own.' And I give him a kiss as I think of Old Woman Bates and how precious our parents are. 'But I might be needing a strong young man.' I raise my eyes upwards.

'Dale?'

'No, Harry.'

I call my son and while I'm waiting for him to appear, I remember I haven't asked after Violet.

'Ah, no, well,' Dad says. 'She's heading towards her expiry date.'

'Dad!'

'What? She's had a good innings and she's ready to go.'

'But it's sad.'

'She's older than the Queen, you know...'

It hovers there, in the kitchen, quivering thoughts of mortality, big questions of life and death, and I know Harry and Lolly need to be told about the divorce and the baby but maybe that's something Mike and I can do together.

Right now, there's someone I must see before going to the museum and Harry's my wing man.

It's been a while since I've been to this house. It used to be his parents' but they've moved to a bungalow the size of Southfork and he's lived here alone since his latest divorce.

I pull up in front of his driveway and cut the engine.

'Nice Jag,' Harry says. 'Isn't this where Dave Barton lives?'

'Yes, it is.'

'So...'

'We're going to have a little chat with him.'

'What are we, the Dingleton mob?'

'No, that's the Bartons and it's about time they gave up their reign of terror and put our town first.'

'Reign of terror? Dave Barton's hardly Robespierre.'

'I'm exaggerating for dramatic effect.'

We get out of the car.

'Right,' he says. 'So what's the plan?'

'The plan?'

'Do we have a script we're working from?'

'This isn't a telesales job, Harry. Just back me up. He won't try any silly business if you're here.'

'Silly business? Does he have a shotgun?'

'Probably. He's always out killing pheasants. But no. It's his hands I'm more worried about.'

'You think he might hit you?'

'No.'

'Oh...' Harry straightens up to his full five foot eight. 'He'd better not try any funny stuff with my mother. Let's go.'

The two of us walk up the driveway. Harry rings the bell. Twice. A dog barks. A big-sounding dog. The door is flung open and a Shih Tzu growls at us.

'OK, big boy. Calm down,' Dave says. 'We have visitors. Harry, you've grown. To what do I owe this pleasure?'

'Can we come in?' I demand. 'I need to talk to you.'

'Sounds ominous.' He stands back, wafts us inside while the dog bares its teeth and we follow him into the front room, or the 'drawing room' as he calls it.

'Drink?' He points at an extravagant trolley full of crystal-cut decanters and chunky glasses.

Tempting as it is, I decline. 'Shall we sit down?'

He looks worried for a second. 'Have you got bad news or something?'

'Just sit.'

He sits on what must be 'his chair' while Harry and I take the sofa.

'So, Jennifer. What can I do you for?'

'I need your help.'

'Do you now. In what way?'

'With Clatford House.'

'You've seen the light and want to sell it on?'

'No, I want your backing.'

'Are you asking for money?'

'Not unless you're offering.'

'I'm not offering.'

'Well, I'm not asking for money. I'm asking for manpower to fix the house. As you must've gathered by now, the storm's knocked it for six.'

'Manpower?'

'Or woman. Whatever. You have a large building firm and masses of contacts and Mike's doing his best to help but it's a bigger job than he can cope with.'

'Mike's helping?'

'Why wouldn't he?'

'Because you're no longer a couple. He left you.'

'Yes, he did leave me. For your niece. But we are working things out together for the future because... because it's what's best for our kids.'

'Plus Melanie's having Dad's baby,' Harry blurts out.

Dave's jaw actually drops as he takes in what Harry

has just said. As does mine. At least my son has the decency to blush.

'How did you know that, Harry?' I ask him, bewildered.

'Dad told me.'

'Right.'

Dave's on his feet now, pouring a whisky, pacing the room, muttering half to himself. 'Mike's got Melanie up the duff? Well, I never. The dirty old dog.' He stops, remembers we're here in the room with him. 'So, Harry.'

'Yes?'

'We're going to be related.'

'It looks that way. A bit. Not close or anything. I'm not going to start calling you Uncle Dave or whatever.'

'Thank God for that.'

'So can you help Mum?'

'Er... I'd like to but no. I don't think I can.' He's saved any explanation by his phone conveniently beeping. And he's rude enough to answer it. 'Sorry about this but I've got to go. It's Melanie.'

'Melanie?' This is too weird. 'Is she all right? Is Mike all right?'

'I'm not sure. She's at Clatford House of all places and wants me to go there right away.'

He's already heading out the door putting on his overcoat, Harry and I on his tail.

286

THE DAMAGE IS worse than I thought. The observatory has lost more tiles. There're great chunks of plaster sprawled across the terrace and one of the bedroom ceilings has pretty much come down so that the air is thick with dust. Jackie, Tish, Miranda, Mike, the spark, the chippy and other blokey mates are getting their hands dirty and I want to cry when I see them all in hard hats and it's difficult not to freak out over the amount of work ahead of us and yet I'm in awe that so many people are pitching in.

Dave is walking round with his hands in his overcoat pockets, examining the walls, ceilings, floors with what might actually be concern on his face. He might've wanted to pimp out this building to a cheap pub chain but he also knew that it would conserve the house. So deep down I don't think he wants to see it go to rack and ruin, even to prove a point.

He catches my eye, looks away when Melanie appears, tugging at his arm, leading him into the library, and I'm tempted to follow but she closes the door behind them. And anyway, what would be the point of that? He's not going to help. Maybe we've got enough help, in any case.

'Right, Harry. Let's get cracking.'

'Yes, ma'am.' He salutes and disappears to help his father while I hunt for Jackie.

I find her upstairs, covered in dust, hauling rubbish across the landing. She's in her element, far more than just a clipboard carrier. 'Don't look so worried, Jen,' she says. 'We've got this.'

At which point Tish appears, like Rosie the Riveter, wielding a plunger. God knows what she intends to do with that. 'Where's Carol?' she asks.

'Working on the gin.'

'She gets all the best jobs,' Tish says. 'Now I must make haste and do mine.' She swishes off, plunger at the ready to do battle.

'Do me a favour, Jen. Can you get me some more sacks, please? They're in the kitchen.'

'Sure.' To be honest, I'm glad to be given a specific task because I don't know where else to delve in so I go downstairs.

As I'm passing the library, the door opens. Melanie comes out, gives me a coy half-smile and disappears fast, leaving Dave standing before me. 'My niece is very persuasive,' he says. 'No wonder Mike fell for her charms.'

I'm about to give him a piece of my mind when he apologizes. Actually says, 'I'm sorry, that was below the belt.'

'Can I help you with something, Dave? Because I'm really quite busy right now.'

He's about to say something, no doubt facetious, when he stops himself. 'Come in here,' he says and I don't have the energy to argue so I follow him into the library, conscious that he's shut the door behind us but confident that there're a lot of burly men and tough women out there if I need them.

'Let's have it then.' I purposefully look out of the window at the finally calm sea rather than at Dave. My heart is beating fast but I have no idea why.

'Don't worry,' he says. 'I'm not going to pounce on you and have my wicked way. I'm offering an olive branch.'

'You are?'

'Don't sound so surprised.'

I'm standing with my hands on my hips, waiting for the naughty boy to own up to whatever this is all about.

'I'm going to help you out,' he says. 'I'll do the job for you at a discounted rate.'

'How discounted?'

'A lot discounted.'

'Really?'

'Really.'

And the surge of relief is enough to have me throw my arms around him in the biggest turnaround of thirty years. But at the brief moment his arms are fast around me, the library door opens. Before I see who it is, the door's slammed shut and there's no one there.

I WALK ALONG the seafront, examining the damage. It's not as bad as the storm a few years back that left the train track hanging above the waves when the sea wall was washed away. Even so, there's a palm tree uprooted and a bench has been knocked over. Sand is scattered everywhere and heaped up against the kiosk and public conveniences. On the beach itself, the tide's out and people are walking their dogs on the shifted sand. Soon Denis will be able to come down here with Bob, once he's had his final jabs.

I keep on walking until I reach Coast Guards Row. The evening is drawing in and there's a light on upstairs. A strange car parked outside. Despite my best intentions, I feel a creeping nausea insinuate itself into my gut.

Who's there?

Only one way to find out. I knock loudly, three times, hoping that this will alert Tom to my presence, hoping he's got nothing to hide. There's a lot of yapping. Betty and Juniper. After a minute or so I'm about to knock again, one last time. Maybe he's not here after all. Maybe he is here but doesn't want to answer the door.

Footsteps approach, accompanied by scurrying scratchy paws and a woman's chiding voice. Then a pause before the door is edged open.

'Hello.' There stands a tall woman with short red hair, holding Juniper under one arm while Betty jumps up at me, tail windmilling, before giving me a thorough sniff-over. 'Jen, isn't it?'

'Er... Sarah? I didn't recognize you without your wig. That's not a wig. Is it?'

'All mine last time I checked. Are you after Tom?'

There are so many ways I could answer this but none of them seem appropriate right now. So I mutter, 'Is he in?'

'Actually, no,' she says. 'You've just missed him.'

'Oh.'

I must look disappointed because she gives me a sympathetic, knowing smile. How I wish I could disguise my emotions more effectively.

'He's gone out for milk,' she says. 'Come in. I'll put the kettle on.' She opens the door wider and Betty skips back along the hallway and through to the kitchen.

I hesitate.

'He should be back soon.'

'Thanks. That would be great.'

Great? How is this great? I shouldn't be here. I'm intruding.

'Sit down,' she says and, when I've sat down, she hands me Juniper. I breathe in her puppy smell and take what comfort I can from this simple pleasure. Has Tom found comfort in Sarah? Would he do that? Would she? If so there's nothing I can do about it. The important thing is to keep him as a friend. What will be will be. Only now I have Doris Day singing '*Que sera sera*' in my head and I might actually be humming it because she is handing me my mug of tea, asking if I'm OK?

'Sorry. Ear worm.'

'You're a fan of Doris Day?'

'Well, my dad is so I suppose it's worn off on me. I blame it on the menopause.'

'Ah, the lovely menopause.'

'You're acquainted?'

'Intimately. My kids tease me about it.'

'How old are they?'

'They're both twenty. Both girls. Both completely different. One's at university, the other's a bookie.'

'How brilliant.'

'It is. I'm proud of the pair of them. Doing their own thing. Tell me about yours.' She offers the biscuit tin and I help myself to a ginger nut.

After a slug of tea, I tell her about my two offspring and what they're up to. Once I'm done I can't stop myself from saying, 'You do have magnificent hair.'

'Er, thank you,' she says. 'It runs in the family. The twins have got it. And so did my sister.'

She looks so sad right at this moment that I can't ignore it. 'I'm so sorry about Claire. You must miss her terribly.'

'God, I do. Every day I wake up and she's the first person I think of. I mean, I always used to worry about her, doing her stuff in war zones, the most dangerous places on earth, but at least I knew she was out there somewhere. Now, I don't know where she is.'

I feel a twist of pain in my stomach and know I must say something, acknowledge this somehow. Words are not enough, not by any means, but they can help, even if you say the wrong ones. Better something naff than nothing at all.

'She's in your heart,' I tell her. 'I don't mean to sound schmaltzy but she'll never die as long as she's there.'

Sarah smiles at me, a smile that lights up her eyes, and I think that if Claire was anything like her then no wonder Tom hasn't been able to get over her. Not that he should have to get over her. But he does need to find a way to live without her and then maybe – selfish, I know – he could squeeze me into a little corner of his heart.

And as if by magic, the front door goes, setting off Betty and Juniper into a frenzy of excitement and tail-wagging and yapping. And there he is standing in the kitchen, taking in the mugs of tea, the biscuit tin.

'Jen? What are you doing here?'

'Now that's a nice welcome,' Sarah chides, only partly playfully.

'I've got something to tell you, Tom.'

'Right, well, I don't think there's any need for that.' He shakes his head. 'I saw it with my own eyes.'

'You saw what?'

'You and Dave.'

'Me and Dave?'

'You were hugging.'

'That's because he'd just told me his firm will help us out with the repairs, mate's rates.'

'You're mates now?'

'It's a figure of speech. We've come to an agreement. With Melanie's help.'

'Mike's Melanie? Why would she help?'

'Because she's Dave's niece and she's having Mike's baby and somehow she wants us all to get on. At least not be at loggerheads. Plus, I think she's feeling guilty for swiping Mike and she was always one of Lauren's biggest fans.'

'Right.' He sits down at the table, rubs his stubbly chin. Looks from me to Sarah and blushes, embarrassed to have his two worlds collide. His old life. His new life. Boom.

Sarah picks up the slack. 'Jen's been telling me all about the museum. How you're going to fund it by selling gin. Genius. Claire would've loved that.'

Is this a test? Sarah saying her sister's name like that? Is it a challenge? Or is she saying it's OK to talk about Claire? That she needn't be the uninvited guest at the table. But Sarah carries on chatting, somehow making this all normal, that it's fine to drop the C-bomb into conversation and there will be no fallout. I'd be happy to stay longer, getting to know this woman, gaining an insight into Claire and, through her, into Tom. But I can't stay because my phone beeps and there's a text from Carol.

Get home quick. Have made perfect gin.

I tell them what's happened, that I have to go. Sarah wishes me luck, offers help with museum curating if we ever need it and then, because Tom is not moving, not saying a word, she sees me to the door.

Right now I'd swap one of his smiles for all the gin in the world.

As I step outside, I'm relieved to find the rain has stopped and I start my walk home but I haven't got very far when I hear my name called out in a hushed shout.

It's Sarah, standing outside the house with a bin bag in her hand. I retrace my steps and she apologizes, says she offered to put out the rubbish on a pretext.

'Pretext?'

'I need to tell you something, without Tom's ears flapping.'

'Oh?'

'You're going to have to take the bull by his horns, if you'll pardon the pun.'

'Excuse me?'

'You're going to have to take the next step.'

'Er...'

'OK.' She grins, realizing she has to spell things out. 'If you want Tom, tell him. Claire had to.'

'Really? I thought he wasn't that bothered.'

'Oh, he's bothered all right. Hot and bothered. I'd go as far as to say he's in love.'

'Who with?'

'You, of course.'

'Really?'

'Really. But he doesn't know it. He's scared and inse-cure and completely hopeless. You'll have to take matters in hand.' She winks, dumps the rubbish into the wheelie bin, and disappears inside.

WE HAVE A late supper by the time we're all gathered together. Dad insists the lamb must be eaten before we test the gin. And it's delicious, cooked to perfection. Dale is in heaven and proper impressed that a man of Dad's generation can cook without a barbecue. All that's missing is Lauren. And I suppose family is like that. For a while, just a short while, if you're lucky, you have a loving partner and kids and your own family unit and, from the day you bring that firstborn home from hospital, you think it will last for ever. You think the hamster wheel will never stop but it slows down when one of them gets off, and stops when the other follows suit. And you're left wondering what that was all about.

And then your family is the same but different. You live in separate places, sometimes across continents, sometimes in Plymouth, but always under the same sky. Then more people get added to your family. You spend more time with friends. And you stop hating your ex-husband for leaving you in the lurch because he has every right to be happy, the same as you do. And Mike is happy. You really think he is. But you don't envy him. He's about to clamber back on the hamster wheel, only this time with dodgy knees and less energy, and you're really quite grateful for that hysterectomy. And for the HRT because it finally seems to be kicking in.

Not only that, Dave has stepped up to the mark with Melanie's guidance and there's the small matter of Tom. Who's allegedly in love with me. But angry and hurt. And I'm just so bloody tired only now I have gin to try in the shed. Carol's handing me a glass.

'Right, Jen. Now we need to do this properly. Sit down,' Carol tells me, all schoolmarmy.

I sit down on one of the deckchairs. The others are my audience.

'Let's start with the nose,' Carol instructs. 'The first sniff. The top notes.'

I inhale deeply.

'Well?' She has a notebook and pen in hand.

'A good gin presence but the juniper doesn't punch you in the face?'

'Good. And?'

I give it another sniff. 'Actually, it's a lovely scent.'

'Be specific.'

'A zesty, floral perfume followed with bright juniper?'

'Excellent. Right, now the palate. Drink it neat. Hold it in your mouth for a bit before swallowing.'

I do as I'm told. 'The juniper's more earthy. And I'm getting the sweetness of liquorice... and orris root... and yes, violet?'

'You've got it.'

'Like a childhood sweet shop. Or a spring garden.'

'All right. You're showing off now. And the finish?'

'A long smooth floral finish with lasting notes of orange blossom?'

She nods encouragingly.

'And hints of apple?'

I get a round of applause.

'But we can't drink it neat. What mixer do you propose?'

'Nothing too shouty,' says Carol, who's wearing the shoutiest of shouty outfits, a neon nineties shell suit. 'We're aiming for light and refreshing so probably a non-quinine tonic, or a soda, or even a bitter lemon.'

She indicates the bottles lined up on the table, a selection of supermarket own brands and bespoke gin mixers. 'What'll you have?'

'The Sicilian lemonade.'

'Excellent choice,' Dad says. 'Reminds me of sere-nading your mother in a hotel in Palermo. Hot sultry nights, with the rustle of the breeze in the olive trees and the ever-present threat of a mafia abduction.'

He helps himself to an olive, as if re-enacting that night. And I'm hoping no one will ask but obviously Dale does.

'What did you sing to her?'

'What makes you think I was singing?'

'Isn't that what serenading means?'

'It's a euphemism for making mad, passionate love.'

'*Dad.*'

He chuckles. So I don't know if he's joking but I suspect he's telling the truth. 'Can we change the subject?'

'All right,' Dad says and veers off on a tangent. 'Did you know that gin was created by Dr Franciscus Sylvius, a Dutch chemist, in the seventeenth century as an attempt to cleanse the blood of those suffering from kidney disorders?'

'No,' we chorus.

'He called it *genièvre*, French for juniper.'

'Maybe that's what we could call the gin,' Harry says. 'Name it after Mum. Jennifer Juniper?'

'Or maybe that's what we call the bar. The Juniper Gin Joint,' Dale suggests.

There's a general consensus that this is a good idea. We'll think on about the gin itself. And, though we're trying not to get ahead of ourselves, we discuss the possibility of producing different gins, with variations on this, our signature one.

'I reckon we should get Jackie and Tish round here

sharpish,' I say, feeling guilty they're missing out on this historic moment.

Carol hunts for her phone in her voluminous handbag and starts punching in numbers.

Meanwhile, there's someone I have to see. Someone I promised would have a bottle of every batch we produce. This might be the only one she gets to try.

'Will you come with me to the hospital, Dad?' I ask.

He understands without me having to spell out why. Which is a first. 'You'll have to drive,' he says. 'I've had an opener, a brightener, a lifter, a tincture, a large gin and tonic without the tonic, a snifter, a snort, a snorter and a snortorino.'

Everyone looks at Dad as if he's finally and completely lost the plot but I happen to know that he's conjuring up the ghost of Denis Thatcher.

'Let's go, Dad.'

'Right with you, Jennifer Juniper.'

And Carol hands me a precious bottle of our Heavenly Devonly Violetty gin.

WE EVENTUALLY REACH the hospital, after Dad directs me on a detour up one of the back lanes, insisting I pull over by the ford to forage for something that he's absolutely sure is necessary right then and there. He's rooting around in the dark by the light of his headlamp

300

while I keep the engine running and the heating on.

Visiting time has long gone but a kind, lovely nurse lets us in to see Ma Bates. She's in a side room with Kev who's snoozing in the chair by her bed. He stirs when we tiptoe in, smiling in recognition when he comes to.

'Evening,' he says, straightening up and wiping the drool from the side of his mouth. 'What you got there then?' He nods at my Co-op bag for life.

When I take out the bottle, Kev's eyes quiver with a spark.

'This is the one,' I tell him dramatically and he nods, knowing exactly what I'm talking about.

'You brought it for Ma to have a taste?'

'I did.'

'Ma,' he says softly, leaning in close to his mother's ear which is nestled somewhere in those soft, grey curls.

Her eyelids flutter open and a smile passes over her lips. You can see how much she loves her son, her weird and wonderful son, who's lost so much and is about to lose more. 'My boy,' she whispers.

I can feel my throat tighten, my grip on today's emotions slipping.

'Our friends have brought something for you to try,' he says.

Dad nears her, so she can see him, and she reaches out her hand to pat the bed next to her. He sits down. She's so tiny, like a child, but with a lifetime's experience flowing through her veins, though the flow isn't what it was. More of a trickle, that'll soon run dry. So why not give her one last taste of heaven on earth before she leaves for the next world and all that has to offer?

He shows her the bottle.

'Is that what I think it is?'

'Yes, Violet. It is.'

'Well, pour us a drop.' She smiles and the room is filled with essence of Devon.

Kev gets one of those hospital beakers meant for water or weak squash and he empties a generous amount of gin into it. Dad moves over so that Kev can hold the cup to her mouth for a sip. A sip that's actually more of a gulp. A snortorino for a tiny woman.

The three of us wait on her verdict. I can actually feel my heart thudding and I have to remove my jumper to counter the flush that's swarming up from my toes, up my legs, over my torso and right on up to the top of my head.

'That's the one,' she says. 'It's lush.'

I try not to whoop but her praise is a real boost. Just what I need.

'I can die happy now,' she says. And she even manages a wink. 'But you two best leave now. My Kevin promised to read to me.'

'Goodbye, Violet,' Dad says and out of the pocket of his tweed jacket he produces a sprig of Devon violets, bluey-purple with those dark heart-shaped leaves, still wet from the hedgerow where he picked them earlier. He lays them carefully on her bedside table where she can hopefully see them and smell them.

Then we slip away, Dad and I, out from that sacred place between mother and son and off into the dark of night.

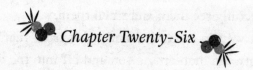

Chapter Twenty-Six

THE MORNING AFTER our visit to see Ma Bates, I woke to find a note pushed through the letterbox, which was strange because neither of the dogs had barked. Bob always barks at the rattle of the door, the brush of the letterbox, footsteps up the path, the wind. But nothing. Both dogs lay fast asleep, Bob curled into my back, Denis on my feet.

The note was almost illegible. It was scrawled on the back of a lottery ticket in a biro that was on its last legs or the writer had been upside down. Anyway, I had to hold it up to the light so I could make out some of the indentations. But I think I knew what the message was. It was from Kev. And he was telling me that his dear old mum had passed away during the night. Dear Violet.

And what of Tom? I went round to see him that afternoon. Only he wasn't there. Turns out he'd gone back with Sarah that morning to Taunton, to see the twins who were both around that weekend. He took Betty and Juniper with him, knowing what a popular uncle that would make him. Only then he got the flu – like proper flu, not just a bad cold – and was in bed up there for the week. And so yet again, the question of Tom and me, us, was left hanging, unanswered.

TODAY IS THE funeral to be held at the Saxon church that's nestled half a mile away from Donker Farm in a bucolic setting, a lush Devon valley. It's one of those churches that has a vicar in rotation with three or four other parishes as numbers have dwindled but you can imagine how many feet have trodden over its threshold, how many knees have knelt in the nave over the last millennium. How many baptisms, marriages and funerals. Christmas, Easter, Morning Prayer, Evensong. Communion and Confirmation.

Today St Martha's is packed with mourners. Church members, villagers, people from the market days, officials from Dingleton, familiar faces dotted everywhere amongst the pews. And at the front, the family. Children, grandchildren, great-grandchildren. The simple oak coffin is decorated with violets. The fragrance surrounds you as you enter the church, comforting and beautiful. Reminiscent of another era.

The vicar's dressed up in his finest, rotund and jolly, with a head shiny as a new penny. We kick off with his hearty welcome and then move straight into 'Morning

Has Broken', a hymn that gets me because Mum had it at her funeral.

Dad and I sit quietly towards the back. I say quietly, but Dad keeps whispering violet facts to me during each lull in the service.

'Did you know that in France, the violet was worn by Napoleon's followers when he was in exile to show their allegiance to him?'

'Funnily enough, Dad, no, I didn't.'

'And Ophelia had them too, amongst other flowers, when she went off her rocker.'

'Sensitively put, Dad.'

'Shakespeare gave flowers meanings and symbolism but I can't for the life of me remember what violets stood for.'

'Death?'

'Really, Jen. You can be morbid sometimes.'

'We're at a funeral. I can't help being morbid at a funeral.'

'No. I think it might be faithfulness.'

'Ssh, Dad. It's time for the eulogy. I hope Kev can keep it together.'

'He'll be fine. I spotted him earlier, hanging around the tombstones having a smoke and a nip from his hip flask.'

Kev walks over to the microphone, dignified and cautious, uncomfortable in a suit that's too baggy and a collar that's too tight. He pulls at it, like he's trying to breathe better. He's bewildered by the technology. The microphone squeals and he visibly jumps. He says, 'S'cuse us,' and has another nip from his flask, bold as you like in front of the vicar who takes it in his stride, even jokes that Jesus liked a drink so all's well.

Despite the Dutch courage, Kev gets off to a shaky start, stumbling over his words and coughing. But then he takes a moment. He turns towards his ma's coffin, touches it with his freshly scrubbed fingers, and somehow scrapes together enough courage to help him start over. And once he gets going, he's on a roll, telling us how much he loved his mother, how she'd kept the farm going through good times and bad. She was born there, left school at fourteen, and worked hard all her life. And what had got her through? Her beloved farm. The support of a good husband. The sweetness of motherhood. And gin.

We laugh briefly, that way you do at a funeral to let out some tension, only then he says something that makes me reach for a tissue. But I can't find the packet of Kleenex I swear I stowed in my bag before we left home, knowing I'd probably end up a snotty mess. Which I have. Which I am. But it's all right. Dad to the rescue. He gives me his handkerchief, which thankfully is clean.

And why am I crying? Because Kev is talking about his lost little lad. How his mum never cast any blame on him, or on his ex-wife for leaving. She just made sure he always had a bed and a hot meal, somewhere he would feel safe, though after what happened I'm not sure Kev has ever felt safe again. I'm not sure that there's any place on earth where he could feel that. And now she's gone, what will happen to him?

Dad understands. Once Kev has finished his homage, there's a spontaneous round of applause and Dad tells me something. He says, 'Did you know Kev can turn his hand to anything? Maintenance and the like? He's his mother's son after all.' And, before I can answer, the organist strikes up 'All Things Bright and Beautiful' which throws me back into childhood, school assemblies and harvest festivals. Mike and Carol. And Dave Barton before he morphed into an idiot. Though everyone can be redeemed, can't they? Even Dave Barton.

The congregation are standing now, voices at full throttle, and when the organist does her final flourish, it's time to go. There's a wake up at the farm and every-one's invited. The least we can do is pay our respects. We owe Violet so much.

THE WAKE IS like one of the best parties ever. There's the usual spread – cocktail sausages, a massive ham, hard-boiled eggs, cheese-and-pickle sarnies, fruit cake, Victoria sponge. And as well as tea and coffee, there's sherry and ale and of course gin. So by the time we've said our condolences to the family, had our fill of food and drink, I'm feeling squiffy. Dad has gallantly been abstemious and I've fully taken advantage of his offer to drive. He didn't seem that disappointed so I've ploughed on.

I duck upstairs to find a bathroom because the downstairs loo is jammed and as I pass a bedroom, trying not to appear like a snooper, I catch a glimpse of Kev, sitting on a bed.

'How do,' he says, looking up. 'I've got something here might interest you.'

'Oh?' I'm intrigued, so I go inside what must've been his mum's room. I don't suppose it's changed much at all since the war, when it was no doubt her parents' bedroom. The sash window overlooks the Devon hills. The curtains are chintzy and sun-damaged. There's a pretty dressing table covered with cross-stitched linen and displayed with an amber-coloured glass set and a tortoiseshell brush and hand mirror. A tin of talc and a WI enamel pin.

The central focus is the bed, a big old Victorian monstrosity with header and footer, a faded rose-pink satin counterpane, white cotton sheets, thick heavy blankets. A bolster lies across the width of the bed under two plumped-up pillows. You could imagine a room staged like this in the museum. Dingleton Farm Life.

'I were born in this bed,' Kev says.

'Really? Wow, that's quite something.'

'Nothing special about that. Lots of babies were born in this bed over the years. There were a few deaths too. It's a pity Ma didn't spend her last moments here rather than in hospital.'

'She was well cared for, though?'

'Can't complain. Just not the same as home.'

I want to ask him what 'home' actually means to him but this isn't the time or place and now he's rummaging in a carved wooden jewellery box.

'Ma asked me to give you this,' he says. 'So here, it's yours.' He hands me a brooch.

'Violets?'

'My father gave it to her on their wedding day.'

'I can't accept this. It belongs in the family.'

'She insisted. It were her wishes.' He puts it in my hand.

It's delicate enamel. Purple-blue petals, green heart-shaped leaves, tied with a white bow.

'She said you'd know what it means.'

'Gin?'

'And something else.'

'What?'

'Don't have a clue. You should ask that Tish woman. She knows all about the old days.'

'I will. Thanks, Kev. I'll treasure it always. But I'd like to ask you something.'

'Oh?'

'We've applied for funding. If we get it there'll be work going. Would you be interested?'

'What type of work? Would I have to wear a suit?' He tugs at his jacket.

'No, you wouldn't have to wear a suit. I hear you can turn your hand to most things?'

'I get by.'

'We'll be needing someone to look after Clatford House. Like a caretaker.'

'A caretaker? I could do that. I don't need money.'

'How about you start as a volunteer and then, hopefully before too long, we'll be able to pay you a salary?'

'I'll do it,' he says, a question in his deep, sad eyes. 'On one condition.'

'Right... What condition?'

'That you sort things out once and for all between you and that Tom.'

'Pardon?'

'It's frustrating for everyone, watching you two dance around each other.'

'Oh, well, I'm sure it'll work itself out in time. There's no hurry.'

'You could die tomorrow. And you're a long time dead.'

'But I'm not sure he's interested.'

'Course he's interested.'

'But I'm not sure he's interested enough to want a relationship. His wife's still very much in his mind and I don't know if I can compete with that.'

'It's not a competition. But if it were, you'd win because you're the one that's here, living and breathing, and he needs a woman that's alive.'

I must look somewhat horrified at this and Kev realizes the implications of his argument.

'That came out all wrong,' he says with a doleful smile. 'I'm not good with words.'

I laugh, a little guiltily. 'I understand what you're trying to say.'

'Good,' he says. 'I don't mean no ill will towards the dead.' His eyes well up and I hold his hand, the two of us side by side on the old farmhouse bed, listening to the sheep out in the field, the hum of talk downstairs.

'I'll tell him tomorrow,' I say. 'I promise.'

'Tell him what?'

'That I have feelings for him.'

'What might they be?'

'Er... Well... That I love him?'

'Do you?'

'Yes. I actually do.'

'Then tell him now. Right away.'

'But he's at school.'

'So drive there.'

'But I'm over the limit.'

'So get your father to drive you there.'

'You don't give up, do you?'

'Plenty of times I've given up.' He sighs, the weight of years on his shoulders. This must be such a hard day for him to get through so if I can do something positive, lighten a little of that burden, then who am I to say no?

TEN MINUTES LATER, Dad and I are back in the car en route to Dingleton. Despite winter weather, we manage to negotiate the track without a repeat of last time's shenanigans when we got stuck in the mud.

'Let me get this straight,' Dad says. 'You want to go up the school to tell Tom you love him?'

'Yes.'

'And do you love him?'

'Yes.'

'You sure you don't just fancy a go at him?'

'Dad!'

'Well, you're a grown woman, Jennifer. You have needs and desires.'

'Dad. Just no.' I have to wrestle off my black woollen coat now. 'I love him and I promised Kev I'd tell him now.'

'You promised Kev?'

'Yes.'

'Trampy Kev?'

'Yes. And can we not call him that any more? It's not very respectful. He's a good man.'

'I never doubted it. So you're going to barge into Tom's classroom and tell him? Just like that?'

'Just like that.'

We're passing along the seafront now and an idea smacks me. Of course. Maybe 'just like that' isn't enough. I need a reason to be in school at this time. I know the staff up there. I go in every term to give talks to some of the classes, depending on what topic they're learning. Until Dave Barton's intrusion they visited the museum all the time. I'm a responsible adult with a DBS check.

'Can you stop at Clatford House, Dad? There's something I need.'

'Your marbles?'

'Funny. I'll be two minutes.' I leap out of the car before he's finished parking on the double yellows and bounce up the steps, hooking out my set of keys and letting myself in quick smart.

WHAT I NEED is in the storeroom and has been for a very long time, awaiting restoration, so I head straight there, acknowledging the workers, saying I'll be back to help in a little while but that I've got something to do.

My footsteps echo up the stairs and the smell of old dust and damp is stronger up here, the air cooler. The storeroom is in one of the old bedrooms at the back, where the curated objects are safe. Captain Clatford's telescope is in an old suitcase, tucked on a shelf behind a case of stuffed Victorian budgies. Poor things.

It's quite heavy but I manage to stagger down the rickety stairs with it and out to the car where Dad has Radio 3 on full blast. Once I'm in, he puts his foot down, sensing the urgency in my body language. We head to the other side of town and Dingleton Juniors. He parks in the one visitor spot and wishes me luck.

I feel bad when I reach reception; I know Mrs Tibbs well and don't like fibbing that Tom is expecting me on a museum visit. But needs must.

'What you got there, Jen?' she asks.

'Captain Clatford's telescope.'

'I thought that was long gone.'

'It's been in store, waiting for funds to fix it. It still works, but it's old and fragile and needs some TLC.'

'Don't we all?' She laughs, including me in this which is fair enough.

I say something or nothing as right now I'm focusing on what the heck I'm going to say to Tom in front of a class of Year Sixes.

'Doing anything nice tonight?' she asks as I'm signing in.

'Tonight?'

'Valentine's Day, dear.'

'Valentine's?' I get myself in a tangle with the visitor's lanyard, almost asphyxiating myself. 'Of course!' I smack myself on the forehead, trying to knock some sense into my block.

February 14th.

Mrs Tibbs buzzes me in and I head down the corridor, past the rows of pegs with coats abandoned on the floor beneath, heaps of backpacks, trails of scarves, and random gloves and plimsolls scattered across the wooden floor. Just because it's Valentine's Day, I won't let this put me off. I will keep going despite the prospect that what I am doing, what I am about to do, all seems a bit... well... staged. Tacky, even.

But. Then again. It's... well... it's romantic, isn't it?

The school is eerily quiet because it must be story time, the calm before the storm when the end-of-day bell rings, chairs go up on tables and the hordes of little people are released from their classrooms to hunt down their outdoor wear, book bags and packed lunch boxes.

I'm outside the Year Six class now. Tom's class. Penguins, they're called. If I stand back a bit and peer sideways, I can see through the glass of the door. There they are, cross-legged on the carpet, gazing up at their beloved teacher as he perches on his chair, telling them a story with props. You're never too old to be told a story with props. And I've got my very own prop though I have no idea how I'm going to tell a story with it or even why the hell I thought I'd be better equipped to bare my soul to Tom with a telescope.

Here goes.

Rat-a-tat-tat.

Thirty-one or so pairs of eyes swivel in my direction. Some look tired. Some bored. Dazed. Excited. Annoyed. Take your pick. And then there's Tom.

'Come in?' he says, all tentative like.

So I go in. And I stand like a lemon next to the display of the Shang Dynasty of Ancient China. 'Nice Pictographs.'

'That's mine, miss,' shouts out Amelia Bond.

'Excellent.' I know I sound like a female, Devonian version of Hugh Grant. I sound ridiculous. I am ridiculous. Completely and utterly ridiculous.

'Everything all right?' Tom asks, now more concerned than shocked.

'Er, yes, thanks. I've just been to a funeral.'

'My dad's gone there. It's Old Woman Bates,' says Jordan Bassett.

'Yes, that's right.'

'Did you see her skeleton?' This from Emma Compton.

'Retard,' says Jordan Bassett. 'It takes ages for a dead body to be a skeleton.'

'Enough of that, Jordan,' Tom says, all teacherfied. 'Apologize now for using that word.'

'Skeleton?'

'The "R" word.'

Jordan Bassett does as he's told and says sorry to Emma Compton.

Emma, perplexed at this whole scenario, looks at Mr Winter for assistance but he can't give her that because he's currently looking at me, perplexed. And I'm looking from face to face, feeling completely and utterly perplexed even though I'm the one who's supposed to know what the heck is going on.

I'll have to wing it.

'Excuse me, Penguin class, I've brought something to show you.'

Now all of Penguin class look perplexed apart from Amelia Bond who is plaiting Emma Compton's hair.

'Mr Winter has been helping us get the museum back open,' I continue, forging on. 'We need to raise lots of money so that we can restore important objects that belong to our town.'

'What you got in there, miss?' This from George Thompson who lives down our road.

'I'll show you.' I open the case, a little dramatically for effect, and take out the telescope. 'I expect you'll know what this is.'

They shout out, 'A telescope!'

Living down here they should flipping well be familiar enough with pirates to know what a telescope is.

'It belonged to a very famous man who used to live in

our town. He was a sea captain, but broke the law and didn't pay his taxes.'

'My dad doesn't pay his tax.'

'Well, tell him he should,' I instruct George Thompson. 'I know your mum, remember.'

George Thompson turns bright red and I feel bad because he's only repeating what he's heard at home so I crack on, diverting attention away from him and back to me and the telescope.

'Anyone know who this man might've been?' I ask. 'No one? Mr Winter?'

Mr Winter does a 'Who, me?' gesture and says, 'Why, I believe you're referring to a Mr Clatford of Clatford House. But why are you showing us this telescope, as interesting and important as it is? History? Science?'

'Ah, well, it's more to do with affairs of the heart.'

'My mum had an affair,' says George Thompson. He can't help himself.

'She don't mean that, idiot,' says Emma Compton, on the ball for once. 'She means biology. The heart.' Everyone is staring at Emma Compton who has never uttered such a sentence in her life. 'That's biology, isn't it, sir.'

'Er... yes?' Tom is uncertain what's going on here.

If Emma can do it, so can I. I will embrace the tackiness which I know Tom will hate because he's a politically correct, right on, do-gooder kind of bloke who probably thinks Valentine's Day is a big con perpetuated by the

319

card companies and Pandora bloody charm bracelets. 'Can I carry on?' I ask Penguin class.

They nod.

'Thank you.' I smile at them, all those fresh-faced ten- and eleven-year-olds. The biggest in the school. The oldest. The prefects and the monitors. It'll be all change for them come September, back to the bottom of the pile. Like a game of snakes and ladders. 'OK, everyone. Bear with me.'

They bear with me. Not a fidget. Not a squeak.

'What I want to say is that a telescope is used to make faraway things look bigger. It doesn't bring them closer to you, but it does make them clearer and you can see more detail. It's like when you meet someone new. You think you know them, then you really aren't sure you know them at all. And what you need is a relationship telescope so that you can examine the other person close up. And they need a telescope too so they can do the same to you.'

My speech has at least had the effect of making the class remain absolutely still and quiet. Most definitely perplexed, at any rate. Tom too. So quiet. Really quiet. And now in my head I sound like Donald Trump which is quite enough in itself to spoil the moment, and still no one's speaking, everyone's staring, but I power on through, touching the violet brooch pinned to my jumper to give me oomph.

'What I'm trying to say, Mr Winter, is...' and I look over the thirty heads of the class to his silver foxiness, 'this telescope needs renovating and then it will be displayed in the museum, up in the observatory.'

'And you needed to tell me this now because...?'

'Because it's an analogy. Have you done analogies with Penguin class?'

'Yes, we've done analogies.'

'Good. Very good. You're a very good teacher.'

'He is a very good teacher,' Emma Compton confirms.

'Thank you?' Mr Winter is blushing now.

'What I'm trying to say, what I'm really trying very hard to say despite what it must sound like, is that I wish I had telescopic vision or at the very least twenty-twenty vision instead of this hyperopia.'

Silence.

'Long-sightedness.'

'You should've gone to Specsavers, miss,' says Emma Compton, on a roll today.

Penguin class think this is hilarious and I realize I only have a very short time in which to grab back their attention before control has vanished for ever and the school bell rings for home time.

'I mean, I wish I could see clearly,' I say loudly. 'Because in my moments of clarity there is something I am completely sure of.'

'What's that, miss?'

'Well, George Thompson, I'm trying to tell Mr Winter that... I love him.'

Emma Compton shrieks but, apart from her dramatic reaction, the rest of the class cover the spectrum from fake vomiting to actual weeping, their reactions not defined by gender, but as individuals. Though the one individual who hasn't said anything is now standing up and walking over to me, picking his way through the huddle of children, trying hard not to tread on any stray limbs, until he's reached the Shang Dynasty of Ancient China where I'm still standing, wobbly-legged, with a telescope held aloft.

'Is that a telescope in your hand or are you just pleased to see me?' Tom asks.

'That doesn't really work. And isn't exactly appropriate, given the circumstances.' We're both very much aware of Penguin class who are now like meerkats, waiting to see what happens next. 'But yes. I am indeed holding a telescope and I am very pleased to see you.'

'I'm very pleased to see you too.'

'Go on, sir. Tell her,' Amelia Bond urges.

'Thank you, Amelia. I'm going to tell her now.'

'Tell me what?'

'Will you give me the chance?'

'Sorry.' I clamp my mouth shut while my heart bounces in anticipation as Tom gazes at me with that twinkle in his eye.

'I love you too, Jennifer Juniper.'

Penguin class erupts into an almighty rumpus. They laugh and scream and shout and clap and whoop and one of them even wolf-whistles, making the most of this moment of joy to make maximum fuss without the risk of being told off. They don't even notice the bell go.

'Nice one, sir,' says Jordan Bassett.

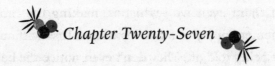

Chapter Twenty-Seven

The Adventures of a Menopausal Gin Lover

08.00: Woken by two dogs licking face and man bearing cup of tea. Can't quite believe that a) I'm fifty today and b) a lovely silver foxy man is bringing me tea in bed.

Am also handed pile of birthday cards.

'Happy birthday, Jen. Here's to a good one.'

We chink mugs. Thinking how nice this is when notice hint of worry about Tom's now very familiar face.

'What's up?'

'There's a letter.'

'Oh?'

'From the Heritage Lottery Fund. If they say no, that'll put a dampener on your birthday.'

Only one way to find out and, since Lauren not back yet, must be brave and open myself.

08.05: Start crying. Big, snotty-nosed ugly crying. Tom alarmed. Reads letter. Yelps in manly fashion. 'You did it!' Yes, we bloody did it. Awarded major grant for Clatford House. Project Gin is a go-go.

09.00: Dale prepares peach champagne cocktails for birthday breakfast slash celebration. 25 ml gin, 25 ml peach liqueur, ¾ glass champagne. Lovely. Lethal. Lush. Dad serves eggs Benedict to soak up booze. Wishes me happy birthday. Puts present on table. Small and box-shaped and wrapped in the pages of *Amateur Gardening*. Mum's eternity ring. Sob.

10.00: Lauren, hair dyed gorgeous shade of violet, love-child of Mrs Pink and Tinky Winky, arrives bearing roses. And boyfriend. Sob again.

10.30: Exhausted. Return to bed for nap. Happy dreams.

12.00: Wake in sweaty panic. Action stations.

13.00: Arrive at Clatford House where Carol, Jackie and Tish already setting up for tonight's launch which they insist will be combined with birthday party. Juniper Gin Joint now ready thanks to Dave's hard-hatted army and troop of volunteers conscripted by Kev. Intend to make splash on local landscape before summer season kicks off. Afternoon of cleaning, finishing touches, party prep starts now.

17.00: Back home and into shower. Wish Tom could join me but at cottage sorting out dogs, including Queenie, now much pampered baby of Tish and Miranda. As hot water pours over my body, offer up silent thanks that am actually here, alive, to enjoy special day. Remind myself to be grateful for family, friends, new love and gin.

17.30: Find Dad in shed, dressed in dinner suit, conducting 'Wow' by Kate Bush. 'Desert Island Discs,' he says. I kiss his cheek and he hugs me, whispering how proud he is and how he wishes Mum were here. 'She liked a knees-up. And a leg-over.' *Dad!*

19.00: Arrive Captain's Parlour which is indeed perfect place for the Juniper Gin Joint, shiny as new pin, glittering in pink sun, setting on horizon of calm and happy sea. Sparkling glasses lined up on the swish bar, ready and waiting for guests to descend to enjoy our gin. Apothecary-style sea-green bottles with cork stoppers displayed prettily with Edwardian-style postcard labels designed by Tish, a sprig of violets and Dingleton Gin in cursive script.

My friends are here. Jackie in M&S, Carol in Marilyn Monroe halter-neck, Tish in dinner suit, smarter than Dad's. I am wearing sparkly violet dress adorned with Ma Bates's purple, green and white brooch. Suffragette colours according to Tish. Feel bloom of pride.

Dale and Harry, our smart bartenders, polish glasses and slice fruit, while Dale Skypes parents, reassuring them investment is safe. Have list of planned delicious cocktails, taking inspiration from library book, *How to Mix Drinks and Serve Them*.

Lauren and boyfriend in charge of music, thankfully not DJ Nobber but suitable for gin-loving menopausal women, i.e. Michael Bublé.

Dad man-marked by Carol but will escape leash at some point. Only hope is get people sizzled before then.

Kev on door, meeting and greeting, his two dogs, Martin and Quincy, in bow ties and on best behaviour.

19.30: First guests arrive with gasps of delight at Gin Joint rather than me reaching a half-century.

19.45: Dave Barton turns up with new beau on his arm, a sheepish-looking Tracey. Reassure her Dave's not the twonk he makes himself out to be. Tracey gives me Mars Bar and coy wink.

20.00: Room is at capacity. Builders, volunteers, family, friends papped by *Gazette*. Tonight a free bar, tomorrow a money-spinner. And in time, room by room, a functioning, wonder-filled museum.

20.30: Dad chinks champagne flute with a knife to grab everyone's attention, which he does when knife cracks glass, sending shards and booze everywhere. While Carol cleans mess, Dad embarks on speech. Stomach fills with jitters.

'Here's to the opening of the Juniper Gin Joint,' he says. 'May all who sail in her, be happy.' Raises newly filled flute and all follow suit with accompanying whoops and whistles and applause. But Dad not finished. Oh, no. 'And here's to my daughter, Jennifer Juniper, who has reached the grand old age of fifty but I know without a doubt that there's life in the old dog yet.'

'*Dad!*'

Room explodes with laughter. Dad rustles up embarrassment when realizes he's just insulted daughter.

Fortunately Tish's Miranda distracts guests by sitting at donated vintage piano and cranking up 'Happy Birthday to You' in the voice of Gracie Fields. Everyone joins in, even soon-to-be ex-husband and partner with bun rising nicely in oven. Despite feeling the love, must sit down. Sob again when my hearts, Harry and Lolly, plonk themselves one on each side of me.

22.00 or maybe 23.00: People start leaving, chattering that way you do after a great party. Ask Kev to follow me next door, to library. Show him display curated by Tish and Jackie, exhibition of Dingleton's Violet Festival with blown-up sepia photograph of the Violet Queen centre stage.

'God bless Ma,' he says.

'Cheers to that.' I give him a hug.

23.50: Tom and I in charge of locking up. Decide to have nightcap first, up in newly restored observatory. He puts pashmina around my shoulders though can't feel cool night because thoroughly warm, not from hot flush but from rush of love. A few months ago, I thought I'd lost everything but it turns out I've found it all. The trick is to keep your eyes open and use that telescope.

'People say life begins at forty,' I tell him. 'But that's not the way it's worked out for me.'

'There's life in the old girl yet?'

'If I didn't know you were joking, I'd get Captain Clatford's telescope and beat you round the head with it.'

'I don't doubt it,' he says.

Then he kisses me and what happens next is not for a menopausal woman to write down. Suffice it to say, gin is this mother's new beginning. And this man her happy ever after.